KATT'S IN THE CRADLE

Ginger Kolbaba & Christy Scannell

KATT'S IN THE CRADLE

A Novel

Our purpose at Howard Books is to:
**Increase faith* in the hearts of growing Christians
**Inspire holiness* in the lives of believers
**Instill hope* in the hearts of struggling people everywhere
Because He's coming again!

Published by Howard Books, a division of Simon & Schuster, Inc.
1230 Avenue of the Americas, New York, NY 10020
www.howardpublishing.com

Library of Congress Cataloging-in-Publication Data
Kolbaba, Ginger.
Katt's in the cradle : a secrets from Lulu's Café novel / Ginger Kolbaba & Christy Scannell.
p cm.
1. Female friendship—Fiction. 2. Coffee shops—Fiction.
I. Scannell, Christy, 1967– II. Title.
PS3611.05825K38 2009
813'.6—dc22 2008025404

ISBN-13: 978-1-4165-4389-3
ISBN-10: 1-4165-4389-9

10 9 8 7 6 5 4 3 2 1

Manufactured in the United States of America

For information regarding special discounts for bulk purchases, please contact Simon & Schuster Special Sales at 1-800-456-6798 or business@simonandschuster.com.

Edited by Ramona Cramer Tucker
Interior design by Tennille Paden
Cover design by Kirk DouPonce

Meet the Pastors' Wives of Red River, Ohio

Lisa Barton is an at-home mom with two kids: Callie, sixteen, and Ricky, fourteen. Her husband, Joel, has pastored Red River Assembly of God for nearly five years. Lisa's parents pastor the Assembly of God in nearby Cloverdale.

Felicia Lopez-Morrison's husband, Dave, pastors the First Baptist Church. They have one child, Nicholas, who is five and in kindergarten. Once a high-powered public relations executive with a top national firm, Felicia now works from home for the company's Midwestern clients. The Morrisons came to Red River three years ago from Los Angeles.

Mimi Plaisance is a former teacher who now stays home with her four children: Michaela, eleven; Mark, Jr. (MJ), nine; Megan, six; and Milo, fifteen months. Mark, her husband, is senior pastor of Trinity United Methodist Church.

Jennifer Shores is married to Sam, pastor of Red River Community Church, where she is the church secretary part-time. They have been married twelve years and have one daughter, Carys, who is eleven months old.

KATT'S IN THE CRADLE

CHAPTER

1

Lulu's Café

Tuesday, March 18

12:05 p.m.

"I can't believe it!" Felicia Lopez-Morrison waved as she ricocheted through the tables, heading toward her three friends seated in their usual booth in the back right-hand corner of Lulu's.

"Did you hear the news?" she asked breathlessly, sliding into the seat next to Jennifer, who pushed her leather purse against the wall and scooched over to give Felicia room.

Mimi laughed. "You mean about the scandal?"

"Who *hasn't* heard?" Jennifer leaned over and gave Felicia a sideways hug.

"When Dave told me, I thought he was kidding," Felicia said. "Kitty hasn't even been in the ground a year."

Lisa nodded. "Well, Norm was probably just lonely. He needed the companionship."

"Then buy a dog," Jennifer suggested. "Of course," she said, getting tickled, "then people would talk about dogs and a Katt living together!"

The other women groaned.

"It would have to be for companionship." Felicia playfully nudged Jennifer in the shoulder. "He just met the woman. He couldn't love her, could he?"

"From what I heard," Mimi said matter-of-factly, "she's more like a girl."

"Ladies!" Lisa smiled but looked a little uncomfortable.

Jennifer knew Lisa was construing this turn as gossipy. *Sweet Lisa,* Jennifer thought, looking at her friend, seated across the table from her. *Always taking the high road. You'd think after three years of us all being friends, we would have picked up some of her good traits.*

"Well, well." A loud, brassy voice interrupted Jennifer's thoughts. Their plump, gruff-sounding waitress, Gracie, was standing over their table, pulling out the order pad from the white apron around her ample thighs. "Glad to see little Miss Señora made it today."

Felicia pulled back in mock offense. "Hey, I'm only five minutes late!"

"Yeah, yeah." A slight smile crossed Gracie's face. She jutted her chin out toward Felicia. "I'm likin' you without all the high-and-mighty outfits and shoes and whatnot."

Everyone at the table laughed. Felicia spread her arms in show and bowed her head, as if accepting a standing ovation. Gracie threw back her head and guffawed.

Felicia certainly had changed in the last year since she'd been working from home, Jennifer realized. Her silky black hair, once curled and neatly laying across the top of her shoulders, was now pulled back in a ponytail. And her high-powered business suits and designer shoes had been replaced by a pair of black jeans and a mauve hoodie sweater. Jennifer glanced under the table—*Well, her boots are still designer,* she thought good-naturedly.

"I like you girls." Gracie pulled a pencil from behind her ear. "You're always the highlight of my every-other-Tuesday."

"Well, thank you, Gracie," Mimi said. "And you're ours."

"All right, enough with the chitchat," Gracie said. "Are we all having the regulars?"

"Yes, ma'am," Jennifer and the others chimed in.

Gracie harrumphed. "I don't know why I keep taking out my order pad and pen for you all. Okay, PWs, I'll be back with your drinks."

Jennifer watched Gracie plod off to her next table of customers, several booths toward the front of the café. Jennifer really liked their waitress—and knew her three friends did, too. Underneath all Gracie's gruffness lay a heart as big as an ocean. And it *was* Gracie who had given the women their official group nickname—the PWs.

When Jennifer, Mimi, Lisa, and Felicia had started secretly meeting at Lulu's nearly three years before, Gracie had been their waitress. She'd overheard them talking about God and their churches, figured out that they were all pastors' wives, and nicknamed them. She'd gotten a big kick out of the fact that the women—all hailing from the southwest Ohio town of Red River—would drive forty miles out of their way every other Tuesday to nosh and chat in this little nothing-special dive. Although the PWs never had explained to Gracie that they met that far from home to avoid nosy townsfolk and their church members overhearing their business, their now-seventy-year-old waitress hadn't taken too long to figure out what was going on.

Now Gracie ambled slowly behind the front counter to the rectangular opening between the restaurant and the kitchen. She pounded a bell sitting on the ledge and yelled, "Order in!"

Felicia unfolded her paper napkin and laid it on her lap. "I just can't believe it," she mused, shaking her head. "Norm Katt remarried. To a woman half his age."

"Whom he just met," Mimi reminded everyone.

Jennifer pulled her eyes from watching the cook grab their order ticket and start to read it. Gracie had interrupted a very important news-sharing moment, and Jennifer didn't want to miss any of it.

"And did you hear her name?" Mimi asked.

"Allison." Lisa shook her head, looking as if she were trying to suppress a laugh. "Ally."

As if in a chorus, the women said, "Ally Katt."

"Does the man never learn?" Felicia laughed. "First, he marries Kitty. And now Ally."

"*Oh,* if they have children!" Jennifer said. "They could name one Fraidy."

Felicia nodded. "Twins, of course, would be named Siamese and Tiger."

"Of course." Jennifer smiled.

"You all are so terrible!" Lisa pushed back her thick, reddish-brown-highlighted hair and fluffed it.

Mimi sighed and patted Lisa on the arm. "Oh, we all know it's just in fun. We really don't mean anything by it, do we, ladies? But you do have to admit, it is funny."

Lisa rolled her eyes and shook her head as if to say, "You silly kids." "Has anybody seen her?"

"Not that I know of—I mean, except for their church," Jennifer said. "I guess Norm and his new bride came back to town only a couple weeks ago."

"Well," Mimi said, "that kid's got a tough act to follow. As much as Kitty drove us all crazy, her church adored her. Wonder how they'll take to a new pastor's wife?"

"I don't know," Lisa said. "But they'll definitely talk. I hope she knows what she's gotten herself into."

"Did *any* of us know that when we married pastors?" Mimi asked.

Lisa smiled. "I guess not."

"I sure didn't!" Jennifer said, thinking back to when she and Sam had married, twelve years ago. She had been attending the church as a relatively new Christian when Sam arrived on the scene as pastor. "Being a church member and being a pastor's wife are two *entirely* different things."

"I didn't marry a pastor," Felicia said. "If you recall, I married a businessman who decided several years into his career that he was called to be a pastor. I didn't get that vote."

Gracie walked toward them, carrying a tray of drinks. She set it down on the edge of their table. "I'm getting too old for this. Can you believe they still make me carry my own trays? And my shoulder all messed up from that fall back in December?"

Gracie had taken a tumble on some ice outside Lulu's one evening after work a few months back and hurt her shoulder and hip.

"Is that still bothering you, Gracie?" Felicia asked.

"I still go to therapy for it, but you know those doctors. You can't trust 'em." She handed Mimi a glass of milk and passed Lisa an iced tea. Felicia grabbed the remaining two glasses, each filled with Diet Coke, and handed one to Jennifer.

"Hey!" Gracie said. "You trying to deprive me of my hard-earned tip?"

"Sorry!" Felicia joked. "But you know I'm working from home now. I need all the money I can get."

"Well, you'd better find a better table. These girls are tighter than a duck's behind with their money." She pulled four straws out of her right apron pocket and plopped them in the center of the table.

"I'll be back." She winked, then pulled up the tray against her chest and trudged away.

"Can you believe it's been a year since Kitty died?" Lisa tore the paper off her straw and crumpled it.

"I know," Jennifer said. "I kind of miss her. All the snarky comments about how insignificant our churches were compared to hers. The patronizing tone. The condescending looks."

"I'm serious!" Lisa said. "It was tragic."

"I know." Jennifer sipped her soda. "Believe me, I wish she *hadn't* died. It wasn't a piece of cake for me—going through that miscarriage and being considered a murder suspect in her death all in the same weekend." *There I go again, making everything about me,* she told herself and inwardly winced.

Felicia rubbed Jennifer's back. *That's sweet,* Jennifer thought, realizing her friends remembered how difficult that time in her life had been. She'd wanted that baby so badly. And to suffer a miscarriage, have an all-out argument with Kitty, threaten her, then have her up and fall down a ravine and break her neck . . . It had been devastating.

"Let's be honest." Mimi dabbed a trace of milk at the corner of her mouth. "We didn't like her. But she didn't deserve what happened to her. Life *has* been calmer and more sane and relaxing since she's been—"

"It was a year ago yesterday," Felicia said. "St. Patrick's Day weekend. At the pastors' wives' retreat."

"That reminds me!" Mimi brightened and reached under the table. She pulled up her large purse/diaper bag and dug into its depths. In her hands appeared two shamrock-and-cross-covered eggs that were the brightest kelly green Jennifer had ever seen. She laid them on the table and reached back in, producing one more. "From Megan. She wanted me to make sure to give these to you. We combined two holidays in one—St. Patrick's Day and Easter, since that's this weekend."

"Carys will like this." Jennifer picked one up and set it on top of her purse.

"I wonder what she looks like?" Felicia took another of the eggs and placed it by her drink.

"Who?" Lisa asked.

"Norm's new wife."

"I wonder if she'll come to the next pastors' wives' meeting at New Life next month?"

"I already called and invited her. She's coming." Lisa tore open a packet of sugar and dumped it into her tea.

The table fell silent as Jennifer, Mimi, and Felicia all stared open-mouthed at their friend.

"What?" Lisa asked.

She really doesn't know why we're shocked, Jennifer realized.

"You've been holding out on us, girlfriend!" Mimi said.

"Spill it," Felicia said.

"What? There's nothing to tell, really." Lisa fidgeted a little in her seat. "I called her last Friday. We didn't talk that long. I just congratulated her on her wedding, welcomed her to Red River and to being a pastor's wife, then invited her to next month's meeting." She looked around the table. "Okay. She did sound young . . . and very perky. And . . . she giggled a lot."

Jennifer, Felicia, and Mimi eyed one another knowingly. *Yep,* Jennifer thought, *this is going to be a fun meeting next month. How in the world did Norm go from hard-edged, superior Kitty to an early-twenties cheerleader?*

"Wonder what Kitty would think?" Felicia asked.

Lisa shrugged. "I'd hope she'd be glad that Norm found someone who loves him and is going to take care of him."

Before Jennifer could say anything, Gracie arrived with their food.

"All right, PWs, quit your yakking and help me unload this thing." Gracie pulled the first plate off the tray and handed it to Mimi. Mimi looked at the tuna melt and strip of cantaloupe and passed it on to Lisa. Jennifer's was next, with her chicken strips and fries. Then Felicia took her Caesar salad. Last was Mimi's hamburger.

They got their food situated, passing the ketchup and salt, then Felicia offered grace.

Mimi shoved a fry in her mouth and savored it. "I love Milo, but I gotta tell you, it's nice to eat a full meal without messy little fingers grabbing something on my plate."

Felicia poured the dressing over her salad. "I know what that's like. Oh, the peace and quiet—and adult conversation!"

Jennifer smiled as she thought of eleven-month-old Carys doing that same thing. But her thoughts drifted back to Kitty and the week following her death. Jennifer had been considered—although not officially—a murder suspect and had had to endure detectives following her around, treating her like a criminal, until they determined Kitty's death had been an accident.

"Remember last year when those detectives were following me around?" Jennifer asked, trying to sound nonchalant.

With their mouths all full, the others could only nod and say, "Mmm-hmmm."

"Well, it's happening again. At least I think it is."

"*What?*" Mimi half choked and plopped her burger onto her plate. She pounded on her chest with her fist as if trying to move the meat down her esophagus. "Detectives are following you around?"

"I don't know who it is. But I keep seeing this black town car everywhere I go. Just glimpses of it, really. But . . ." Jennifer knew the whole thing sounded crazy. And verbalizing it made it sound even more outlandish. *Maybe I'm just making this up*. "Never mind. It's . . . probably nothing." She tried to laugh it off. "Just my overactive imagination. You know, with all the sleep deprivation and everything."

"Oh, yeah, I can relate," Mimi said. But she tilted her head toward Jennifer. "You okay? I mean, if somebody *is* following you . . ."

"Why would somebody follow you?" Felicia asked.

"That's just it." Jennifer swirled her chicken strip in her barbecue sauce. "I don't know. I can't think of one plausible explanation."

"Maybe it's a church member trying to dig up dirt on you." Felicia smiled and patted Jennifer's arm.

Jennifer laughed. "No, that would be Lisa with that problem."

Lisa lifted her napkin to hide her face, then let it droop to just below her eyes. Wide-eyed, she looked around the diner frantically. They all laughed, but Jennifer knew Lisa was trying to put up a good front. Lisa had lost fifteen pounds in the last six months, and the sparkle in her hazel eyes had lost its shine. *Poor Lisa,* Jennifer thought. *God, take care of this situation at her church. They don't deserve this. They're good people.*

"What's going on with your church?" Jennifer asked, partly to take the focus from herself, and partly because she hadn't heard an update in a while.

Lisa dropped the napkin back to her lap and shrugged. "Same old, same old. At least Joel is still the pastor—though I don't know for how much longer. He's meeting with the head troublemaker next week to confront him."

That's not going to be easy. Although Jennifer and Sam had had their share of church member issues, they'd never gone through major conflict, as Lisa and her husband, Joel, were now. She ached for them.

Lisa continued. "I just wish . . . you know, if these people are so upset, why do they cause such trouble? Why not just leave? Why make it into a huge power struggle?"

"Because"—Mimi leaned over until her shoulder was touching Lisa's—"and you should know this better than any of us, Miss Assemblies of God, this is called spiritual warfare. The enemy doesn't want the church to be vibrant and powerful in the community. He'd rather take down a church from the inside out than have it succeed."

"Oh, sure, look at it from a spiritual perspective, why don't you?" Felicia smiled gently.

"It's hard to do that, though, isn't it?" Jennifer asked. "Especially when the hurt is so deep."

"Well, sweetie, you know you're in our prayers." Mimi wrapped her arm around Lisa and squeezed.

Lisa just nodded and looked down. Jennifer could tell her friend was embarrassed, because she'd quickly wiped at her eyes.

"How are things in your life?" Jennifer asked Felicia, trying to take some of the pressure off Lisa.

"Actually, can't complain right now." Felicia swirled around some more dressing in her salad but didn't look anyone in the eyes. "My clients are happy. I mean, there are challenges working at home. Mostly because everybody thinks that since I'm home, I'm, you know, sitting around watching *Dr. Phil* and just waiting for someone to put me to good use."

"Oh, yes." Mimi laughed. "Been there. Everybody thinks that we live to serve, huh? Okay, well, we *do,* actually—at least that's what my kids tell me—but still!" She laughed again.

"So that's been a bit of a challenge. But other than that, things are . . . good." Felicia held up crossed fingers. "Enjoy the peace while I can, right?"

Jennifer waited to see if Felicia would say any more. She got the sense something else was going on with Felicia but knew her friend would speak up when the time was right.

Lisa must have thought the same, because she turned to Mimi. "And how about you? How's Dad doing?"

"Awwk." Mimi rolled her eyes. "As ornery as ever. One of the conditions for Dad staying with us is that he's supposed to attend his AA meetings. He's still attending, but he's also still drinking. He does it on the sly, as if he thinks we don't notice. I don't know what to do, honestly. We can't kick him out; he's got no place else to go."

"Where's your mom?" Felicia asked.

"She's down in Kentucky, staying with her sister. She's *definitely* not interested in taking him back. And I don't blame her. Life with my father has never been easy. But when he ran off to California with that woman . . . I can't say I'd take him back either, if he were my husband."

"So instead," Jennifer said, feeling a little bitter, "you, the daughter, have to take him in and parent him."

Mimi half chuckled. "Yep. My sister made it clear she wasn't interested. So I'm it."

"Doesn't that tick you off?" Jennifer said.

"Sometimes, yes. But you know, *I'm* the responsible one." She tucked her short, blond hair behind her ears, something she did whenever she was stressed or frustrated about something. "Plus, Mark and I have been trying to look at it from a spiritual perspective. He's my dad—and he needs the Lord."

Just like my mother. Jennifer tried to push the thought aside.

"Is he going to church with you yet?" Felicia asked.

"No, that's one thing he refuses to do. But we keep working on him. It's really cute to see Megan reprimanding him about not attending."

Jennifer could picture Mimi's precocious six-year-old giving her grandfather a lecture about loving Jesus and getting saved.

Gracie reappeared and dropped the check on the table. "Here's your parting gift, ladies. Hope you have a good week and those preacher husbands of yours treat you all right."

"Hey, how's your sister doing, Gracie?" Lisa asked as Gracie started to turn away.

Gracie grimaced and a shadow crossed her face. Jennifer knew Gracie's sister had been diagnosed with breast cancer a year ago and had gone through surgery and chemo.

"Not good. She just went to the doc last week. It's back, and vicious."

"I thought she had it beat," Jennifer said.

"We thought so, too, but when she went in for a checkup, they found it. It's in her bones and I don't know where all."

"Oh, Gracie, we're so sorry." Mimi touched Gracie's hand. Gracie squeezed it and held on.

"Oh, Gracie," Jennifer murmured.

"That's terrible," said Lisa.

Felicia just shook her head, her face concerned.

"I'm flying down to Florida next week to be with her," Gracie said. "So I guess I won't see you next time."

"We'll be praying for your sister—and for you," Lisa said.

Gracie nodded and let go of Mimi's hand. "I know you will. If God hears anybody, I know it's you four women. Pray hard, will ya? Maybe he'll take pity on an old, crotchety woman and her sister." She winked, then turned and walked slowly away.

Jennifer and the others looked at one another but didn't say anything for a moment.

"I had no idea." Felicia's eyes followed Gracie as she tended to her other customers on the opposite side of the restaurant.

"She didn't let on at all that something was up," Mimi said, looking amazed by how well Gracie had covered up her pain.

"Maybe we should pray for her and her sister right now," Lisa suggested.

Jennifer and the others agreed. There was no better time and place to pray.

CHAPTER 2

Jennifer

Wednesday, March 19

5:15 p.m.

Jennifer pulled her silver Toyota Corolla into the driveway, eager to haul in the groceries before Sam got home with Carys. He'd volunteered to pick up their eleven-month-old from the babysitter so Jennifer could have time to shop and get dinner started since they had to be back at Red River Community at seven for prayer meeting.

We need to start those all-church suppers on Wednesdays like Mimi's church does, she thought as she lifted one plastic sack of produce and another with milk and a frozen lasagna from the backseat. Even though the PWs tried to avoid talking about church when they were together, it was an unavoidable topic of conversation—especially how to streamline responsibilities. Their lives were so tightly wound around their congregations' activities that they couldn't help but talk shop sometimes. Most often, Jennifer enjoyed hearing about the way the other PWs "did" church. Not that she necessarily wanted her church to compete with the other churches, but she knew staying relevant was part of the ministry effort. Mimi's Methodist church's Family Night Dinners seemed a fabulous way to get people out for the midweek meeting (and keep Jennifer from having to rush around!).

At the front door, she stopped to grab the mail protruding from the box, but the plastic sacks around her wrists caused her to drop an envelope. She leaned down to pick it up, taking in a sharp breath when she saw the return address: *Bozeman, Montana.*

There was only one person she knew in Montana: Jessica, Carys's birth mother. The last time Jennifer had seen Jessica, a twenty-something she'd counseled at the Red River women's shelter, was at the hospital, shortly after Jessica had given birth to Carys, the biracial child she'd conceived while having an affair, cheating on her abusive husband, Ron. When Ron had said he wanted to try again on their marriage, Jessica had agreed to place Carys for adoption with Sam and Jennifer, who had been unable to conceive.

Jessica had made it clear she wanted no further contact with the Shores family. *So why is she writing now?*

Jennifer loosened the bags from her arms and set them on the stoop, lowering herself onto the cold pavement next to them. She ripped open the letter.

Dear Jennifer,

Yes, it is me here in Montana. I no I said I wouldn't write or call, but I no the baby will be one next month and I wonder if U would send me a picture of her. Don't worry—I'm not trying to be her mom or nothing. I just want to see what she looks like. I no U and Sam are taking good care of her. We are fine here. Ron got that job with the sheriff's. I am working down at Bessy's for the lunch shift. Ron comes in every day for lunch. He says he wants to keep an I on me. I am so luckee to have a man who cares about me that much, doncha think? He still pushes me around sometime but I no it's only because he loves me and wants things to be good. We're even talking about hav-

ing a baby. Well anyway if you can send a picture that would be good. Send it to the address on the envelope. That's Bessy's and she will C that I get it so Ronny don't no.

Your friend,
Jessica

Jennifer hung her head in her hands as she reread the letter on her lap. *A photo? That means she still thinks about her. Am I going to turn around in Wal-Mart one of these days and find her standing there?*

Wanting to dwell on her worry but knowing she didn't have time, Jennifer reluctantly stood, tucked the letter in her pocket, and reslung the grocery bags onto her arms.

Before going inside, she glanced down the street to see if Sam was coming. Instead, she saw a black town car parked two doors down—the same car she'd spotted behind her a couple times in the last week. Its driver seemed to be watching her . . . although when she focused on him, he lifted a newspaper as if reading it.

I'm really starting to lose it, Jennifer thought as she turned back to go inside the house. *Why would I think that guy is following me? Has this letter from Jessica made me paranoid now?*

Reaching the kitchen, she put away the groceries, pondering the black car for a moment longer. But it was the letter that earned a more prominent spot in her thoughts. What if Jessica wanted to have a place in Carys's life? Could she allow that? Would she? And what would Sam say about all of this?

9:17 p.m.

Sam was robotically flipping TV channels when Jennifer, carrying the envelope from Jessica, found him in the living room. She knew he was in his post-church "zone," trying to decompress, so she dreaded having to bring him the letter and even considered not showing it to him at all. She had wanted to share it with him earlier, but the dash through dinner and back to church left no opportunities.

With Carys down for the night, she figured it was now or never.

"Sam." She hesitated, standing in the archway between the hall and the living room.

He didn't look up but did stop clicking the remote as he stared at the screen. "Hey, that show is on—the one you like with the chef guy who fixes bad restaurants." He glanced over to her for approval, but she didn't move, causing his expression to go from casual to concerned. "What's the matter? What have you got there? Did we get another wrong insurance bill?"

His guess made sense. The insurance company the church used was prone to mistakes. Ever since Carys's adoption, they'd had problems getting the company to pay for her charges. Although Jennifer knew it was just computer errors, every time a bill came back marked *Patient Not a Known Dependent,* it made her stomach flop. The conversations that ensued when she called customer service (a misnomer, she thought) were equally annoying, particularly when one agent asked why she saw no charges for prenatal care in Jennifer's history, as if the employee were trying to discredit Carys from the family.

"Because she is adopted," Jennifer had had to tell her. Though the woman had gone on to apologize for the error, Jennifer was left feeling once again that she was second class—a familiar distinction to her, since Sam was a widower and she was his second wife. But she hadn't expected to experience it again with Carys.

Now here was another reminder: the letter from Jessica.

Jennifer shuffled over to Sam, the letter against her Ohio State sweatshirted chest.

"No, not the insurance company this time. It's a letter . . . from Jessica."

"Jess—" Sam started to question it and then the name sank in. His eyes narrowed behind his wire-rimmed glasses and his face became grim as he tossed aside the TV control, stood slightly, and reached over to grab the letter from Jennifer's hands.

She held it back. "Now don't get mad, Sam. She means well."

He leaned out farther and ripped it from her grip. "Don't tell me how to react, Jen. This . . . this . . . *woman*"—Jennifer could tell that wasn't the description he really wanted to use—"told us she would stay out of our lives. And now she's writing less than a year later?"

Sam sat back down on the edge of the couch and grew quiet as he slipped the letter from its envelope. He shook his head and *tsked* twice while reading, then folded the letter, stuffed it back in the envelope, and tossed it on the coffee table in front of him.

Jennifer watched as he lifted the remote control. "Well, aren't you going to say anything? What do you think?"

He avoided her gaze, studying the TV, so she stepped in front of it, arms crossed.

"Jen, come on. Can't I just relax here for a few minutes?" He jutted his head left and right as if he could see around her.

Jennifer was used to his avoidance tactics, but she sensed something different this time. She didn't budge.

"Tell me what you think, Sam," she pleaded. "Should we be worried?"

He shook his head. "Nah. What could a picture hurt? She already knows where we live anyway."

She slipped over to the sofa and perched on the arm next to him. "Do you think she's having second thoughts?"

"I really don't care if she is or not," he said matter-of-factly, still channel-surfing. "Our agreement is legal and binding."

While she could tell his concerns were deeper than he was letting on, she also knew he wasn't one to get overly emotional. They made a good pair that way since most of the time she was like dry kindling waiting for a spark.

"That's true," she said, but her words weren't as reassuring as she'd tried to make them sound.

Jennifer could see Sam wanted to process this on his own, and she sensed she was escalating the situation by being there, so she left the room and went into the kitchen. One thing she had learned in twelve years with Sam was to turn off the pressure. If she let her emotions get the best of her, he would look at her with the "are you flipping out like your mother?" look that made her feel even more off-kilter.

That's why she didn't mention the town car she'd seen following her off and on for days now. If Sam heard her tell that story, for sure he'd think she was "going Jo Jo," as they called it, after her mother.

The thought of her mother made Jennifer stop opening the Twinkie she'd pulled from the box as a sugar salve for her anxiety. She'd been so caught up with work, church, and Carys that she hadn't realized it had been a few weeks since she'd heard from Jo Jo. *Maybe she'll have some insight on this Jessica thing.*

She dialed the number, the same one she'd grown up with at the same house where she'd been raised.

"Hello?" The voice was soft and meek.

"Mother, did I wake you?" Jennifer had forgotten it was a bit late.

"No, no, I'm not sleeping much these days."

Jennifer's heart sank. She knew that tone and what it meant. "Are you depressed?"

She heard her mother sniffle before she responded, "I guess so."

Taking the phone receiver to the dinette table, Jennifer eased herself into a chair. *I should have known better than to think she would be here for me when I need her. It's never about me—it's always about her.*

While Jennifer tried to make conversation with her mom, disguising her disappointment, she inwardly scolded herself for her lack of compassion. Still, she couldn't help but yearn for a parent, someone on whom she could rely for counsel.

Jennifer knew Jo Jo wasn't that person—and never would be.

CHAPTER 3

Felicia

Thursday, March 20

10:03 a.m.

It had been about a year since Felicia had begun working at home, but she was still adjusting. Having Nicholas at full-day kindergarten was helpful—even if she did have Becky Cohen, her weekly housekeeper, as a babysitter backup—if for no reason other than that she didn't feel guilty being at home and carting Nicholas off to Becky's house, as she had before he started school. It seemed strange to her to have him away from home when she was there, but she knew she couldn't get anything done with a child running around. And since her public relations agency had closed the Cincinnati office, working from home was her only option.

So now with Nicholas in school rather than banished from his own home, she had one less thing about which to feel guilty. And she had a solid six-hour block, from nine until three, when she could work.

That was it in theory, but that wasn't really it, she'd discovered. In reality, her being home meant something different to everyone but her. While she saw office time as just that, friends, relatives, and especially church members saw her only as "at home." No matter what she said or did, no one could seem to understand that her working from home was no different from her going to an office forty miles away. While she hadn't minded the calls, and even did some quick errands to help with church business sometimes, she still felt a lot of pressure to maintain her workload.

Dave tried, but even he was duped by her presence. She'd noticed not long after she established her home office that he'd stopped making the bed in the morning, as he'd always done, and his dishes didn't seem to make their way into the dishwasher anymore. These weren't big things, she knew, but they were signs to her that he viewed her four-step commute to their third bedroom as a wink-wink kind of "job."

If he only saw my voluminous e-mail, she thought, scrolling through the last few days' communications and realizing she hadn't answered nearly as many as she'd thought.

Hearing the phone ring, she hesitated before answering. She knew she really didn't have a choice—their home phone was her office phone as well—but since people at the church slowly had found out she was working from home, they didn't hesitate to call. And not everyone had caller ID. She'd thought about installing a separate phone line, but it seemed overkill, considering she did most of her interaction via the Internet and fax.

She picked up the cordless next to her. "Hello?"

"Hi, Felicia. It's Pam, from church."

Felicia smiled in relief. Pam and her husband, Tim, were a favorite couple of Dave's and hers. In their late thirties like Felicia and Dave, Pam and Tim were the kind of people who made them feel "normal" when they were around—not like the pastor and his wife on a pedestal. The two couples had been to each other's homes for meals, and Felicia and Pam occasionally met for quick cups of coffee on Saturday mornings.

"Hey, Pam. What's up?"

"I know you're busy, so I won't keep you."

If I only had a dollar for every time someone has said that in the last year.

"I just wanted to invite you guys over next Saturday night, the twenty-ninth. I'm doing a little birthday thing for Tim—you know, snacks and cake."

"Oh, sure. Sounds fun. Let me check with Dave and I'll let you know."

After they said their good-byes, Felicia got to thinking about Dave's upcoming fortieth birthday on May 24.

Should I have a party? Who would I invite?

She knew she had a problem on her hands. If she threw a get-together to celebrate, she'd want to invite some people from the church—those to whom they were closer, like Pam and Tim—but she was well aware that the pastor (or his wife) inviting a portion of the congregation never worked. Even the times they'd had Pam and Tim over, she'd felt as though she needed to whisper about it to Pam at church for fear of someone overhearing her and feeling left out.

No, there is no way we can do a party without inviting everyone.

Everyone! That would mean cramming two hundred people into their house.

We could have it at the church, she thought. Their church loved having parties—especially if it was for their pastor. But that would mean involving other people in the planning—and Felicia was *definitely* against that. She already knew Dave was dealing with the whole aging thing, and if there *was* to be a party, he'd want something more intimate, not something where the entire congregation would have an official occasion to give him "over the hill" presents and gift bags.

We can't do that. No one would have fun, especially not Dave and me.

But what could they do to celebrate? It occurred to Felicia that they didn't have any other friends in Red River aside from people at church. She had the PWs, of course, but since their husbands didn't know about their "secret" lunches, she couldn't really invite them. She and Dave had smile-and-wave relationships with their neighbors, but certainly nothing deep enough to celebrate a birthday together. Maybe she could get some of their old friends from L.A. to come out, but she doubted it. They all had young children, too, and that five-hour plane trip would be difficult for them, not to mention the time off from work and the expense. Plus, the Morrisons had just been to L.A. right after the holidays, so she'd seen everyone.

I guess I'll ask him what he wants to do, she decided.

She knew there was something else the two of them needed to discuss, a topic she had avoided but couldn't much longer: a second child. She would be forty herself next year, yet they had never committed to adding to their family.

Felicia thought about Nicholas and the struggles they'd had with him and biting. *Could we handle another one? And how would I do that and work?*

Another guilt pang hit her. *We have a good life, and we easily could provide for another child. And Dave has mentioned several times how fun it would be to have a little girl, someone we could dress up and have tea parties with. Plus, won't Nicholas be spoiled growing up as an only child?*

Still, she knew in her heart she didn't want to start over with a baby. Their lives were so much better now that Nicholas was a bit older.

Is it wrong to take the easy way out?

CHAPTER 4

Lisa

Tuesday, March 25

10:26 p.m.

Lisa Barton stood in the master bathroom and spit her toothpaste into the sink. She'd just changed into her nightgown and was brushing her teeth, thinking about her husband and wondering—but deep down, already knowing—if he was succeeding at what he'd set out to do that evening.

Joel Barton, senior pastor of Red River Assembly of God, was in the midst of a crisis. A mutiny in the church, actually. And tonight he and two elders were visiting one of the mutineers.

Joel had been very concerned about handling the situation according to Matthew 18—the believers' guidelines to dealing with a Christian who has sinned.

As such, several weeks prior Joel had paid a visit to Tom Graves. Tom was a longtime member of the church and youth Sunday school teacher who'd been caught sneaking out of adult bookstores and who'd had an ongoing relationship with someone other than his wife. Although he'd claimed the out-of-state relationship was platonic, *miraculously* it had produced a child.

In the one-on-one visit, Joel had begged Tom to see the error of his ways and to repent. Tom would have none of it.

Now Joel was taking the next step; he'd invited several elders to go with him to again talk with Tom. Before Joel left home, he and Lisa had spent a half hour in their bedroom praying that all would go well, that the outcome would be pleasing to God and that it would grow and strengthen the church.

But several hours later, Lisa was going through her bedtime routine, and Joel still wasn't home. She weakly thought that Joel and the elders might have gone out for coffee and to debrief afterward. But the reality was more likely that he and the elders were still talking with Tom.

At least he hasn't kicked them out. There is that to be thankful for.

Downstairs, Lisa heard the front door shut. She quickly spit out the last of the toothpaste, rinsed, and scurried to meet her husband.

Lisa found Joel in the kitchen, rummaging through the refrigerator. He pulled out a can of generic-brand cola, popped the top, and took a long swig. He was still wearing his jacket and his hair was tousled from the night wind.

"Well, you don't have a black eye," she said, trying to keep the conversation light—at least to begin with. "That's something. The elders intact?"

"A little the worse for wear, but yeah." He sighed and leaned against the closed fridge. "He just isn't interested, Lisa. His heart is harder than a steel girder. Somehow he's twisted this all around to be my problem, my fault, my sin!" He took another drink and lightly belched. "Sorry."

"So he didn't respond at all?"

"Oh, he responded all right. He told me that he had a lot of friends in town who could 'watch' me. And I needed to make sure I remembered that."

"Watch you?" Lisa was confused. "What do you mean, 'watch' you?"

Joel raised an eyebrow.

What? she wondered. His subtle cue was a little too subtle for her.

How was she supposed to figure it out? They lived in a small town and he was the pastor of a church—*everybody* was watching them. They lived in a fishbowl, for crying out loud.

"Think about it, Lis," he said, sounding mildly irritated. He moved to the right side of the kitchen and peered down the hallway. "Where are the kids?"

Now she just felt stupid. He was asking about the kids, and she was still trying to figure out what he was telling her.

"They're upstairs," she answered. "Callie's probably on the phone with Theresa. Ricky's either doing his homework or playing video games."

Joel took a few steps toward Lisa and looked intently into her eyes, as if to see whether she was getting the seriousness of what he was saying. She looked back at him. *I got nothing here.*

He lowered his voice. "He threatened me."

She blinked and tried to take in his words. They sounded dangerous. Then understanding slammed into her mind. *So that was what "watch" meant?* She wanted to lift her fist to her head and thump it. She should have known what that meant. But why would she? How many parishioners blatantly threaten their pastor? She had to stop being naive. She knew they did—a lot more than people realized. So why was she being so thickheaded?

But just as quickly as she had that realization, twenty questions started colliding with one another in her mind. *What do you mean he threatened you? What kind of threat exactly? Threaten you how? Was he serious? Do you really think he'd do something to hurt us? Are you sure? Should we pack it all up and leave town? Should we call the police? Are the kids safe?*

No, she wanted to tell herself. *No way. He's just all talk. He's . . .*

"Oh, my goodness, Joel," she whispered frantically. "The fire. You don't think . . ."

Joel shook his head, but the flicker of fear that passed over his face said it all. Fifteen years before Joel and Lisa had taken the pastorate at Red River Assembly, the church had been set on fire. The tragedy had come on the heels of a dispute between a group of parishioners led by Tom who, against the wishes of the pastor at the time, wanted to remodel the church. Right after the pastor gave his final refusal to support the plan, the church was a victim of arson. Afterward, Tom's construction company did the rebuilding—for twice what the other bids had been, it was discovered later, even though no one did anything about it. Some attributed Tom's success to the fact that his daughter-in-law, Alaina, was church treasurer at the time. Not long after, the pastor ended up leaving.

"Nothing was ever proven, Lisa."

"But it certainly looks suspicious, doesn't it? Now he's threatening you. What's he going to do? Set the parsonage on fire? Have one of his 'friends' run over Callie or Ricky?"

"Lisa, let's not blow this thing out of proportion. He was just angry and spouting off." Joel's calm words didn't reflect his tone or body language—he was clenching his fists, and his shoulders were tightened almost to his neck.

"Okay, fine," she said, trying to match his words. "But he did threaten you in front of the elders."

Joel pinched up his face. He clearly wanted to tell her something but was fighting within himself over whether or not he should. After eighteen years of marriage, she knew her husband too well.

"What?" she asked him. "What are you not telling me?"

He picked up the soda can and fiddled with it.

"Joel."

"He threatened them, too," he finally admitted. "Called them my patsies. They didn't take too kindly to that," he rushed to add.

"What did they do?"

"Well . . ."

"They didn't really do anything, did they?" Lisa already knew the answer before Joel shook his head. "That's why this church is in this mess—because the leaders aren't stepping up to the plate. Well, what did *you* do when he threatened you?"

"I said, 'Are you threatening me?'"

"And? What did he say to that?"

"Nothing. He just smiled and shrugged."

"Okay." Lisa walked to the kitchen table and sat. She tapped her fingers lightly on the table, as if they were a gavel and she was trying to impose some order. "Let's back up a minute. What happened that made him threaten you?"

"Well . . ." Joel followed her to the table. He groaned as he sat, as if the weight he'd been carrying was too much to handle. "I called him to repentance."

"But you've done that before—"

"It's a little different pointing out someone's sin in private versus bringing in several other people to overhear."

She nodded. She could understand how that could be off-putting. "That was it?"

"No," Joel said. "I called him to repentance, and when he scoffed at the idea, I issued an ultimatum."

Instinctively, Lisa knew what was coming next.

"I told him he had a choice. He could resign from his positions at church—including the Sunday school teacher position—stop what he was doing, and get help. Or *we* could remove him from all the positions, and he stops what he's doing and gets help."

She could picture the scene. "Tom probably rose from his chair, turned bright red, pointed his finger in your face, and said, 'How dare you? I helped build this church, and I'll be here long after you're gone.' That about it?"

"More or less." Joel smiled weakly. "You forgot to add the part where he said, 'Who are you to tell me to resign? You think you're God or something? The almighty Pastor Barton!'"

"Were you like, 'Well, Tom, as a matter of fact, I *am* God's messenger. And the Bible *is* pretty clear about calling sinful behavior into accountability'?" She knew that wouldn't have been Joel's response—even though it easily could have been.

Leaning back in her chair and sighing, she thought about the passage from Hebrews 13 and mentally recited it to herself. *Obey your leaders and submit to their authority. They keep watch over you as men who must give an account. Obey them so that their work will be a joy, not a burden, for that would be of no advantage to you.* She knew that didn't mean her husband should hold absolute control over the congregation. And she knew that wasn't her husband's style anyway. He truly loved God and wanted to build God's kingdom through the local church. That was what she wanted, too. Unfortunately, not everyone in the congregation felt that way.

"It's too bad that Tom hasn't read Hebrews 13 lately," she said.

He chuckled. "It seems to me that Tom isn't all that concerned with what the Bible says—in Hebrews or anywhere else."

Lisa shivered from nerves. "He won't really do anything to hurt us or the kids, will he?"

Dread washed over her when Joel didn't answer right away. "*Will* he?" she pressed.

With his eyes focused on a point somewhere near the foot of his chair, he quietly said, "He can do damage. The truth is, there are worse things than something physical that he can hit us with."

CHAPTER 5

Mimi

Sunday, March 30

12:17 p.m.

"Would you *stop* using illustrations from our marriage?" Mimi grabbed the seat belt and snapped it into place.

Mark looked surprised. "What?"

"Oh, no, you don't. Don't you do the 'What?' routine again. I'm serious."

Mark grinned and started the car. "You mean the little story I told about when we took the kids to the zoo and you accidentally left MJ behind but took someone else's kid?"

Giggles came from the back of the minivan.

"I forgot about that, Mom," Mark Jr., better known as MJ, called from behind her. "That was pretty funny. I was standing there watching the whole thing."

Mimi ignored her son. "Yes, that story. And every other story you feel the need to share with everybody in the church to make some point in your sermons. Can't you pick on somebody else?"

"Hon, I'm not picking on you. Those illustrations are great for making spiritual connections. And they make you more relatable to the congregation."

"Well, stop it. I don't need to be more relatable."

"Then you remember, Dad," MJ continued, "how Mom backed into that goat in the petting area? And he butted her?" MJ started to laugh hard. "And she fell into that pile of poop!"

Mark, Michaela, their older daughter, and Megan, their younger girl, joined the laughter.

"Can we focus here, please?" Mimi could feel her blood pressure pulsing. She was in no mood to have her embarrassing past revisited.

"Look on the bright side, Mims," Mark said lightheartedly. "At least I didn't bring up *that* episode."

"Very funny. Is everybody enjoying themselves at Mom's expense?" She was getting nowhere trying to make her point.

Suddenly Milo, the newest—as well as the noisiest—addition to the Plaisance household decided to join in and began to whimper.

Oh, no. Mimi cringed. She knew the routine. First the whimper, then . . .

Milo's voice burst forth in a loud, shrill yell.

Mark exhaled heavily. Obviously he, too, knew it had been coming.

"Michaela," Mimi said, "would you grab his toy truck out of the diaper bag?"

Mimi could hear Michaela rummaging through the bag. "I don't see it."

"Look in the front pocket. I know it's there."

"Mom, tell Milo to knock it off," MJ complained.

If it were that easy, kiddo, I'd bottle it and be a millionaire.

"Found it!" Michaela said triumphantly. "Here you go, Milo."

"Hey!" Megan yelled.

"Mom, Milo just threw it at Megan," MJ announced.

"Let him throw his fit," Mimi said. She had bigger issues she wanted to deal with.

"Dad, can we go to the Clucker House for lunch?" MJ asked. "I'm hungry."

"No," said Mimi and turned back toward Mark. "I mean it, Mark. The church already knows more than enough about our personal life without you spilling everything. How about a little privacy?"

"Guess what I learned in Sunday school?" six-year-old Megan said. "Did you know Noah and Mrs. Noah took two animals in a big boat and it rained for forty-two nights?"

"Nuh-uh," MJ said.

"Uh-huh, too!"

Michaela sighed. "Megan, it was two of every kind of animal and it rained for *forty* days and forty nights."

"That's what I said," Megan said defensively.

"No, you didn't, dummy face. You said forty-two days." MJ always resorted to name-calling when he wanted to make the point that he was right about something.

"MJ," Mark yelled to the back, "what did you just say?"

"When?"

"I mean it," Mark said.

MJ sighed. "Nothing."

"Say you're sorry. You know better than that."

"Sorry."

"The next time I hear you calling somebody a name, you're grounded."

"I'm hungry!" MJ said.

Mimi was used to the after-church scene on their way home. The kids would expend so much energy trying to be good during church that by the time they got to the car after the service, they'd reached their limit. But she was also afraid that their antics would make her lose her battle with Mark. And she was tired of losing. She decided to drive her point home.

"I'm through, Mark. If you don't knock it off, I'm going to stop doing anything for you."

Mark laughed. "Mimi, it's no big deal."

"It *is* a big deal. You talk about me without my permission! And you tell things that don't need to be told. I just want some respect and some privacy."

"Well, I'm sure the church won't remember it after a few days anyway."

"I don't care," Mimi said, growing more frustrated as she watched Mark's grin. *He's not about to stop using us as illustrations,* she realized.

"I need to make my sermons relevant. You know that."

"Find some other way."

"Hey, Dad!" MJ interrupted. "Remember that time we went to Kentucky and we stopped to go to the bathroom and Mom walked into the men's room?" He started to laugh again.

"I remember that," Michaela joined in. "We all waited to see if she'd—"

"That's it," Mimi announced, tossing her hands in the air. "I'm done."

"Ah, come on, honey," Mark said.

"No. I'm done cooking. I'm done cleaning. I'm done doing your laundry." Mimi took a breath and pulled out the wild card. "And I'm through with *you know what*."

"What?" MJ said.

Mimi glanced ahead of her to the stoplight that was turning yellow. Mark didn't seem to notice. "Are you going to stop?" she said, shoving her feet on the imaginary floor brakes. Her body propelled forward against her seat belt as Mark stomped down to bring the van to a halt.

"Never mind, MJ." Mark glanced at Mimi and smiled slyly. "Come on, Mims."

"Ha!" She wagged her perfectly manicured finger at him. "*That* should give you a good sermon illustration."

Mark started to speak when a horn blared beside them. Mimi glanced next to her to find the Magruders, a family from their church. *Great,* she thought as she remembered the last "traffic" encounter she'd had with them. It had been a little more than a year before, when she'd been pulled over by the police. It had been innocent enough—she'd fallen asleep at a red light when trying to soothe her colicky baby, Milo, by driving him around for hours. The Magruders had driven past *twice,* then proceeded to alert the rest of their church—and the entire town—that Mimi had had a run-in with the law.

Slowly she pasted on her sweet pastor's wife smile as she rolled down the window. "Well, hello, Magruders," she said, her voice as light, fluffy, and sweet as cotton candy. "Going our way?"

Bud Magruder, the patriarch of the clan, chuckled. "That was an awfully jerky stop you just had there, Pastor. Did the missus forget another of your kids?"

Mimi forced a laugh as Milo's yells floated from the minivan.

"The light was almost red," Mark said cheerfully and quite loudly, leaning forward to see past Mimi. "Didn't want to run a red light—especially on the Lord's day."

MJ cut in. "Mom was yelling at—"

Mimi reached quickly into the back and snapped her fingers—the Plaisance family signal for "Keep your mouth shut." She laughed again, but more pained this time.

Bud chuckled, as if he could tell what they'd been discussing. "Good sermon today, Pastor. My wife and me just love those stories you tell."

I'll bet.

"Thanks, Bud," Mark said cheerfully. "See you this Wednesday?"

Blessedly, the light turned green.

"Wouldn't miss it! Have a good day," Bud said as he pulled away.

Why can't we live in a large city? Chicago, maybe, where no one would know us or our business, Mimi thought wryly.

As she pondered pleasant, faraway places, her eyes took in her current surroundings. They were headed in the direction of the Clucker House, her least favorite restaurant. For the life of her, she couldn't grasp the love affair her family had with this run-down, cheesy chicken joint.

"Why is it that whenever I'm upset, you drive me to the Clucker House?" she asked to no one in particular.

Mark grinned. "Well, two reasons, really. One, it gives you a break from having to cook. And two, you're already in a bad mood, so I figure you can't get in a worse one."

Mark had apparently recovered from the recent threat Mimi had leveled at him.

"That's great logic," Mimi said. "So rather than putting me from a good mood to a bad one by coming here, you just wait till I'm already put out and plan it then."

"Right!"

Mimi rolled her eyes.

"I like the Clucker House." MJ clearly felt the need this day to add his opinion to everything.

"You like Buster's dog bones, too," Michaela said, laughing, referring to their black cockapoo.

"Isn't there some other place we could go? Especially since you owe me?" Mimi came back to the subject at hand.

Mark looked at her. "I owe you?" he said in a surprised tone.

"That story you told?"

Mark pulled into the Clucker House parking lot. It was already packed with other churchgoers. She could see the Christian fish-and-cross bumper stickers plastered on many of the cars parked there.

"Well, we're here now," he said. "We might as well just stay."

Mimi sighed and shoved her blond bob behind her ears. "Fine." *Why do I even bother?*

"Would you rather just go home?"

"No," Mimi said. "With Dad home, who knows if the house is still even standing. Michaela, would you take care of Milo?"

"Great," Michaela said sarcastically.

"Never mind," Mimi said.

Milo had worked himself into one grumpy-kid mood.

"I'll get Megan," MJ said cheerfully.

Megan, who was petite even for six, had a few pounds to go until she would be liberated from traveling in a car seat.

"No!" Megan, Mark, and Mimi said in unison.

"The last time you 'helped' Megan out, you ended up giving her a black eye and a bump on her head," Mark said.

"That was an accident," MJ said. "If she'd stopped wiggling, I could've gotten her better."

Mimi wished she could say her older son was a kind, gentle, helpful boy. But mostly, he was destructive—even when he tried to be helpful. Like the time he'd accidentally set their shed on fire when he lit a match for light.

"I'll take her." Mark got out of their minivan and moved to the side door.

"Did you see my picture?" Megan said, excitedly pushing an ark drawing at him.

"That's really pretty." He unbuckled Megan and lifted her to her feet. "Let's leave it in the car, though, okay?" He tousled her hair playfully and she skipped off toward the restaurant entrance.

Meanwhile, Mimi was hoisting Milo from his car seat. She cut off the fleeting thought encouraging her to stick her hand over his mouth. The problem was the kid now had teeth—that he wouldn't hesitate to use.

Mark locked the doors and silently walked ahead of Mimi. She followed her family grudgingly through the glass restaurant doors, past the giant six-foot rooster that looked suspiciously like Foghorn Leghorn from Looney Tunes. As she walked past, Foghorn greeted her with a crackled, "Cock-a-doodle to you! Cluck right over and get yourself some goodies from the Clucker House!" She cringed . . . her usual response.

She moved quickly to the end of the ordering line, where Mark was stationed, waiting their turn. MJ, Michaela, and Megan had immediately gone to the playland. Milo squiggled and squealed, also wanting to play, until finally Mimi walked him quickly to the play area and dumped him.

"Michaela, MJ, watch your brother." Michaela, eleven and eager to be a "real" babysitter, as she termed it, dashed over to grab her littlest brother's hand. Fortunately the play area was enclosed, so Milo could yell his lungs out and the adults wouldn't be interrupted. Mimi smiled as she returned to Mark, still in line.

The counter was crowded and loud, with the noises of the kitchen fryers and the drive-through speaker. The dining area wasn't much better, with laughing or screaming children, and adults deep in conversation. *A nice, quiet meal would be good,* she thought as she glanced at the menu hanging above the cashier stations. It looked like it had been hanging there since 1972. *Maybe in Tahiti, with just me.*

"Well, lookie who's joined the ranks of average folks," a gruff, gravelly voice that sounded as if it had smoked too many cigarettes called out, cutting across the room.

Mimi didn't even bother turning around. She glanced at Mark, who wore what she could only assume was the same grim expression as her own. *Dad.*

Instinctively, she pushed her hair behind her ears. Slowly she turned to watch her thin, stoop-shouldered father swagger over to them.

"Buying me lunch, are you?" He laughed and smacked Mark on the back.

"Dad, what are you doing here?" Mimi whispered loudly, almost choking on the smell of quaffed beer and stale cigarettes emanating from her father, Archie Gibson. *You reek. What is wrong with you?*

He looked as if he hadn't changed his clothes from the day before. His thinning gray hair was matted to his head, but it appeared he'd at least pretended to comb some of it. He motioned to a woman behind the counter.

"See that lovely lady there?"

Mimi caught sight of a female employee in her red, yellow, and white uniform. The woman grinned slightly as she shoved fries into their container. Mimi was surprised by how much she resembled Mimi's mother.

"That there's Peggy. I've taken a liking to her, so I'm waiting for her to get off her shift, and then we're going out on a date."

Mimi exhaled heavily. *Great. More fuel to the fire of the town gossip.* "You know, Dad, you could get her in trouble, hanging around here like this."

"I'm not causing any trouble."

"Did you even bother to take a shower this morning?" she said lower, her voice clipped.

"Yes."

Mimi's eyes narrowed.

"I . . . I," he stuttered as he rubbed his hand against his gray-stubbled chin. "I washed up a bit."

"Have you eaten anything today?"

"I'm not that hungry."

Of course not, she thought bitterly. *Why would you be? Your belly's full of beer. Wouldn't want to ruin that buzz!*

Mimi glanced at Mark as if to say, "Would you handle this?"

Mark put his hand gently on his father-in-law's shoulder. "Hey, Dad, how about we get you some chicken? Then after we all eat, you can come home with us and get cleaned up for your date. You want to impress Peggy, don't you?"

Archie hesitated. His pungent beer stench hung in the air.

"Dad," Mimi said, a little softer, "go save us some seats and we'll take care of ordering, okay?" *And this is the topper for my great meal here at the Clucker House. If we'd just gone somewhere else, like I asked . . .* She stopped herself, feeling guilty. This was her father, after all. But it had also been a year since he'd shown up on her doorstep, escorted by Officer Dan McCarthy. He'd had no place to go, so he was now staying with her family. And continually, belligerently, breaking all their rules.

She watched him trudge back to his spot in the crowded dining area.

"I have to be honest, Mark," she said slowly, inwardly struggling with her dilemma. "I don't know how much longer I can take him."

Mark sighed and stepped closer to the counter. "I know, honey. Maybe it's time for a family boundary meeting."

"Like another one will do the trick this time?" Mimi shook her head. She lowered her voice to make sure no one standing near them could overhear. "I know we're supposed to turn the other cheek—especially since he's my father. I'm really trying to honor him. But I feel like I'm destroying myself and my sanity in the meantime. How much are we supposed to sacrifice for him? If he were appreciative or even attempted to respect our family, that would be one thing. But . . ." She trailed off. Standing in line at the Clucker House was not the place for this type of conversation. She was desperate, but still, even she knew the inappropriateness of it.

"I know," Mark said. "We'll come up with something."

"Well, we'd better." Mimi glanced back at her father, who was busily shoving sugar packets into his pants pockets for no good reason. "Soon."

CHAPTER 6

Jennifer

Friday, April 4

4:15 p.m.

"One step, two steps, oops!"

Jennifer lifted Carys off the driveway at her mother's white clapboard house. The tot had squirmed—apparently eager to try walking again—when Jennifer had hoisted her out of her car seat and into her arms. Two to three steps were about her limit, although she'd only been doing that for a few weeks.

Jennifer planted Carys on her hip and kissed her cheek. Carys's milk-chocolaty baby skin was so soft.

"Nice job!" she said as Carys tried to worm her way back out of her embrace. "Now let's go see Grandma."

They climbed the four steps. A couple of knocks at the door earned no response.

"Wonder where Grandma is?" Jennifer asked Carys, who was disinterested, continuing to battle her way out of her mother's arms for another shot at her new skill.

"I'll put you down when we get inside, peanut," Jennifer said absentmindedly while she leaned around the door to look in a window. Nothing. Jo Jo's car was in the driveway. Maybe someone had picked her up?

Just then she saw a shadow through the sheer curtains covering the door's window, followed by a short struggle to unlock the door.

"Hi, Moth—"

Jennifer stopped when the door opened all the way and she saw what stood before her. Then she looked quickly around the living room. A wall, half painted in lavender with yellow trim, was the background for a folding table strewn with craft supplies. Shopping bags, some still full, were stacked on the floor among boxes of what appeared to be small appliances, tools, and kitchen gear.

Jo Jo wrapped her fuzzy green bathrobe more tightly around her, not bothering to smooth her reddish hair, and looked nonchalantly at Jennifer. "I wish you'd called first so I could have cleaned up."

It would take a truckload of Merry Maids to clean this up.

Carys was continuing to squirm, so Jennifer stood her on her feet but leaned over and held her hands. "Mother, what is going on here? Why are you still in your robe at four? Are you sick?"

Jo Jo waved her off, crouching down to look Carys in the face. "How's Grandma's baby girl?"

She lightly tickled Carys's stomach, which elicited a stream of giggles. Hearing Carys laugh lifted Jennifer's spirits momentarily, but when her mom rose again and Jennifer looked at her face, she knew what she was dealing with. Jo Jo's eyes—the googly ones—were the telltale sign.

"Mother, are you taking your medication?"

Jo Jo didn't answer, instead motioning for them to sit on the couch. Jennifer had to lift Carys off the floor to keep her from whacking into the piles of boxes and bags, not to mention paint cans. Once they were settled, she pulled some Cheerios out of her giant mommy purse for Carys to munch on.

Sitting across from them, Jo Jo seemed oblivious to the chaos in her house.

Jennifer looked again at the purple wall, doing an internal head-shake, before she pressed on. "Seriously, Mother, you're worrying me. Tell me what's going on."

"Oh, Jennifer, I get so tired of you being judgmental. Can't you just let me be?"

"Let you be! Are you kidding me?" Jennifer felt fire rising into her neck. "If I had 'let you be' when I was growing up, you'd probably be living in a gutter somewhere."

Jennifer regretted having been so blunt when she saw her mom's face fall, but she knew she had to shock her to get her to talk.

"I'm off my meds," Jo Jo said sullenly, not lifting her head. "And I quit my job."

Don't get emotional. At least she is being honest. "Why are you off your meds? Don't you remember, you feel better when you're on them?"

Her mother looked up at her vacantly, as if she were deaf and needed Jennifer to sign her thoughts.

Carys tried to slide off the couch, but Jennifer slid her backward, reached into her bag, and dug for the light-up cell phone, Carys's latest toy of choice.

"I guess I know what you're saying," Jo Jo finally admitted, "but I was feeling so good, I—"

Jennifer handed Carys the toy and turned back, exasperated, to Jo Jo. "When are you going to learn? How many times do you have to go off the meds and end up like this until you get it?"

"You don't know what it's like, Jen," Jo Jo said in a near whisper as she stared down at her hands, her thumbs twirling wildly. She seemed to Jennifer to be in a tailspin—depressed one minute, herky-jerky with manic energy the next. Not unusual behavior during an unmedicated phase, she knew.

Jennifer looked around the room again. *How much is an adult child responsible for a parent? Where does the liability end?*

"No, you're right, Mother, I don't," Jennifer said matter-of-factly. She wanted to show compassion, she really did, but it felt dulled and unreachable after all those years of dealing with her mom's illness. "But I do know you function better on the pills. So where are they? Let's get you going again."

Jo Jo got tears in her eyes. "Please, Jen. I hate how I feel when I'm on those. It's like I'm in neutral all the time. I don't feel sad, and I don't feel happy. I'm just—"

Jennifer didn't hear the last part of what Jo Jo said because she was already in the kitchen, shaking pills into her hand from two bottles, and pouring a glass of water. She came back into the room to find Jo Jo on the couch, holding a bewildered Carys, as Jo Jo heaved with tears.

Jennifer stood over them—her child and her childlike mother—and wondered if ever there would be a day she wouldn't worry about one or both of them.

"Here, Mother, go ahead." She handed Jo Jo the water and the pills, which she immediately put in her mouth.

While Jo Jo drank a few sips of water and took some deep breaths to help calm herself, Jennifer poked around the living room. *So much stuff! And no job? How could she afford it?*

She slid into the sky blue upholstered chair across from the sofa. "Mother, if you aren't working, how are you paying for all this? Are you in serious debt?"

Jo Jo again wouldn't allow her eyes to meet Jennifer's as she answered. "I think we've dealt with enough today. Let's save that topic for another time. I think I need to go lie down now."

Hearing that her mom's financial situation was a "topic" caused Jennifer's stomach to twist uncomfortably. How much trouble was she in this time—and what would Jennifer have to do to get her out of it?

CHAPTER

7

New Life Church

Middletown, Ohio
Saturday, April 5
9:45 a.m.

Felicia shifted in her generously padded folding chair, moving her arm just right so she could peer at her watch without, hopefully, anyone seeing her do so.

Nine forty-five. Crud.

This was the sixth southwest Ohio pastors' wives' fellowship meeting since the PWs had restarted it last June. The irony was not lost on her—and she presumed the other three women—that they were now running the gathering from which they had *gone* running three years ago due to the plastic facade Kitty Katt had given it. But after Kitty's death, and weighing the strong bonds the PWs had formed as pastors' wives fellowshipping at Lulu's Café, they decided it might be time to revisit the idea of bringing pastors' wives together to contemplate their unique ministry role and, hopefully, to encourage one another in that role.

Finding a location—it didn't seem right to do it at Kitty's church now that she was gone—proved to be a challenge. But once they'd selected a more central location for the region—Middletown, which was halfway between Dayton and Cincinnati, the two main cities in southwest Ohio—the choice was obvious: New Life Church, congregation 7,500. Not only did New Life have a room devoted to women's ministries that was as large as Felicia's church's entire fellowship hall, it had a coffee bar and catering kitchen where they could order in beverages and pastries, giving them one less thing to worry about. Of course, Mimi still brought a large tray of muffins each time anyway, always a different flavor. Felicia had been particularly fond of the chocolate-peppermint version at their Christmas meeting.

Part of the deal in securing New Life's nifty space was that the church's senior pastor's wife, Henrietta Styles, had to host the meetings.

"We lead ministries, we don't team-lead them," one of New Life's facility coordinators had told Felicia when she'd called to see about holding the event there.

Fine, she'd thought at the time. *Less work for us.*

But when she'd reported the requirement to the other three, they'd been concerned that Henrietta, whom they'd seen on television plenty of times with her popular husband, Pastor Shawn Styles, would be another Kitty.

"That hair!" Jennifer had gasped when Felicia told her. "It's so . . . so *perfect.*"

Henrietta did have golden hair that fell from her head in ringlets, reminding Felicia of Rapunzel.

"And have you seen her makeup and her clothes?" Mimi had asked. "She always looks like she just walked off the runway. Reminds me of a movie star."

"She's never even been to our fellowship before, and now she's going to run it?" Lisa had exclaimed.

"Host it," Felicia had corrected.

As it turned out, they had nothing to worry about. Henrietta Styles—"Etta," as she encouraged everyone to call her—was about as down to earth as anyone Felicia had met in her three years of living in Ohio. Sure, she had nice clothes, but she didn't flaunt them. In fact, she showed up at every pastors' wives' meeting in jeans, running shoes, and a cute but not over-the-top blouse. Even her hair and makeup were appropriately softened.

I wonder if she purposely dresses down so she doesn't make people uncomfortable? Felicia thought, reflecting on the times she'd had to tone down her wardrobe so as not to offend parishioners. Either way, she figured, it worked.

So now here was Etta up front, leading a devotional on why God allows problems in people's lives. "People are like tea bags," she said. "To find out what they're made of, you have to drop them in hot water. Who has experienced some hot water lately?"

Felicia looked around. Not one woman of the fifty-two attending raised her hand. Most looked down or away, like a class not wanting the teacher to call on them.

After Etta didn't get an answer to her question, she told about a time when New Life was just a house church and how the small group wasn't sure if they would ever raise enough money to build a church for worship and growth.

Although it was an interesting story the way Etta told it, Felicia recognized it as yet another dodge in almost a year of meetings. No matter if it was during Etta's teaching, the group's prayer time, or even the one-on-one fellowship before and after, Felicia saw a lack of candidness among the women. They could talk forever about how busy they and their churches were, but no one ever said, for example, that they wished some of their demanding congregation members would go jump in a lake. Or leave them alone. Or leave their kids alone.

And that's what bugged Felicia and made her look at her watch. *This is becoming another waste of time, just like it was when Kitty ran it.* She hated to admit it, but the PWs' reenergized attempt at a pastors' wives' fellowship was limping to the finish line.

She looked over at Lisa, standing off to the side after refilling her coffee cup. *How she could use some of these women to tell her everything will be okay, that church splits can have happy endings.*

Then she saw Mimi, her eyes partially glazed over, fixed on Etta, who was now on to God using problems as a way to build character in his people. *Mimi must have character beyond measure by now, considering what she's been through with Milo and her dad.*

Felicia couldn't spot Jennifer, but figured she was sitting behind her, away from the buffet table, since she was always trying to lose weight. *I need to remember to tell her how nice she looks next time I see her. She's so insecure and has no reason to be.*

A few minutes later, Etta closed in prayer and the women stood and stretched. Some headed over to warm their coffee from the urn, while others made a second pass by the table still brimming with doughnuts, Mimi's muffins, and miniquiches.

Felicia turned to see Jennifer, her strawberry blond hair pulled into a jaunty ponytail, across the room. She was wearing black capris and a long-sleeved green knit shirt that set off her fresh, freckled skin, and was quite slimming, Felicia thought. Jennifer waved her over, but before Felicia could join her, someone else strode up to talk with Jennifer. So Felicia joined a nearby conversation.

"I've never been to that conference," a tall, slender lady in purple jeans and a white sweatshirt with an Easter cross on it said.

"Me neither. That's why I decided to sign up. I've heard they share some great ideas on how to reach out to seekers, and we have plenty of those in our neighborhood," said a woman Felicia knew was Ruth, a PW from Dayton. "And it's just over in Indianapolis, so we can drive. The pastor's wife from another Baptist church across town is going with me. Should be fun."

Hearing *Baptist,* Felicia piped up, "What conference is that?"

The two turned to her. "It's called ARMS of Love," Ruth said eagerly. "The A-R-M-S stands for something, but I can't remember what. Guess I'll find out next month!" Then she leaned in and whispered, "But I have to admit, I'm mostly looking forward to a weekend away at a hotel—no dishes to wash, beds to make, or runny noses to wipe."

Felicia and the other woman chuckled knowingly. *That does sound nice.*

On the other side of the room, Felicia spied Lisa and Mimi huddling together—and Ally Katt, sporting two thick braids, a denim miniskirt, and too-high heels that made her teeter when she walked, closing in on them fast. Felicia had seen Ally arrive earlier and introduced herself, pretending not to know who Ally was until she'd said her name, even though Felicia had suspected she was Norm Katt's very young and quite bubbly new wife.

"Excuse me," Felicia said pleasantly to Ruth and her friend, gently touching each of their shoulders with a hand. "I think I see someone who needs me over there."

By the time Felicia got to Lisa and Mimi, Ally had thrust what appeared to be her wedding book—a white leather, padded scrapbook—on them. Several other women gathered behind Lisa and Mimi to look at the photos while Ally narrated.

"That's me getting out of my princess carriage," she said, pointing to a photo. "My daddy got me that because he said I'm a princess who deserves to be taken to her wedding in a grand carriage."

Some of the women emitted "awwws" at Ally's description, but Felicia saw Mimi lift her head just enough to reveal crossed eyes. Felicia covered her mouth to keep from laughing.

Ally continued her explanation of each picture as Lisa and Mimi held the book between them. Mimi turned each page with increasing speed, causing Ally to hold on to the pages from one side so Mimi couldn't flip them until she had finished recounting each element.

"Oh!" Ally squealed, pointing at about the tenth page. "That's our cake. My dream wedding cake."

Standing in front of the book, Felicia twisted her head to see the picture. Front and center was a five-layer white and yellow—*yellow!*—wedding cake, fountains coming off it on four sides. Bride and groom

Precious Moments figurines held court on top of the cake, which was surrounded by Precious Moments paper cups and plates on what appeared to be a Precious Moments–stitched tablecloth. It was striking, but not in a good way, Felicia thought. And she couldn't believe Norm would allow Ally to use yellow so prominently in their wedding when his first wife, Kitty, was known to favor it as her signature color, wearing it on some part of her body at all times (usually her shoes, which made her feet look like bananas, Felicia had always mused).

Felicia heard Mimi take in a breath as she absorbed the photo, clearly unable to comprehend the coming together of a wedding and a children's birthday party on one table.

"Keep going," Ally urged. "I want you to see our beautiful honeymoon shots."

A few pages later, blue skies and palm trees were the center of several photos. "Hawaii." Ally sighed, raising a hand to her heart. Felicia had to admit, the pictures were gorgeous.

And then a shot featuring Norm appeared. He was humped over but smiling. One arm was around Ally while the other supported his back.

"What happened to Norm?" Lisa asked, alarmed. He did look to be in pain.

Ally moved her hand from her heart to her mouth. "My Normy got a little . . . frisky." She snorted.

Normy?! Felicia caught Lisa and gave her the "She calls him 'Normy'?" glance.

"I guess he and Kitty hadn't been . . . active . . . for a while," Ally continued. "And before we knew it, his back was acting up."

Mimi quickly shut the book in an obvious attempt at shutting down Ally's story, causing the other women to back away a bit since there was nothing to see, but that didn't stop Ally.

"Oh, girls," Ally nearly hollered, tossing back her blond braids and waving her arms in the air, "that man was . . . is . . . an animal." Felicia could see many of the women raise their eyebrows at one another and begin to pull away to other conversations, clearly uncomfortable with Ally's tale. "First, it was four times a day. Then it was three. And now—"

"Ally," Felicia cut in, "would Norm really want you telling those things in public like this?"

In a nanosecond, Ally's expression changed from proud to crestfallen. "But I don't consider you the public," she said innocently, her eyes wide as saucers. "You are my . . . my mentors. I'm going to need you older ladies to help me learn what it means to be a good pastor's wife. I mean, I know I have the natural abilities—that's what my Normy tells me—but I think I can learn a lot from your years and years of wisdom."

"Aw, honey," Lisa said as she sweetly hugged Ally, but the bemused face Lisa made mid-embrace made Felicia laugh. Yes, Ally had a lot to learn. But Felicia—and she assumed the other three would agree—did not consider herself a sage at the ripe old age of thirty-nine. Besides, as these women had discovered, there is no training course for being a pastor's wife. That manual would fill a semi—and then some.

CHAPTER 8

Jennifer

Saturday, April 5

2:04 p.m.

"Stop reaching for the wheels or you're going to pinch your hand," Jennifer told Carys as they motored along the path at the Southwest Ohio Regional Park, Carys in her heavy-duty stroller and Jennifer pushing from behind. She'd seen the stroller in an ad a few weeks earlier and convinced herself that if she bought it, she'd get back to walking again now that the weather was breaking. Their other stroller was so flimsy, she'd used that as an excuse not to walk, when in fact Sam could have been with Carys while she walked alone.

Better late than never, she assured herself.

Jennifer glanced around as they moved, hoping to see Father Scott, as she had two Saturdays before. She had taken Carys to see him at the church when Carys was a few weeks old, but he seemed particularly delighted with her now that she was a bit older. "Oh, now look at that beautiful daughter of yours," he'd said as he'd lifted her from the stroller. "Babies are wonderful, you know. But they're really fun to have around when you start to see their little personalities blossoming."

Jennifer noticed with pleasure how easily Carys had taken to him, just as Jennifer had when she'd seen him for counseling a few years ago. His warm, easy manner was an instant comfort to her, so she was intrigued to see Carys have a similar reaction.

Eager to meet up with Father Scott again, she continued walking a little longer than her normal thirty minutes, but after forty she called it a "workout" and headed to the car. Carys whimpered, as if she wanted to keep going, when Jennifer took her out of the stroller.

"Listen, peanut, Mommy can walk for only so long before she needs a handful of Pringles and a Diet Coke," Jennifer said, buckling her in. Carys seemed to understand the joke—a sweet smile crept across her face.

Jennifer kissed her, then shut the backseat door, opened hers, and hopped into the driver's seat. As she pulled away from the parking space, she glanced in the rearview mirror to check on Carys, but something else caught her eye: the black town car was following her.

Is that the same guy? she wondered, trying to look back and drive at the same time. The afternoon sun was angled just right on the town car's windshield, so she couldn't quite make out the driver's face.

Her mind raced. *Maybe it's just another car. But how many town cars are there in Red River? Should I call Sam? No, he doesn't even know about this. Maybe it's just a coincidence. But what if it's not?*

Jennifer stuck her hand in her purse and rifled through it for her cell phone. *I'll call 911. But what will I tell them? "Town cars are following me around"?*

As they got closer to her house, Jennifer started to panic. *What if we get out at home and they steal Carys?* Assurances and fears tumbled through her head like corn in a popper.

Then an inexplicable calm, spiked with resolve, strengthened her body. Passing a street she knew was a cul-de-sac, she took a hard right. The town car followed. When she got to the end of the street, the car still behind her, she made a move she'd seen on *Cops,* trapping the car in the curve.

Without even giving it another thought, Jennifer jumped from her car and ran to the driver's side of the town car. When she saw the stout man trying to hoist himself from the seat, she felt some relief.

Even I could outrun him.

Then reality set in. *I can't believe I'm doing this. Especially with Carys in the car.*

"What do you want with me?" she screeched from about fifteen feet away when he finally emerged. Then she held up her cell phone. "And you'd better not lay a hand on me because I'll . . . I'll call the cops."

Perhaps you should have done that already, Citizen Psycho.

The man smiled. He appeared completely nonthreatening, which allowed Jennifer to drop her guard a bit. She noticed that a couple of kids riding by on their bikes had stopped to watch the scene.

"I'm a private detective," he said, moving closer and handing her a business card. "Why don't we get our cars out of the way here before we really cause a scene?"

Jennifer eyed him suspiciously. "You won't take off?"

"I won't," he answered. "Besides, I just gave you my card. You'd know where to find me."

"Oh . . . yeah." Jennifer looked over to the car, where she could see Carys had—amazingly—fallen asleep. "Okay, let's pull over there."

The man looked to the curb where Jennifer had pointed, nodded, and squeezed himself back into the leather driver's seat. Jennifer jogged over to her Corolla and turned it so he could pull to the side.

They met again outside their cars.

"So who is your client?" Jennifer asked. "Does this have to do with my mother? Some debt she owes? Because we don't have the money to pay it, and . . . or does this have something to do with Kitty Katt's death last year? The cops already cleared me of that—"

The man started to answer her, then hesitated. "Wait, you were accused of killing a cat and the cops got involved?" He whipped out a pad and jotted a note.

"No, no, I was just accused but—" *Why am I bothering to explain it to this stranger?* "Look, buddy, tell me right now who your client is. I can't take you following me around anymore. I have a child! And I'm a pastor's wife!"

She wasn't sure why she'd added that last part but it seemed relevant.

"That's why we're called *private* detectives," he said wearily. "I can't reveal who my client is. But I will tell my client I've done enough surveillance on you. I'm sure they'll be contacting you soon. Have a nice day."

And with that he turned to go back to his car, leaving Jennifer next to hers with her hands on her hips. She glanced in at Carys, who was snoozing away, then ran to catch up with him.

"But wait," she said pleadingly. "I'm just supposed to go along like nothing's happened?"

He opened his door. "I guess you'll have to." He shrugged, then lowered himself onto the seat.

Jennifer watched him pull away, not sure if she should cry or laugh. *Who would spend money to trail me? I can't even imagine that report: went to Kroger, stopped at dry cleaner's, sneaked into Baskin-Robbins. Why would someone want to know about my boring life?*

After she got in her Corolla, Jennifer picked up the business card she'd thrown to the seat beside her when she was moving her car out of the cul-de-sac. She caught her breath when she read it closely:

Red River Detective Agency
P.O. Box 1000
Red River, OH 44321

No name. No phone number.

Jennifer stuck the card in her pocket as tears welled in her eyes. *This guy could have been a serial killer! How could I have been so reckless, especially with Carys? Oh, Lord, please forgive me for not turning to you and instead taking this into my own hands. I know you've entrusted this child's precious life to me. Help me make better decisions.*

Then she wiped away the tears—but she knew she'd be looking in her rearview mirror a lot more.

CHAPTER

9

Mimi

Saturday, April 12

10:23 a.m.

Michaela walked into Mimi and Mark's bedroom as Mimi was changing the sheets. "Mom?" Michaela asked hesitantly. "You may want to come take a look at something."

"What is it?"

"Grandpa's in the backyard."

That's all it took. Mimi stopped tucking in the sheet corner and looked at her daughter sharply. "What's he doing now?"

Michaela backed up a step and shook her head. "You'd better just look."

"Watch Milo for me," she said, nodding toward her fifteen-month-old who was amusing himself in a corner with a PlaySkool Weebles play set. She walked past Michaela, toward the back of the house where MJ's room was. She would be able to see more quickly and clearly from there.

MJ's room was covered with comic books, Matchbox car sets, school papers, and clothes. There was a small path to the bed, which was unmade. Disgusted, and reminding herself that she needed to whip her son and his room back into shape, she gingerly stepped through the mess, trying not to step on anything, but squashing a toy truck in her rush to get to the window.

A year ago, Mimi never would have allowed any room in her house to look like such a pigpen. But that was a year ago. One year can change a lot of things. A year can suck the energy right out of a person. A year ago, she was dealing with a colicky newborn. A year ago, she didn't have her father living with them. Her alcoholic, ornery, belligerent, waste-of-a-man father.

Mimi pushed the Spider-Man curtains to the side and peered down into the backyard to see what damage he was up to now.

Not to disappoint, there he stood, at the base of their giant oak tree next to the garage, holding a hatchet with a rope tied to it. *What is he doing?*

As if in answer to her thought, Archie leaned back, hurled the hatchet up into the tree, and then ran to get out of the way as the weapon raced its way back to the ground.

"Call your father," Mimi yelled to Michaela as she rushed down the hallway. "Tell him he needs to get home *right now*." Mark liked to go to the church on Saturdays to pray over the sanctuary and to finish up any last-minute details for the next day's service, but that was going to have to wait. Mimi had a father who was trying to kill himself, one of her kids, or their garage roof.

"Dad!" Mimi was shouting after running down the stairs and through the back door, narrowly missing little Megan, who was standing on the back porch watching her grandfather. Mimi took her steps two at a time and hit the grass running. Off to the side of the garage, just out of hatchet range, stood MJ, wide eyed and mouth agape. It looked as if MJ wasn't sure whether to laugh or be afraid. Seeing him so close by made Mimi even more upset.

"Dad!" Mimi called again. "What are you doing?" She walked up to him just as he let the hatchet rise again. Quickly she ducked and ran over to grab her son, trying to protect him and hoping that was a safe spot—but with her father's aim, nowhere in Southwest Ohio seemed too safe.

"Whoa, there!" Archie laughed heartily, as if the whole incident were a giant game of tag.

As soon as the hatchet fell back to earth, Mimi straightened and gently pushed MJ toward the house. "Go inside, son."

"Mom," MJ started, "Grandpa's—"

"I know," Mimi said shortly. "Just go and wait inside. Try cleaning your room."

Archie retrieved the hatchet and was again taking aim.

"Oh, no, you don't! Stop!" Mimi walked, hand out, to a face-off. "What are you doing? You could kill somebody. You could have killed MJ!"

Instead of apologizing and realizing the error of his ways, her father smiled and chuckled as she watched, incredulous. "Aw, darlin'," he said, "he was all right. He was out of the way."

His cavalier attitude infuriated her. "That's not the point, Dad. Give me the hatchet." Mimi jerked it away from him. "What were you thinking?"

He chuckled again and pushed a large, calloused, worn hand through his greasy hair. "I was just trying to help."

"Help? *Help?* By throwing an ax into a tree?"

He shrugged. "I heard Mark telling you the other day that he needed to cut down those dead branches so they wouldn't fall on the garage roof." He smiled again and shoved his hands into his pockets.

Mimi waited. Of course he was going to give some other explanation. Of course he was going to say it was an error in judgment and he was sorry. Of course he was going to stop his odd behavior and become a normal, caring, loving, strong father and grandfather.

Unbelievable, she thought when he remained silent.

They stared at each other for a few moments. Her face felt hotter than fireworks blazing on the Fourth of July. Her father's face remained impassive.

"So let me get this straight," Mimi said finally when she realized there would be no more explanations or apologies. "You threw an ax—"

"Hatchet."

"A *hatchet* into our tree in order to cut down the dead branches."

He nodded.

She blinked hard. "And how's that working out for you?"

Archie chuckled again and moved from one foot to the other. "Well, not so good. But then, you interrupted me, so I'm not—"

"Dad!" She glanced over at the back porch. There stood MJ, Megan, and Michaela, holding little Milo. Even their dog, Buster, was hanging out with them, waiting to see what would happen next.

Breathe, Mimi. Get a hold of yourself. The kids are watching. Your neighbors are watching. The entire town of Red River is most likely watching by this point. The Magruders are probably even going to drive by at any moment.

"Dad," she started again, hoping to sound calmer and less agitated. Then she stopped and sighed. What *could* she say? What could she possibly say to get through to him that throwing a hatchet into a tree was unacceptable? And what could she possibly say to her father that would still "honor" him? And what could she say that would ensure there wouldn't be some verbal backlash against her personally?

"This is so wrong," she said quietly, not sure if she was talking to him or to herself.

She looked him in the face. He looked haggard and old. His skin looked like beef jerky.

"I was just trying to—," he started.

She lifted her hand. "Just stop it. Mark will take care of the branches. Just . . ."

She exhaled deeply. A dull ache was beginning at the top of her head. It felt as if maybe that hatchet had actually landed there. Resignedly, she dropped the hatchet to her side, turned, and walked back toward the house.

11:07 a.m.

"This is out of control, Mark. He was throwing an *ax* into the tree—with MJ standing right there!" Mimi pointed at the garage, less than twenty-five feet away. "He could've been killed."

Mark looked up at the tree and then down at the side of the garage. Mimi watched the color drain from his face, leaving in its wake a dull grayish hue. Then, just as suddenly, his face burned bright red. It matched the red polo shirt he was wearing.

"Where is he now?"

Mimi shook her head. "After I confronted him about it, he left in a huff. Said he was just trying to help out and that he was unappreciated and disrespected."

"Call his sponsor," Mark said.

"You think he's still attending AA?" Mimi asked in disbelief. "You think he's not drinking but the side effects of the years of alcohol in his system leave him still doing stupid things?"

"Then call Dan."

Mark's suggestion did seem like the best choice. Since the first day Officer Dan McCarthy had brought her father back into her life after a fifteen-year absence, Dan had been nothing short of a godsend to them. He could have thrown Archie in jail a hundred times over—deservedly—but instead, Dan let him sober up in a holding cell until his shift ended, and then he packed Archie into his car and dropped him off at Mimi's on his way home. And especially prized to Mimi was that he never spoke a word of it to anyone—they didn't even discuss it on Sunday mornings at church.

But she was hesitant to ask him to get involved in this, too. She feared it was too much of a good thing—and she didn't want to cross that line.

"That's not fair to him," she said as she shook her head. "The poor man has already done enough to help us out."

"Then we'll call another—"

"And have our business broadcast all over town?" Mimi shook her head. "It's bad enough what he's doing to our family—there's no need to make it worse by embarrassing us with the church and town knowing, too."

"Well, what do you want me to do, Mimi?"

What *did* she want him to do? *Throw him out to the curb!* she wanted to yell. But what would that solve—except to make her feel guilty and a failure because there was something in her life that she couldn't control.

She felt defeated and helpless. "I don't know."

"Why don't you call your mom?"

Mimi wanted to laugh. "Are you kidding me? When I called her after he showed up on our doorstep last year, she said she wasn't interested in taking him back. Ever. His hatchet attachment surely isn't going to make her change her mind."

"Well, what about your sister?"

"Mark, we've been over this a hundred times. We're it. Nobody in my family wants anything to do with him."

They looked at each other as Mimi's words sank into her brain. She hated saying that. *Why couldn't I have a loving family? A normal family? Or at least a sober one?*

Mark looked back up into the tree where dead branches hung dangerously about twenty feet off the ground.

"He really threw a hatchet and a rope into the tree to cut off the branches?"

"Yep."

"What was the rope for? To pull in case the hatchet got stuck?"

"Apparently."

Mark smiled slightly. "Your dad is a real piece of work."

"Yeah, that's the understatement of the year."

"Well, at least nobody was hurt—we can be thankful for that."

"Thanks for that insight, Mr. Optimism," Mimi said testily.

"And at least he didn't damage the garage."

"Don't give him any ideas."

Mark reached for Mimi's hand as they walked back to the house. She could hear the kids in the kitchen rummaging around for food. As usual, MJ was the ringleader. "Grab me a pickle, Megan. I want to add it to your peanut butter sandwich. You'll really like it." Michaela groaned.

"Promise me we'll get this situation under control. I don't want my kids to have to deal with him like I had to."

"I promise. Things will work out."

She wanted to believe her husband. He always meant well—and he did always seem to be right. She only hoped he'd be right about this, too. But an uneasy feeling settled in her stomach.

CHAPTER

10

Felicia

Saturday, April 12

2:05 p.m.

Felicia walked into the church fellowship hall where the baby shower was about to begin. As she placed her present on the table, she glanced around at the ladies seated in a circle of chairs and immediately recognized that she had overdressed for the occasion. Now that she didn't have to put on "clothes" for work (and no more runny hose!), her only opportunity to wear her collection of suits was on Sunday. So she'd decided to put on one of her favorites that day, a matching purple crepe jacket and skirt with a cream blouse, complemented by cream spectator pumps that had a purple toe cap the same shade as the suit.

"Wow, you're putting us all to shame," called Tonya Lancaster, one of the hosts of the working women's Bible study Felicia attended.

Felicia tried to laugh it off as she joined the dozen women seated in a circle. "Well, y'know, now that I can go to work in my robe and slippers, I can't let these suits get all dusty."

The others chuckled, but Felicia sensed some of them were only being polite and really couldn't relate.

Tonya shook her head. "Lucky dog. The last thing I want to wear on the weekend is high heels." She stretched out her tennis-shoe-covered feet and shook them in example.

Thank God for someone who understands. What was I thinking, getting all dressed up like this for a Saturday-afternoon shower here?

Felicia had always been careful about not shoving her big-city California sensibilities down the throats of those at First Baptist, where her husband was the pastor. She knew the church members initially eyed her suspiciously, with her designer clothes and high-end handbags, and even though she felt they understood her better now after three years, she didn't want to stir up any ideas in their heads about her being condescending or ostentatious. Those sentiments didn't jell with being a pastor's wife.

Heather Dodge, the guest of honor, waddled her way to a plush chair the shower coordinators had placed for her in the circle, nearly stepping on a couple of toddlers coloring on the floor because she couldn't see them over her belly. She was clearly in the final weeks of her pregnancy.

Oh, I don't miss that time, Felicia thought, remembering how uncomfortable she'd been her last month of carrying Nicholas. September was often the hottest month of the year in Southern California, and that September five and a half years ago had been no exception. With Dave in seminary, she was the sole breadwinner for the family, so she'd worked right up to her due date, even making calls from her living room sofa before she left for the hospital after she'd gone into labor.

"Now I know you ladies are going to be disappointed when I tell you this," Nancy Borden, one of the shower hosts, said, "but we aren't going to play any games at this shower."

Some of the women cheered while others erupted in mock boos.

Oh, thank God. My kind of shower.

Nancy raised her hands and shrugged in obvious disappointment. "I know, I know. But I was outvoted by the other shower hostesses. So—"

Tonya spoke up. "I know when my Jakey was born"—Felicia knew "Jakey" was now a college sophomore—"it was part of the deal that you had to go through those games at showers. But these younger girls are smarter now and they just do the fellowship and gifts part . . . and that's what everyone likes best anyway, right? And we're all so *busy* nowadays it's probably better if we just cut to the chase."

Got that right. Felicia saw several women nodding. It made her wonder why no one had taken that stand earlier. But she also recalled laughing until her face hurt at some showers back home during those crazy toilet paper and melted chocolate games. So maybe it wasn't all bad.

"Okay, then," Nancy said. "Let's say a blessing, then you can help yourself to as much cake and punch as you'd like"—she pointed off to the side where the food table was piled with finger sandwiches, cake, nuts, mints, and punch—"meanwhile we can fellowship and watch Heather open her presents."

As people crisscrossed, some going to fill their plates and others hauling gifts closer to where Heather was sitting, Felicia remembered her own shower. It had been given in her aunt Ofelia's expansive Orange County backyard (her aunt's first husband had died, and she'd met and married a wealthy real estate agent shortly after) on a sultry day in early September. Nearly fifty of Felicia's family, friends, and work associates were there, sitting on Aunt Ofie's deck and sipping mock mimosas. Felicia had never been much for babysitting growing up, so some of the gadgets she received were unfamiliar to her. Afterward, Dave had come to help her load the car—the guys had gone to a movie during the event—and she'd revealed to him how scared she was.

"I don't know if I can do this," she'd told him, leaning against their car. "I mean, what if he needs something and I don't know what it is?" They already knew they were having a boy.

Dave hadn't had any more experience with babies than she had, but he laughed and hugged her. "People have been having babies since the beginning of time," he said into her hair. "I think a couple of UCLA grads can figure it out."

His confidence had been a boost to hers. She considered that as she again thought about having a second child.

Maybe I'm back where I started. I didn't believe I could handle one baby, and now I'm talking myself out of another one.

A child's cry zapped her back to the present. She turned around to see Bettina Robins, who had a new baby, Cora, and another little girl, Mabel, who was a few months younger than Nicholas. Bettina had just come through the door, trying to balance baby Cora's carrier while holding Mabel's hand, but Mabel was trying to squirm away. When Bettina wouldn't let go of her hand, Mabel let out a yell and fell to the floor, dragging Bettina's arm down with her.

Although Felicia jumped up to help Bettina by taking the baby carrier, someone beat her to it, so she returned to her seat. As she watched Bettina patiently crouch down to reprimand Mabel, Felicia saw herself: one screaming kid hanging off one hand, and a helpless infant in the other.

The thought of that lack of control gave her a chill. And that's when she noticed it: the beginning of a run in her hose, right down the side of her left calf.

CHAPTER

11

Lisa

Monday, April 14

6:23 p.m.

"These are Christians!" Callie said, splashing her hands in the soapy dishwater and pulling out a dinner plate stained with spaghetti sauce.

"No, honey." Lisa pulled a glass from the dish drainer, dried it, and put it in the cabinet next to the sink. "These are people who *call* themselves Christians."

This now seemed to be a nightly conversation. Dinner came, and with it, more talk about what new rumor or slanderous comment had been made about the Bartons. Not liking that her family was focused on such negative issues, Lisa would always do her best to change the subject. Discussing those things wasn't productive and only made the wounds that much more painful.

Joel had been right. There were worse things than taking a physical hit.

Church members had whispered to people all over town about her family. And they were all lies. First it started with the gossip that some "prominent" members of their church suspected Joel of embezzling tithes, and that, because of it, the church was struggling. Never mind the fact that anybody who patronized Ace Hardware on most weekday afternoons could find him stocking shelves to help support his family since the church had cut his salary in half.

Then there was the rumor that Joel was a sex addict; that he'd made sexual advances to several women in the church—and in the youth group. He also had anger issues, had hidden away another family somewhere in Arkansas, and abused prescription painkillers. He also abused his wife. Plagiarized his sermons. Purchased cigarettes for minors. And was secretly involved in a satanic cult.

The rumors didn't stop at Joel. Apparently, Lisa was on the verge of a nervous breakdown. She verbally and physically abused Ricky and Callie. She routinely stole flowers from her neighbor's prize rosebush. She had been fired from twelve jobs—and that's why she didn't work. She had an eating disorder. Had propositioned a man in their church to try couples swinging. And had gotten pregnant by another man and covered it up by having an abortion. She also abused dogs.

But the worst rumors were about their children. Callie was a drug addict. Ricky fondled small boys and bullied children at school, taking their lunch money.

This evening's dinnertime gossip debriefing, offered by Callie, who had overheard one of her classmates discussing it, was that Joel and Lisa hadn't been married when they'd conceived Callie.

Overly concerned that Callie might think it was true, Lisa told her, "Think about it, sweetheart. Your dad and I were married a full two years before you were born."

"I know, Mom," Callie said exasperatedly.

Joel just tried to blow it off—as he attempted doing with each new wave of malice by making light of it. "Wow, Lisa, you had a longer gestation period than an elephant!"

Ricky, who was younger than his sister by fourteen months, tried to follow his dad's lead on how to react and made jokes about it all. "Mom, were you and Dad married when I was conceived?"

"All right, that's enough," Lisa said. "Let's change the subject. What did you learn in school today—other than that rumor?"

Unfortunately, her success was short lived and once supper was finished and they were cleaning up, Callie started in again.

"Why does God let these people get away with what they're doing?" Callie asked.

Lisa paused. If she allowed herself to be truly honest, she sometimes wondered that same thing. She'd often prayed, *How long, Lord, will you allow this to go on? How long will you stand by and watch your servant and his family smeared in the community and at church? When will you show up and do something?*

But she wasn't about to confess those thoughts to Callie—especially right now. Doing so would serve only to fan the flames. And she wasn't about to do that with her daughter. Her baby girl. She turned from the cabinet where she'd placed another glass and took in the frame of her child. Callie's long, straight brown hair was grasped in a ponytail and her body was filling out into that of a young woman's. Her pink glasses were sliding down her nose as she leaned over the sink full of dishes.

Lisa's heart filled with love and pain at the same time. How could people be so cruel? And how could she possibly protect her daughter? It wasn't fair. They were trying their best to be obedient to God and what was it getting them? Her daughter didn't deserve this. And she certainly hadn't asked to be in a pastor's family. She was stuck. Innocent and helpless.

Across the room, the phone began to ring. Lisa could hear Joel yell, "I'll get it."

"Why doesn't God strike them down?" Callie asked. "I mean, seriously? He did it in the Old Testament. Why doesn't he do it now?"

Callie's words brought Lisa back to the discussion.

Lisa smoothed her daughter's hair. "He will, baby girl. In his time."

"Well, he needs to speed it up. I can't stand having to listen to this stuff and not be able to fight it."

Ricky strolled into the kitchen and opened the refrigerator. "The

Lord will fight for you; you need only to be still," he said, pulling out a cheese stick and an apple. "Exodus 14:14."

Out of the mouths of babes . . . Lisa thought proudly of her son. She hoped he really took that Scripture promise to heart. They all needed to.

"Oh, shut up!" Callie hurled her dishrag through the air and it smacked her brother in the ear.

Ah, yes, out of the mouths of babes. She sighed and smiled in spite of herself.

"Hey!" Ricky flinched and threw the rag back. "Score!" he said when it landed in the sink, splashing water all over her Red River High School T-shirt.

"Your brother is right, you know," Lisa gently reprimanded Callie. "Ultimately, we do need to trust that God sees and that he will take care of us in his time."

Callie and Ricky joined her as she said "in his time."

"I know, Mom," Callie said defensively, wiping the suds off her cheek and glasses. "But does he have to be such a know-it-all?"

"I believe the correct word is *smug,*" Ricky said, bowing.

"Learn a new word in school today?" Callie said, adding a sweetness to her tone. "How about this one? *Dork.*"

"As a matter of fact, the teacher showed *your* face for that one."

"Guys, come on. We have enough people calling us names," Lisa said. "We don't need to do it to one another."

Lisa spied Joel walking toward them from the living room. Once he got to the doorway, he stopped.

"Who was it?" she asked, knowing it probably wasn't good news.

"That was Amos Milner. Jean's been in the hospital for the past three days. She had a stroke." Amos and Jean were members of their church. Jean was in the opposition camp. Amos tried to sit on the fence.

"What? And he's just calling you now?"

"Apparently, Jean made it clear that she didn't want me anywhere near her. She told him not to allow me in the room. Not even to pray with her."

Lisa's mouth dropped open. "How's she doing?"

"Not well. That's why Amos called. He wants me to come—only I can't actually visit Jean. He wants me to go to the waiting room and pray with him."

Lisa couldn't believe what she was hearing. Jean could be ushered into eternity to face her Creator and she was still holding on to anger and a harsh spirit?

"Are you going to go?" Callie asked.

"Whatever hurt feelings I have toward them, I'm still their pastor, their spiritual leader. I have to do what I can."

The thought of Jean being face-to-face with eternity made Lisa forget her anger about what the Milners had done to her family. Now she was filled with pity and fear for Jean. *Oh, God, help her repent—before it's too late. She doesn't want to go in front of you with this hanging over her head.*

She glanced over at Callie. *Well, baby girl, you may have gotten what you just wished for.* Lisa believed in the power of prayer. She also believed in the power of a hardened heart. And a part of her was afraid for Jean. Very afraid.

CHAPTER

12

Lulu's Café

Tuesday, April 15

11:56 a.m.

Mimi walked through the front door of Lulu's Café and immediately checked out the familiar booth in the back to see if any of the others were there. Although she hadn't seen their cars parked outside, she didn't want to take for granted that they hadn't arrived yet.

Seeing the empty booth, she next glanced around to see if Gracie had returned from Florida. She and her family had been praying for Gracie and her sister.

No sign of her either, Mimi thought as she slowly snaked her way through the tables toward the back booth and took a seat.

As soon as she settled in, facing the door, Lisa and Felicia walked in together, each looking springy in their light khaki capris and blue, short-sleeved blouses.

Mimi noticed that they seemed to do the same thing: look around for Gracie, then spot Mimi, wave, and walk toward her.

Jennifer followed within a few minutes, wearing dark khaki capris and a royal blue short-sleeved blouse.

Mimi glanced down at her own outfit. Light khaki capris and a robin's egg blue, short-sleeved, button-down blouse.

"I guess we all got the memo," Felicia said, laughing, and lifting up the shoulder corners of her blouse.

"I've heard that women who spend a lot of time with one another usually get on the same monthly cycle," Jennifer said, sliding in next to Mimi, "but I didn't know it also applied to clothing choices."

Though they spent a few moments joking about what they were wearing, something didn't feel quite right to Mimi. Everyone's tone seemed a little too forced.

She knew her mood could be summed up by the stress in her household caused by her dad, but she wondered what was causing the others to be donning the "pastor's-wife persona." Especially this group—they were all friends. They'd been through terrible times with one another, supporting and being vulnerable. What was going on today?

The group fell silent. Lisa straightened her knife and fork, while Jennifer busied herself by smoothing her napkin over her lap. Felicia looked around the restaurant.

"Any sign of Gracie?" Felicia asked.

Mimi shook her head. "I haven't seen her since I arrived."

"I hope everything's okay," Jennifer said.

"Me, too," Mimi said. Everyone fell silent again, all looking preoccupied. *Such a contrast from the day.* Outside, the weather was an unseasonably warm seventy-five degrees. The sun was shining brightly, *happily,* she thought.

Just then, Gracie pushed through the kitchen door and nodded over at Mimi's table. She walked straight to the Coke dispenser and started filling glasses with ice and drinks.

Mimi nudged Jennifer.

"Yep," Jennifer said. "Wonder how she's doing?"

Lisa and Felicia turned slightly in their seats to better get a view. "I can never tell with Gracie," Lisa admitted.

"It looks like she's getting our drinks," Felicia said as Gracie poured a glass of milk, Mimi's drink of choice.

"Here you are, ladies," Gracie said, plodding over with their drinks. "I took them for granted and just brought what you normally get."

"That's great, Gracie," Felicia said, smiling widely.

I know that smile, Mimi thought. *That PW I'm-having-a-terrible-day-but-your-needs-are-more-important-than-mine smile.*

"My sister died, if that's what you're getting ready to ask," Gracie said, even more gruffly than usual, as she passed out the drinks.

Poor Gracie. She must be trying to hold her emotions in check. Mimi knew Gracie and her sister had been close.

"Now I'm it," Gracie continued. "The last one standing. Here's your iced tea."

Lisa reached across Felicia and grabbed the glass.

"We're so sorry to hear that," Jennifer said. "How are you do—"

Gracie cut her off. "I'll make it."

She probably doesn't want to talk about it, Mimi thought. *I can understand that.*

"I've got a carry-out order I need to work on. I'll be back to get your orders—unless you all want what you usually have."

Mimi and the other women nodded. "That's fine," Mimi said. "Don't worry about us. Do what you need to do."

The women silently started in on their drinks, each seemingly lost in her own thoughts. This was so unusual!

"Okay, what's up?" Mimi finally blurted out. "This isn't like us. This is like what we were when we first started getting together here three years ago. This is like the wives' meeting at New Life we just had. Come on."

Like puppy dogs getting caught digging in a flower bed, Lisa, Jennifer, and Felicia each smiled slightly.

"Just preoccupied, I guess," Felicia admitted sheepishly.

Mimi crossed her arms. "And?" She wasn't going to allow her friends to wiggle back into their cocoons. No way. She needed to hear about somebody else's troubles for a while, since she'd had to focus solely on her own and she was sick of it!

Felicia bit the inside of her lip. "Well . . . I've been feeling the clock ticking lately. . . ."

"And . . . you're not sure if you want another baby," Lisa said.

Felicia nodded.

Another baby . . . I can definitely understand how that can bring on a whole level of anxiety.

"You can always have one of mine, if you decide you want another," Mimi offered. "Really. I know it would be a sacrifice on my part. But you're my friend, and I'm willing to make that sacrifice for a friend."

"Why is it that I think you'd pass off Milo or MJ?"

Mimi shrugged. "Like I said, the sacrifice I'm willing—"

Felicia threw back her head and laughed. This time it felt genuine. "I'm thinking of having another baby. You send Milo or MJ my way and I may change my mind and have Dave and me both sterilized!"

"Oooh!" Jennifer laughed. "She goes for the kill."

The walls are coming down, Mimi thought. It felt good to laugh and be with her friends. "I'd even throw in my father, if you'd like."

Felicia shuddered. "Uh, no thanks. I've got my own quirky family members."

"So which way are you leaning?" Lisa asked.

"That's just it. I don't know."

"What's Dave think?" Jennifer asked.

"We haven't really had a chance to talk about it yet."

"Well, what's your heart telling you?" Mimi asked.

"It rocks back and forth worse than our bushes during a spring storm. I went to a baby shower and felt that pull, but then my head goes through all the practical stuff—the midnight feedings and diaper changes and teething and mess and craziness."

Jennifer raised her hand. "I'm there. And believe it or not, Sam and I have started talking about adopting another baby."

Mimi laughed. "I have a wonderful child I'd be willing—"

"Nice try," Jennifer said.

"Wow," Lisa said, "lots of baby stuff today."

"Well, I'm pleased to announce that I am not pregnant," Mimi said. If she laughed enough, she figured, she could forget about what she was going to do about her home situation.

"Thank God," the other three chimed in.

"I just don't know what to do," Felicia admitted.

"Sometimes there is no answer," Lisa said, patting her hand. "That's probably not what you want to hear, I realize, but . . ."

"No, it really isn't," Felicia said, laughing, but Mimi could tell Felicia was genuinely struggling and wanted some concrete answer—after all, that was Felicia's character. Make quick, decisive judgments and roll with them.

This must be throwing her for a loop.

"Keep praying about it," Lisa said. "God will give you an answer eventually."

Felicia nodded, but again, Mimi sensed that wasn't the response Felicia wanted.

Felicia looked at Jennifer. "So, you two know for certain you want another child?"

"Well, not for certain. I mean, with adoption it's not as if we can run down to the local convenience mart and pick one up."

Mimi was impressed that Jennifer seemed to be in good spirits about another adoption. Jennifer had been through so much trying to get pregnant. They had even had some brief tension in *their* relationship when Mimi had announced she was pregnant with her fourth—the oopsy child.

Mimi could hear the jingle of the entrance doorbell. Jennifer gasped and elbowed her. Mimi's eyes shot over to the front counter where the customer was now standing.

"What is it?" Lisa said. "Your eyes are the size of grapefruits." She turned in her seat. "Oh, my goodness. Is that Seth?"

"I can't tell," Felicia said. "He looks so . . . clean . . . and neat."

A man in his midthirties stood at the counter. He was in new-looking Levi's and a solid, charcoal gray button-down shirt that was untucked, but neat and pressed. His brown hair was clipped close to his head. He pulled a thin stack of cash out of his pocket.

Felicia jumped from her seat and waved, trying to get his attention.

Mimi blinked, trying to make sure that really was Kitty Katt's "secret" son whom she'd put up for adoption when she was a teenager. The PWs had discovered her secret two years ago in this very café. They'd originally thought she was having an affair. But when they learned the truth, they had promised to keep her secret.

I hope that is Seth, or Felicia's going to look awfully funny.

"Seth!" Felicia said, waving again.

The man turned to face their group. A slow smile crept over his face and he greeted them with a nod. He dropped the cash on the counter, thanked Gracie, and walked toward them, holding his bag of takeout.

"Hello," he said, his voice cracking a little. His self-confidence still seemed a little shaky. "I haven't seen you here for a while."

Felicia grabbed a chair and pulled it to the end of their booth.

"Wow, Seth." Mimi couldn't get over how different he looked. "It looks like you've really pulled yourself together."

"God did it, to tell you the truth," he said, barely loud enough for Mimi to hear.

Did he say, "God"?

"What have you been up to?" Jennifer asked.

He smiled.

I think that's the first time I've ever seen him smile. He looks handsome when he smiles. A nice-looking person.

"After my mom died," he said, setting his bag on their table, "I had a difficult time. I blamed God and the church and her husband and everybody else I could. I was even upset with her. But then a friend of mine invited me to a small church in the neighborhood. I liked the pastor, and he talked to me for a long time about my anger and what had happened in my life. The more I talked to him, the more everything my mom had told me about God started to make sense. So when the pastor asked if I wanted to commit my life to God and let him take control of my life and decisions, I realized that was really what my mom had tried to do when she found me. She wanted me to know what her faith was all about."

Mimi was impressed. *There goes Kitty again. We just get into not liking her, and she goes and does something sincere and good. Even after she's dead.*

"I bet your mother would be proud to know the choices you've made," Lisa said, tearing up a little.

Seth smiled. "Yeah. I've really gotten involved in the church. It's small, you know. Nothing like Mom's church was. But it suits me."

"This is so wonderful!" Felicia squeezed his arm. "Your mom planted the seed and invested in your life—and God didn't let it go in vain. He took your mother's love and work and grew it in you. What a testimony to her life."

"That's what my pastor said, too. Listen, I can't stay long. I'm actually grabbing lunch and heading with my buddy to go to Cincinnati. We're volunteering at a shelter down there—the one I used to stay at before I moved here." He pointed across the street to the two-story apartment building where he lived.

"Well, it was good to see you," Mimi said. "God is doing some great things in your life."

"Yeah, thanks. I still miss my mom, though. I didn't think I would miss her as much as I do, but people from the church have been great. So that's helped a lot. And I feel close to her when I read the Bible she gave me."

"Excellent," Jennifer said. "Keep it up."

"Definitely." He rose from the chair and grabbed his lunch. "I'll see you guys later."

He passed Gracie as she was walking to their table.

"Well, he's definitely done a one-eighty, hasn't he?" Gracie placed the tray with their lunches on the table. "What a mess that kid was."

"He just became a Christian, Gracie," Lisa said. "He's doing really well."

"Hmmph. All right, take your food. I'm not here to camp, you know."

The women grabbed their plates and thanked her. Mimi watched her trudge off toward the kitchen. She wished Gracie could grasp more strongly how much God loved her. But she knew it would all happen according to his timing.

"Okay, you're up," Mimi said to Jennifer after she'd offered the blessing for their meal. "What's going on with the person following you?"

Jennifer looked sheepish. "I had had enough—I felt like he was always in my rearview mirror—so I made him pull over and talk to me." She told the women the details of the cul-de-sac confrontation, drawing reactions at her boldness from all three.

Mimi shut off her imagination when she considered what could have happened had the man attacked Jennifer or Carys.

"And I can't figure out," Jennifer continued, "what interest someone would have in me. A detective agency? Unless this has something to do with my mother—she's way off her meds again and I made her go back on. That's why I didn't tell Sam. He doesn't understand her, and this would make it worse. Anyway, now I'm just waiting to hear from this agency or the guy who hired him and it's driving me crazy," she half whined. "Why can't life just be easy?"

"Oh, I hear you!" Lisa said.

"I don't want to talk about my stuff," Jennifer said. "What's going on with your dad, Mimi?"

Mimi had known this moment was eventually going to come. "It's getting worse. He turned on the water in the tub to take a bath. But he fell asleep on the toilet—drunk, surprise, surprise—and the water overflowed. It ruined the bathroom floor and ran down the walls to the first floor. My blood pressure rises every time I think about it, so I'm with Jennifer. I'd prefer not to go there."

"So I suppose that leaves me, huh?" Lisa said, smiling, but it seemed pasted on. "We have a woman named Jean in the church who is in the other camp. Or *was,* I should say. She died. She wouldn't let Joel visit her in the hospital, preferring to have the main troublemaker with her, praying her into eternity. And she told her husband—the fence-sitter—that she didn't want Joel to handle the funeral either. Can you imagine having that kind of anger walking into eternity and meeting God? I'm scared for her. I just don't understand that."

"There are a lot of things people in the church do that I don't understand," Felicia said. "How did Joel take it?"

"Well, it hurts him, obviously. But he's not going to push his leadership on to someone who so clearly doesn't want it. He prayed with the husband. And he's prayed a lot for the family. But it's like he told me, it's in God's hands."

"Any new developments with the church?" Mimi asked.

Lisa shook her head. "Just the usual rotten gossip and mean-spiritedness. But what really gets me is that"—her eyes filled with tears—"for several months now, we've tried to get pastors' wives together to share their struggles and offer encouragement, and nobody opens up. We're all dealing with these same types of people, and we all act like we aren't! It's so deceptive. What's it going to take for these women to open up?"

Mimi nodded. She knew the strong passion that Lisa had for pastors' wives. And at the time she desperately needed these women to come alongside her and provide strength, she was the one pouring it out into them.

Mimi touched her hand. "I know, sweetie. We all feel that. It might never happen. That's why I'm so thankful to have you three. You understand me. And we're here for you. We can't take away what's going on at your church. But we're supporting you and we know that you and Joel are standing for what's right. We're not going anywhere."

Lisa lifted her napkin and wiped her eyes. "Sorry."

"For what?" Jennifer said. "For feeling passionately about the pastors' wives' get-togethers? For loving your church and your husband? For feeling such intense, helpless pain, watching what your husband has to endure? Honey, there's *nothing* to be sorry for. In fact, you just let it out and have yourself a good old cry if you want to." She handed Lisa her own napkin. "Here's another, if you need it."

Lisa looked down at the napkin Jennifer was offering her. It was covered with barbecue-sauce stains.

"Well," Jennifer said sheepishly, "turn it over. Don't use that part."

Gracie walked over and dropped their tab on the table. "Oh, good grief. Are you at the crying stuff again? You girls shed more water than any women I've ever seen." She started to walk away, then turned back. Her pursed lips seemed to give away the fact that she wanted to say something else.

"All right, spit it out, Gracie," Mimi said.

Gracie narrowed her eyes. "I know you gals are supposed to say yes, but . . . well . . . do you *really* believe there's a heaven? I've never believed before. You know how I feel about churches telling you things just to get your money and all. But you four have always seemed to be the real thing. So . . ."

Mimi was stunned. For three years the PWs had prayed for Gracie to turn her life over to God, and for three years Gracie had never been interested. Was her sister's death the thing God was going to use to show himself to her?

Jennifer seemed to find her voice first. "Yes, Gracie. I believe with all my heart—and my friends do as well—that there is a heaven. And the Bible is clear that there is a heaven."

Gracie harrumphed again. "Well, I'm not too sure about it. But losing my sister . . . and I'm almost seventy, you know. I don't know how much longer I've got. Might as well cover all the bases, right? Well, I've gotta check on my other customers."

What other customers? Mimi looked around. Everyone was taken care of. What could be more important than talking about the God who created us for a relationship with him?

"You know, you can ask us anything," Mimi said. "We'd be more than happy to answer any questions you have."

"And we won't even hit you up for any money for the church either," Jennifer joked.

Gracie chuckled. "You PWs. You're something else."

Could it be that God was starting to tear down some of the spiritual blinders covering Gracie's eyes?

CHAPTER 13

Felicia

Tuesday, April 15

8:32 p.m.

Felicia hit the mute button on the TV remote.

"Hey, what are you doing?" Dave asked, lifting his head off the sofa where he was lying, so he could look at her. "It's *American Idol*."

She laughed. "You don't care about this dumb show."

"You're right." He rolled his legs off and spun around into a sitting position. "What's up? It must be important if *you're* willing to miss *Idol*."

"I'll set the DVR. I'm afraid if we keep watching, you're going to fall asleep."

He yawned dramatically. "You're probably right."

Felicia pointed the remote at the TV to record the rest of the show. She couldn't figure out why she liked it so much, but she thought it had to do with that Simon guy, who was so confident, obnoxious, and almost always right.

"Okay," she said, tossing the remote on the coffee table and taking a deep breath, "I think we really need to make a decision about whether we want to have another baby or not. You're going to be forty soon."

"Don't remind me." He shook his head dramatically.

"And I'm right behind you. So it's time to fish or cut bait."

"That's a great way to put it." Dave rolled his eyes and smiled.

"Sorry, I don't mean to make it sound like I'm not taking this seriously." *You're not, Felicia. You've already decided.* "But, uh, what do you think?"

Dave ran his hand through his blond hair. "I don't know. Obviously I've mulled it over. We did have quite a run there with Nicholas and the biting."

Oh, good, he agrees with me.

"But in the grand scheme of things, that time is nuthin'. Look at him now! And wouldn't it be great if we had a little girl you could dress up like your little mini-me?"

Oh, no, he doesn't.

"Of course I don't know what we'd do about child care," he continued. "And it would be tough on Nicholas after being an only child for almost six years."

Maybe he's changing—

The ringing phone interrupted Dave's decision-making tennis match. They gave each other the "are you going to get it or am I?" look before Felicia rose to swipe the phone from its holder.

"Hello?"

"Hi, Fifi. I hope I didn't wake anyone." It was her mother calling from Los Angeles.

"No, Mama. You know Nicholas sleeps like a log, and it's only eight-thirty, so we're still awake." She saw Dave do another dramatic yawn and stretch, and motioned to him to stay put so they could finish their conversation.

"With him sleeping so well, you should have time for another baby." Her mother, Lupita, said the last part of her "suggestion" in a singsong voice.

Felicia rolled her eyes. "Yeah, that's a topic of conversation now."

After a few minutes of catching up, Lupita launched into the reason for her call. "I was looking at my calendar and saw Dave's birthday is coming up next month. It's his fortieth, right?"

"Yes," said Felicia, eyeing him flipping channels even though the TV was on mute.

"That's what I thought. Your father and I were thinking about coming out for a visit since we've never been there. Miguel is doing a good job running the bakery and we think we can leave him for a few days."

Felicia's parents had owned a bakery for more than forty years with only a few vacations. With Felicia's encouragement, they had hired and trained a family friend—Miguel—to manage the business so they could take more time off.

"Oh," she tried to say brightly, though she was caught off-guard. She loved her parents, but the idea of them staying with her for several days was a bit daunting. "I guess we can have a party then."

"Weren't you going to have a party?" Lupita asked with surprise.

Felicia sighed. "Yes. We just hadn't decided what kind or who to invite."

Her mother was silent for a moment. "I don't understand. Why wouldn't you simply invite everyone?" In Mexican culture, carried over to become Mexican-American tradition, birthday parties were large events. Even children's parties included adults, and the food went beyond cake to several entrées and side dishes, plus a piñata.

"People don't do that here, Mama." Felicia tried to be deferential, even though she felt her mother's bossiness coming on. It was a trait among the women in their family. "And I can't have the whole church over," she said, defending herself.

Her mother clucked her tongue. "Nonsense. I will help you. It's a good thing I'm coming, Fifi. You're going to need me."

Felicia got Dave's attention from across the room and pretended to punch the phone. "Mama, I don't know if we will have a big party like you're thinking," she said quickly and calmly. "It's too much. And I'm not sure it's what Dave wants." She saw him nod as if to say, "Good thinking—put it on me."

"But I want to meet your friends and your church people," her mother said, nearly whining. "And of course it's what Dave wants. This is a big birthday. It deserves a big party!"

No one could wear down Felicia like her mother. Although she'd learned ways to deal with her mom's control tendencies over the years, ultimately she found it easier to give in rather than fight it out like her sister Gina always had.

"You know what, Mama? Maybe you're right. With you two coming out, this does call for a fiesta. But that means I definitely *will* need you to help me. Can you get here a few days beforehand?"

Dave shot her an "are you crazy?" look. She gave him an okay sign and nodded to calm him. He shrugged and went back to channel-surfing.

"Not a problem, Fifi." She could hear how pleased her mother was, which momentarily eclipsed the dread sinking into her bones. Felicia loved to entertain—but the thought of that many people coming and going in one day, and the planning necessary to have food, drinks, chairs, plates . . . the scope was overwhelming. And it would have to be at their house. There really was no way she could handle trying to plan a party at the church with all the women *and* her mother making decisions for her.

Felicia was listening to her mother roll through a monologue of menu ideas—"Chicken enchiladas, his favorite. But we must have tamales, too, for a party"—when she saw Dave hit the off button on the remote and rise from the couch. He offered a little wave as he slinked off to their bedroom, clearly wiped out.

Maybe it's just as well that our conversation ended there for now, she thought as her mom chattered on. *Now that I know he is leaning more toward another baby, I can try to figure out how it would work. After all, if Dave wants another baby, we should have one.*

Allowing herself to really consider a second child made Felicia's heart beat faster—the pregnancy, the infant years, trying to work, Nicholas's reaction. For the first time in more than a year, she started hearing in her head the jets screeching to a halt on the runway.

At least there was one silver lining to her angst over having another baby: it made planning Dave's birthday party seem like toasting a Pop-Tart.

CHAPTER 14

Jennifer

Wednesday, April 16

3:24 p.m.

"Haven't your meds kicked in yet?"

Jennifer had given her mom nearly two weeks for the medication to take effect before visiting again. She'd talked to her by phone, but Jo Jo had seemed to cut short their conversations, as if she were afraid that if she talked too long, she might say something she shouldn't.

As much as Jennifer didn't want to, she couldn't help but be concerned. So she'd swung by, only to find the house in further disarray.

Jo Jo, sitting across from Jennifer in the living room, reached down to pull up a sock that had sagged below her sweatpants cuff.

At least she's dressed.

"Yes, I am taking them, if that's what you're implying, Jen," her mom said, making Jennifer feel as though she were prying.

"Then what is all this?" Jennifer did a Vanna White arm sweep. "I would have thought you'd put this stuff away by now."

The shopping bags and boxes were stacked but still taking up more than half the combined living/dining area. To Jennifer's dismay, not only was one wall fully painted in lavender now, a facing wall was covered in green and had the beginnings of a mural on it. In addition, one corner of the dining room had no carpet and was instead home to a small section of wood-tile flooring.

I'm so glad I left Carys with Sam this time.

"I . . . well, there isn't much place to put it away," Jo Jo said. "You know this is a small house."

"Exactly. That's why I'm wondering why on earth you'd go buy all these things." Jennifer wanted to sound less biting, but she couldn't find an even tone. "And more important, I'm wondering how you could possibly afford them without a job. How are you even paying your bills? Are you living off credit cards again?"

Although Jennifer had cut off contact with her mother after leaving home at eighteen, she had reestablished the relationship a little more than a year before. Jo Jo had told her that three years prior to their reconciliation, she'd had to refinance the house because she'd run up twenty thousand dollars in debt.

"No, Jen, I told you I'd never do *that* again." She kept her eyes averted from Jennifer, which made her wary. She knew her mother's illness—when she wasn't on her medication—caused her to lie, among other things.

"So what then, Mother? Did you win the lottery?" Jennifer started to chuckle but stopped when she saw Jo Jo's head snap up as if she'd hit a nerve.

"No, not exactly," Jo Jo replied.

"Just what does 'not exactly' mean? You 'sort of' won the lottery?"

Jo Jo reached down to the coffee table, rifled through a bowl of leftover Easter candy Jennifer had brought (to get it out of the house so *she* wouldn't eat it!), and opened a foil-wrapped bunny.

Her words were a bit muffled by the chocolate. "I'll tell you when I can. Just don't worry about me."

Yeah, right.

Jo Jo brightened. "Now what did you come over to talk about? You told me something was bothering you. It's not me, is it?"

Well, yes, but that's an ongoing problem. "Someone is—or was—following me."

Jennifer had decided to confide in her mom about the town car, figuring she of all people would not think Jennifer was crazy. So she filled her in on all the details, ending with the cul-de-sac confrontation.

Hearing about Jennifer's "chat" with the detective, Jo Jo's eyes grew as big as saucers. "Did you call the police?" she asked breathlessly.

"No, and I don't know why." Jennifer eyed her mother warily. *Why is she so emotional about this?* "I haven't even told Sam, because I don't want to hear how he thinks I'm cra . . . a bad mother doing that with Carys in the car. I guess I figure as long as I don't see the guy again, everything is okay. But since he said someone would be calling me and they haven't, I can't say I'm not a little concerned. Of course, who knows with that weird business card."

"Mmm . . . I'm glad you didn't call the cops," Jo Jo said almost under her breath. Then, seeming to catch herself with her guard down, she added, "Because it might have caused you more trouble."

Before Jennifer could ask what she meant, Jo Jo had leaped from the chair and bounced into the kitchen. "You want a Coke?" she called.

"Sure," Jennifer yelled back. "But what do you mean it would have caused me more trouble? Do you know something about this, Mother?"

"I can't hear you in here. Let me get these drinks—I'll be back in a minute."

Perturbed, Jennifer started into the kitchen to follow up, but as she walked by the dining room table, she noticed Jo Jo's new computer setup with its super-large screen—part of her manic haul. As she leaned in to look at the screen's energy-saver picture, a captivating undersea montage, she accidentally tapped the space bar.

"No, Jen—"

Jo Jo had emerged from the kitchen, but it was too late. Jennifer had spotted what her mom didn't want her to see: the sign-on page for a poker website, one Jennifer had seen advertised repeatedly on TV as having "the highest stakes of any poker site on the Internet."

She turned from the computer to see her mother, a glass of soda in each hand, with a look of terror on her face. "Jen, that's not . . . I swear it's not—"

Jennifer wasn't going to stick around for her mother's excuses. She brushed by her, grabbed her jacket off the couch, and started for the door. But just before she clutched the handle, she stopped and turned.

"This is really it this time, Mother," she said through gritted teeth. "And don't expect me to bail you out of whatever mess you're in. I've helped you for the last time."

CHAPTER

15

Felicia

Friday, April 18

2:45 p.m.

Felicia was just reaching for her keys off the hook by the kitchen counter when the phone rang.

Let it go, she told herself. But her conscientiousness won out. *It could be a client.*

It wasn't.

"Hi, Maria," Felicia said when she heard her younger sister's voice. "How are you guys?"

Maria and her husband, Javier, lived not far from Felicia's parents in Los Angeles. Javier, whom Felicia really liked because he was laid back and laughed a lot, was a butcher. He and Maria had met as teenagers when Maria delivered bread from the family bakery to his family's meat market.

"We're good!" Maria said energetically. Felicia could hear Estella, her sister's three-year-old daughter, chattering in the background.

She looked at the clock. "Hey, Maria, can I call you back? I'm on my way to pick up Nicholas from school."

"I'll be fast," Maria said, instantly frustrating Felicia, who hated to be late anywhere. "I was talking to Mama, and she said they are planning to come out for Dave's birthday. Well, I was telling Javier about it and he said we should come, too. You know—a real family thing. We've never been out to see you, and Estella is old enough now to make the flight easier. Anyway, I checked online and there's a good deal on airfares, so I wanted to see if you thought it was okay."

Felicia felt a mix of delight and apprehension. She loved her sister and wanted to see them, but her house would be bursting at the seams with those three plus her parents.

Surely they're planning to stay in a hotel.

"We'd love it if you could come," Felicia said in a tone bereft of any misgivings. She wasn't sure if it was being in public relations for so many years or being a pastor's wife, but she had perfected sounding one way and thinking another.

"Would it be a problem if we stayed with you?" Maria asked, as if she could read Felicia's mind.

How could she turn away her own sister? "Of course not!" Felicia said. "We'll have to get creative with who sleeps where, but we can manage." *No, we can't! It's going to be chaos!*

"We can always put the kids in a tent out in the backyard," Maria said jokingly.

The kids are the least of my worries. "We'll figure out something," Felicia said. "Is that all you wanted? I've got to get going."

"Mmm . . . I probably should tell you something else," Maria said ominously.

"What?" Felicia was losing patience.

"Javier's not speaking to Mama right now," she said. "He thinks it's wrong the way she's been to Li, so he's mostly just avoiding her. But there have been a few times when we're in the same room and he doesn't talk to her at all."

This was some juicy news! Her mother hadn't mentioned any rift the last time she'd spoken with her. "Are you at home?" she asked Maria.

When she said she was, Felicia told her she'd call her right back from the car. She couldn't wait to hear what had caused Javier—Mr. Nice Guy—to get so riled up he wasn't speaking to Mama.

None of them was a big fan of Li, her older sister Gina's boyfriend. Felicia had met him when she was in L.A. on business last year, and had her doubts about his character. Besides his tattoos and the smoking, he didn't seem like a good match for Gina. Then again, Gina had always been the one of the three girls who did things unconventionally, even in choosing her boyfriends. Felicia had been the first to bring home a non-Mexican guy when she started dating Dave, but that was about the only rebellious—if it could even be called that—thing she'd ever done growing up. Maria was even more compliant, learning the family business, marrying, and settling down in the same neighborhood where they were raised. But Gina—she was the one, when they were teens sharing a bedroom, jumping out the window at night to go meet some guy. Even as an adult she wandered from job to job and apartment to apartment, never following any particular direction. Although Felicia wanted to shake some sense into her sister, she knew all she could really do was pray for her.

Once in the car and backing out, Felicia plugged into her hands-free device and called Maria back.

"Okay, so fill me in," she said.

"There's really not much to tell. Mama invited us over for a barbecue for Papa's birthday last month. When we got there, Gina wasn't there. So after a while, when she didn't show up, I asked Mama about it and she said she wasn't coming."

Felicia took in a breath. Family birthday parties weren't "optional" in her family, especially for her father. Not that *he* probably cared; it was her mother who did.

Maria continued her story. "I thought she was sick or something—you know how you have to be on your deathbed to miss one of Mama's 'soirees.'"

Felicia giggled at Maria's choice of words.

"But Mama said Gina had 'chosen'—that was how she put it—not to come. I knew something was up then."

Felicia maneuvered her car down the street toward Newberry Elementary School. She was relieved to see there weren't any children on the sidewalks yet. "Did you have to drag it out of her?"

"Sort of. I asked if she wasn't there because she and Li had plans, and I heard Mama say under her breath, 'Yeah, moo goo get man.'"

Felicia burst out laughing. "She didn't!"

"Mmm-hmmm." Maria seemed to savor telling the story. "So then Javier got on his soapbox and said, 'Lupita, did you tell Gina she couldn't bring Li?'"

"What did she do?"

"Oh, you can probably guess . . ."

"The shoulder shrug and walk away?"

"Yep. Then I couldn't believe this. Javier picked up Estella with one arm, took my hand with the other, and said, 'We're leaving.' And we did."

Felicia saw a few students trickle out of the school's front doors. "You left without celebrating Papa's birthday?" Although her mother's antics made her laugh, she didn't want to be doing it at the expense of her father.

"That's just it. On the way out the door, Javier put me and Estella in the car and then went back in the house. I was worried he might be running his mouth some more—but he wasn't in there for more than a second when there he was again, carrying the packages of steak. And Papa was behind him!"

"What?" This story was getting confusing. "Papa came with you?"

"Yeah!" Maria said proudly. "Javier told Mama we were cooking at our house, and she was welcome to come, but he was calling Gina and Li to come over. He told her Gina shouldn't have to miss her daddy's birthday just because her mother's a racist."

Felicia put her hand over her mouth. "He didn't! Oh, no one talks to Mama like that!"

"Javier did!" Maria said exuberantly. Then she lowered her voice. "But that may be the last time he talks to her. You know she doesn't take well to being told what to do."

Felicia saw Nicholas running toward the car, dragging his book bag behind him. "Maria, Nicholas is coming, so I should go. But listen, try to get that worked out between them, okay? We can't have a house full of people not talking to one another." *As if it's not going to be crazy enough.*

They ended their call, and Felicia reached across the passenger seat to open the door for Nicholas. He tossed his book bag on the floor, then slid in and buckled his seat belt.

"Hey, Nicholas Nickleby. How was school today?" Felicia asked as she always did.

While Nicholas carried on animatedly about a story his teacher had read the class, Felicia had trouble concentrating. *Eight people in one house for four days? CBS might want to send over some cameras—I'm sure there will be enough going on for a whole season of some reality show.*

CHAPTER 16

Felicia

Monday, April 21

12:14 p.m.

Dave had slipped away from the church for a quick meal at home with Felicia. They'd been enjoying these occasional "lunch dates," as they'd been calling them, since Nicholas started school. It gave them a few minutes in the middle of the day for just the two of them—a rarity with a five-year-old, Felicia's job, and all their church responsibilities. And since both of them were morning people, the time after Nicholas went to bed typically was not conducive to anything but trying to stay awake until the ten o'clock news.

Felicia slid a bowl of leftover chili in front of Dave, who was sitting at the breakfast nook table, then set a bowl of chicken noodle soup at her place and seated herself.

"So how's your morning been going?" Dave asked after he blessed the food for them.

Felicia blew on a spoonful of soup. "Work is fine. But Gina called a while ago."

"Oh, brother," Dave shook his head and dropped a pinch of grated cheese from a bowl on the table into his chili. "Let me guess: she's coming, too?"

"Yep," Felicia said, raising her hand, "but she and Li are staying in a motel."

"Well, that's good, because if we take in any more people that weekend, we're going to be sleeping in the car." He looked at her. "Are she and your mom talking yet?"

Felicia crumpled some crackers into her soup. "Yes, they're talking. It's Mama and Javier who aren't speaking."

"Wait—you mean Javier and your mom aren't talking because of something to do with Gina and Li, yet Gina and your mom are carrying on like nothing's happened?"

Felicia shrugged. She knew Dave didn't understand her family's dynamics. "What's between Mama and Javier is between them. Besides, Mama and Gina have never really gotten along that well anyway. Maria was always Mama's girl. Gina was Dad's favorite."

"What about you, *mi amor*?" Dave rubbed her hand lovingly.

Felicia thought for a moment. "I guess I've always tried to be both. I never felt as if I was more connected to one or the other."

"I always wondered what it was like to be the middle kid. With Don and me growing up, one of us could always get Mom or Dad. But when there's three, it seems like someone would always be odd man out."

"It did feel like I didn't have a place sometimes," Felicia admitted. "Gina was the older, bossy one who did what she wanted, and Maria was the baby everyone took care of. I suppose I just tried to stay out of the way since the other two needed so much attention."

Felicia had never given her birth order much consideration. Now hearing herself analyze her childhood, however, made her feel the tiniest bit indignant. *How come I always got the least attention?*

Dave interrupted her thoughts. "We never finished our conversation last week about having another baby."

Taking a sip of water, Felicia tried to act nonchalant, although she was well aware they hadn't picked up that discussion where they'd left off. She never dreamed he'd be the one to revisit it.

"Mmm, that's right," she said, feigning indifference.

Dave dropped his spoon in his empty chili bowl and chugged the rest of his milk before speaking. "Well, I've made a decision."

Felicia raised her eyebrows and looked at him. "You have?" she said, gripping the table's underside brace where Dave couldn't see her hands.

"Yes, well, sort of. I think you should decide, Felicia. I'm good either way—another child or just Nicholas. Either one sounds fine to me, but I think another child has much more of an impact on you. So I think it should be your choice."

Felicia was relieved for a millisecond—until it hit her. *I have to make this monumental decision and live with the ramifications?*

She shook her head. "No, Dave. That's not fair. I don't want us to be sixty and you say you wish we'd had another one. That's too much pressure for me to handle."

Dave stood and came around behind her. Leaning down, he wrapped his arms around her and said in her ear, "I won't second-guess you, *mi amor,* or throw it in your face." He kissed her on the cheek. "If you decide you want to go for it, just let me know when and where I need to be to . . . do my part."

She swatted him playfully. "I don't think I've ever needed to ask you to 'do your part,'" she said, smiling. "You seem to be pretty good at figuring that out yourself."

Dave let go of the embrace and she turned to see him looking at the clock. "Speaking of which," he said, "I don't have to be back until one—"

Felicia laughed. "Get on out of here, Casanova," she said, pretending to shoo him out the door. "I've got to get some work done before it's time to pick up Nicholas."

Dave wore a mockingly disappointed expression. "Too bad. I was hoping maybe we could get that baby-making thing started today." He reached for his windbreaker.

Felicia rose and took their bowls to the sink. Though it was generous of Dave to allow her to decide on expanding their family, at the same time she felt as if he was copping out on her. She suspected he did feel more strongly about it than he let on. His eagerness to launch into "baby-making" only confirmed her fears.

"See ya later," Dave called from the back door before heading out. "And hey, don't feel like you have to decide about the baby thing *today*. We've still got plenty of time."

"Yeah, thanks," Felicia answered sarcastically. "See you 'round five."

Rinsing the bowls and dropping them into the dishwasher, Felicia wondered how she would make this decision by herself. She was always quick to decide on business matters, using facts as her guide, but this time there were no facts. Just emotions. *How can I make a solid decision with nothing to go on? What if I regret it?*

The discomfort of it all—especially the potential for failure—caused her to stop and close her eyes on her way back down the hall to her office.

"Lord, show me your will in this," she prayed. "Because Dave sure hasn't, and I need to know that what I'm doing is the right thing."

CHAPTER

17

Mimi

Thursday, April 24

11:13 a.m.

Officer Dan McCarthy pulled up beside Mimi in his squad car and honked.

She was on her way home from the grocery store. It had been one of the most peaceful, enjoyable times she'd had in months. Milo only screamed to have a few brightly colored objects (her other three kids were at school), she was able to save almost twenty dollars in coupons, and she didn't run into anybody from the church nosing into her cart to see what she was purchasing. Yes, she'd say it had been a banner day so far.

Mimi rolled down her window.

"Hey, Mimi," Dan yelled over to her. "Pretty quiet nights for you lately. Archie staying home?"

She smiled despite herself.

"Yeah. Mark and I had a long—what I'd like to call 'diplomatic'—discussion with him, in which we reviewed the law of our land, so to speak. He's trying to behave."

"Glad to hear it. How long do you think it will last?"

"About as long as this light we're sitting at."

Dan laughed. "You got a few minutes?"

"Just a few," Mimi said. "I'm coming from the grocery store, so I have frozen stuff I need to get in the freezer."

"Understand. You want me to follow you home?"

"No!" she said a little too quickly. Having him show up at her door at night was bad enough. She didn't need a police officer parading over to her house in broad daylight. She might as well just hire a giant float and megaphone to announce her business to the neighbors. "I mean . . ."

"That's okay," he said good-naturedly. "I don't think I'd want an officer at my house during the day either. It gets people talking. If you'd rather, I can turn on my siren and lights and pull you over."

" 'Cause that would be so much better! No thanks, you've already done that once before, as I recall. I'd like not to have a repeat performance."

She'd met Dan a little over a year before—he was the officer who had pulled her over for napping at a green light while she was driving around trying to get fussy Milo to fall asleep.

Reminded, she glanced in her rearview mirror to check on her youngest. He was occupied with spitting down his chin, but at least he was quiet about it. For now.

"How about meeting me at McDonald's?" Dan suggested. Mimi could see the large golden arches down the street a few blocks to their right. It was MJ's favorite place to eat—other than the Clucker House. "I get free coffee there."

Mimi rolled her eyes dramatically. "Yeah, yeah. Rub it in."

The light turned green.

"Race you?" Dan asked and laughed as he nudged ahead of her.

In McDonald's Mimi settled into a plastic yellow seat and opened her milk container. Milo was in his car seat next to her, half chewing, half gumming some Cheerios she'd pulled out of his diaper bag.

"Milk?" Dan asked as he plopped into the plastic seat across from her with his coffee.

"It does a body good," Mimi said, holding up the container and smiling as though she were the official dairy spokeswoman.

"I love their coffee," Dan said. "I'm glad they give it away free, or I'd be broke. I drink so much of it."

"Mimi!" a high-pitched, breathy voice rang out across the otherwise quiet restaurant.

Inwardly Mimi groaned. *What is it with Katt women? They always seem to turn up at the most inopportune times.* "Hi, Ally."

Ally Katt bounded over to their table and sat down next to Dan, eyeing him up and down. She was dressed in a silky black and yellow blouse and jeans. The blouse looked a little too tight and low cut, especially for a pastor's wife. Her blond locks fell over her shoulders perfectly, as if she'd just come off a modeling shoot.

Norm sure knows how to pick 'em.

"This doesn't look like your husband," Ally said pointedly.

Thank you for that brilliant observation.

"No, you're right. This is Officer Dan McCarthy. He attends our church. Officer McCarthy, this is Ally—Allison—Katt. Her husband is pastor of First Presbyterian."

Dan's eyes widened slightly when Mimi said Ally's odd name combination, but he held his own. "Nice to meet you."

"Does your husband know you're here with a church member of the"—she leaned in and whispered—"opposite gender?"

Is she becoming Kitty? Mimi thought and noticed Ally *was* wearing yellow, Norm's first wife's trademark color.

"No, ma'am," Dan piped up. "It's nothing like that. We're just discussing some unfinished business about a mutual friend."

"I could help!" Ally sounded like an excited teenager. "I have *lots* of friends."

"Ally," Mimi said, hoping to change the subject, "what brings you to McDonald's? I thought you were anti–fast food."

"Well," Ally said, smiling as though she had a wonderful secret, "my Normy loves their French fries."

Normy! I'll never be able to hear that without giggling.

Dan looked confused.

"I just can't say no to that man," Ally continued, oblivious. "His first wife, Kitty, never let him eat *anything*. So I say, if he wants fries, give him fries. You know what they say: the way to a man's stomach is through his heart."

"Is that what they say?" Mimi knew she should correct Ally, but couldn't help herself. This was too much fun.

"Oh, sure," Ally continued. "You've never heard that saying? It's older, probably from your generation or something. Anyway, since I don't cook, the least I can do is drive over and pick these up for him." She twisted the small white bag. Then, as if seeing Milo for the first time, Ally jumped up and bent over him. "Is this your baby? Oh, he's a cutie! Normy and I are going to try for a baby. Well, I want to, but he's not so sure—already having his kids and all. Did you know his daughter's a year older than me?" She giggled. "I don't make her call me Mom or anything, though. That would be too weird, don't you think?" She looked at Milo again. "Hi, sweetie peetie. You sure are a looker. You gonna grow up and be a pastor, too?"

"He's got the vocal chords for it," Dan said and sipped his coffee.

"That's funny!" Ally said. "I'll have to tell my husband that. Well, I should really go before these fries get cold. See you in a few at the pastors' wives' meeting. Those are so nice! You older women really put on a good time. Gotta run! 'Bye!"

Mimi felt as if she'd just run a marathon trying to keep up with Ally's cadence. *And what was the crack about my generation? And older women?*

"You older women are really something," Dan said, as if reading her mind. He grinned widely, brightening his mildly sunburned face. His light brownish-red hair and fair skin didn't react well to being in the sunshine all the time, even when he wore his police officer's hat.

He should wear sunscreen or something, she thought, then caught herself. *Ugh. I* am *getting old! I'm starting to act like his mother! And he's not that much younger than I am.*

"Okay, watch it there, youngster," she said, trying to play along.

Dan laughed, then took another sip of his coffee. "Listen, I can't stay long. I do have a job—catching speeders and other breakers of the law."

Mimi could tell he was trying to keep the conversation light.

"Your dad is supposed to be attending AA meetings at the Elks Club, right?"

Mimi nodded. "He quit going, but we told him he had to start back up or he couldn't stay with us any longer."

"Well, there's probably a good chance he's going to quit again. He seems to have a follow-through issue."

"You could say that."

"I drive right by the Elks Club every night on my way home. If you want, I could pick him up and drop him off some nights for meetings. I wouldn't be in the squad car. I'd make sure it was real quiet and all."

Why is he doing this? "Oh, Dan, that's really thoughtful of you, but I can't ask you to do that. You've already done so much."

"It's not a problem. Really. Plus, you're not asking; I'm offering."

She paused for a moment, suspicious and wondering if she should dig deeper. "Why?"

"Excuse me?"

"Why are you offering?"

"Because you're the pastor's wife."

Mimi laughed.

"What's so funny?" Dan asked.

"Well, most people don't offer that kind of support to a pastor's wife."

"Really?" He looked genuinely surprised.

"Really. Oh, most people love to bring over a casserole if the pastor's sick. They'll offer advice for a troubled pastor's kid. But you're really going out of your way to help—in a very ugly situation. Most people won't do that. So why are you offering?"

"As you know, I admire and respect your husband. He's a good man. A godly man. The real deal."

"I completely agree."

"I mean, since I've been a Christian, he's taken me under his wing, so to speak, and helped me understand what faith is all about and why hope is such a good thing. I owe him a lot."

Mimi had been amazed when Dan started to attend their church a year ago. He'd come at the pressuring of his aunt, a faithful attender of Trinity United Methodist. It almost seemed like he showed up against his will, but he appeared to soak up Mark's teaching. When he finally became a Christian after six months there, Dan totally changed. He couldn't get enough of reading the Bible and wanting to talk about God. In fact, every chance he got, he'd begun to witness to people. When handing them speeding tickets, he'd try to work in a comment about eternity. When arresting people, he'd slip them friendly Christian tracts and ask Mark to come visit. In fact, Dan had easily doubled Mark's schedule with visitation opportunities.

"And I know you've been under a lot of pressure. What with all those kids and all the baking and volunteering you do. And then with little Milo here and what a ruckus he made the first several months of his life."

Get to the point. Where's this going?

"Your family has had it tough. And I know Archie hasn't made life any easier for you. But I admire how you've stuck with him—even when I'm sure you've wanted to throw him out on the street. But instead you've continued to show him Christ's love."

If you only knew how much I haven't done that! she thought, now feeling a little guilty.

"Anyway, this is my opportunity to serve you and your family. To give back a little of what you've given me."

"But, Dan, this is too much. Really."

He shook his head and pinched at the coffee lid. "My dad was an alcoholic, too."

Mimi leaned back in her chair, stunned. "You never told me that."

"It's not exactly something that I'm proud to go around announcing."

She understood that all too well. "Where is he now?"

"Dead," he said heavily.

"I'm so sorry, Dan."

"Thanks. He basically drank himself to death. His liver couldn't take it anymore. He died four years ago. I was pretty angry with him at the end. When he didn't drink, he was great. A great dad. A lot of fun. But that was mostly when I was little. When he drank, he became useless. Then he lost his job and drinking became his profession. But the worst part was that I never told him I loved him. I was too ashamed of him. In the last year, since I became a Christian, I've really dealt with that—and I think your dad has brought it to the forefront for me."

Mimi turned her attention to Milo to keep from crying. When her dad died, would she have to deal with this same emotion? But she had taken him in, right? She was doing right by her father. Right? The hole in her stomach wasn't reassuring her.

"Is helping my father maybe a chance for you to make it up to your dad?" she said, still not looking at him.

He tapped the side of his coffee cup a few times, then inhaled loudly. "Maybe it is. Either way, I'd like to help. It's what Jesus would do, I believe."

For some unknown reason, Mimi suddenly found herself pouring out her feelings to Dan. "When you first started attending Trinity, I didn't like you very much. I blamed it on the fact that you'd given me that ticket. But Mark saw right through it, and he confronted me about it. And he was right. It wasn't the ticket. Okay, well, it was the ticket. But it was something deeper. My dad was arrested when I was eight years old. He shot our neighbor in his butt. They'd gotten into an argument over the backyard fence, of all the stupid things. So my dad went down to our basement, dusted off his BB gun, and fired away. I hid behind the basement door when they came to arrest him. He was angry and mean and fought the policemen. Looking back on it now, I think as an eight-year-old I didn't really understand what my dad had done and I didn't want to believe he could be a bad person, so I turned it on the police. It was their fault. And somehow I never got over that. I thought I'd pushed it down, but"—she shrugged—"apparently not down far enough. Because it came back to nail you."

"I understand."

"No, it's not right. I spent the first several months not liking you—and feeling guilty about it. When all you'd done was your job. Now you were on my turf—the church—and you were seeking answers about God. And I didn't want to give them to you. That was so wrong of me. I'm really sorry. A pastor's wife shouldn't be that way, huh?" A tear trickled down her cheek.

Looking uncomfortable, Dan shifted in his seat and stared intently at his coffee. "Don't worry about it," he said finally to break the silence. "That's why we all need a savior—even really spiritual people. That's what my aunt used to tell me before I became a Christian."

She smiled weakly. She knew this guy was on fire for Christ. She had forgotten what it was like to be a new Christian.

"Well? Would you like me to pick him up?"

"I'd like that. But only as long as it doesn't become a hassle."

"No problem. I can handle Archie."

Yeah, well, I sure wish I could. "Thanks, Dan. You're an okay guy."

His radio, attached to the side of his belt, crackled awake. "McCarthy, can you check out a stalled car on Washington?"

Dan smiled at Mimi and grabbed his radio. "Looks like my coffee break's over. I'll see you Sunday. Say hey to Pastor for me."

"I will. See you." Just then she remembered her frozen food, probably half thawed by that point. *Oh well,* she thought, picking up Milo. *Guess tonight's meal will be all that not so frozen food.*

CHAPTER 18

Lisa

Friday, April 25

11:47 a.m.

Breaker Hill Pancake House was packed when Lisa arrived. She stepped through the crowd of people crammed into the waiting area about the size of a postage stamp and scanned the tables to find her mother. When she didn't see her at any of the tables or booths, she looked at the others waiting with her.

This is a first, she thought, proud that she'd made it to their weekly lunch date before her always-ten-minutes-early-to-everything mother.

She squeezed her way between an obese man with a walker and a tiny, frail woman wearing too much makeup and way too much Opium.

"Two for Barton," she told the hostess, trying not to choke on the perfume. *Wow, they need to have a perfume and a nonperfume section in restaurants now.* Just as she turned to make her way across the waiting area and as far from the Cologned Wonder as she could, she heard her mother's commanding voice.

"Well, this is a surprise."

Lisa tried to smile brightly as she watched her mother, Lydia

Jenkins, walk regally toward her. She was dressed in a gray silk button-down blouse, a black skirt that fell to just below her knees, and black pumps. Her salt-and-pepper hair was neatly pinned in a bun at the nape of her neck, a style she wore when out in public. Lisa had always thought her mother could be pretty if it weren't for the harsh crow's-feet around her eyes and the constant half frown she wore.

"Hi, Mom." Lisa formally hugged her mother. It wasn't a hug of affection, more of duty.

"I don't think you've ever beaten me here. What happened?"

"Oh, I don't know. Just lucky, I guess."

Her mother pursed her lips as if she were about to say something, then smiled politely. "Did you put our names in?"

"Yes, just a few minutes ago. But I can't believe how busy it is today."

"Well, it is Friday. You know it's always busy on Friday."

"Yes, that's true. How was your drive in?"

"Fine. Nothing particularly noteworthy." Lydia lived in Red River's neighboring town, Cloverdale. It wasn't far, but the drive between the two was all country roads.

"The weather's been holding up nicely," Lisa said, sorry that the best the conversation could get was to discuss the weather. Pretty pathetic, considering it was sunny and fifty degrees.

"It's spring. Of course it's going to be nicer than winter," her mother said, pulling some hand lotion from her purse.

Lisa turned slightly so she could gaze out the front windows. She loved her mother; she just didn't love their relationship. She wanted it to be more . . . more affectionate, more girlfriendy, more fun.

From the outside, Lisa knew that people would think their relationship was strong, one of mutual respect. After all, they got together every week at Breaker Hill for lunch. They were both pastors' wives. People probably thought they got together to encourage each other in their ministry and do some mother-daughter bonding.

But it was more complicated than that.

Mainly, Lisa met her mother every week out of respect and to honor her because her mother had requested it. It was the thing to do. And above all, she knew her mother valued the commandment that said, "Honor your mother and father." She'd reminded Lisa of that on more than one occasion.

But Lisa also continued to meet with her mother because deep down within her soul, Lisa had a well of eternal hope that promised that *one* day her mother would change. That Lydia would remove that mantle of pastor's wife—the mantle she wore even at home around her children and grandchildren—and would become the mother Lisa longed for her to be in their relationship. A mother who wanted to go shopping, who fussed over Lisa, who encouraged her. Who told her she loved her.

Rationality would sometimes overcome Lisa and she'd realize, *My mother is sixty-five years old. She's not going to change.* But then hope would chime in, *Anyone can change. It's not too late for my mother.*

Maybe today was the day Lydia would surprise her. It hadn't gotten off to a promising start—pretty predictabley, really. But after a little noshing, maybe?

"Barton, party of two," the hostess called out above the din of the crowd.

Thank you! Lisa smiled cheerfully at the hostess and followed her.

They were fortunate to get a booth by the windows. The sun beaming through would keep Lisa warm—at least on the outside.

"We won't need those," Lydia told the hostess, nodding toward the menus. "We already know what we're going to have."

They settled into their booth and within a few moments, the waitress came to their table. Lisa blinked several times in disbelief.

In a bright pink, short-skirted uniform and matching pink high heels, stood Allison Katt.

"Oh, my goodness!" Ally threw a hand to her hip. "Lisa Barton! How are you? I didn't know you came here. And this must be . . ." She turned toward Lydia and put out her hand to shake.

"This is my mother, Lydia Jenkins. Mom," Lisa said, still shocked by this turn of events, "this is Allison Katt, Norman's wife, from over at First Pres."

Lydia's eyes grew large for a moment before she regained her composure. Then she smiled and graciously took her waitress's hand. "It's a pleasure, Allison."

"Oh, call me Ally. Everybody does."

"How are you"—Lydia seemed at a loss—"getting settled into church life?"

"I love it—"

"Miss?" The customer from the booth behind Lydia leaned over to Ally to get her attention.

Keeping her eyes focused on Lydia, she waved her hand at the customer. "I'll be with you in just a minute. Everybody's been so nice to me at the church. They all still miss Kitty, I know. But they're just sweet as can be."

"Ally," Lisa asked, "why are you working here?" Ally didn't seem the type: (a) to work or; (b) to work as a waitress. And she couldn't believe Norm would be that fond of the situation. His first wife, Kitty, had always been clear about the fact that her husband was the pastor of the largest church in the county. She never would have deigned to take a *job*. Now Ally was waitressing? What was going on?

"Oh, I know!" Ally said lightly.

"Miss?" The voice drifted over to their booth, this time a little more frustrated.

"Just a sec," Ally said. "I'm taking an order here."

Lisa could hear the man behind her grumble to his companion, "It sounds like she's more interested in chatting with her friends." Lisa started to feel uncomfortable. She didn't want to get Ally into trouble.

"Normy threw a fit about it . . ."

Lisa didn't think she'd ever get used to the senior pastor of a formal church like First Pres being called Normy, even by someone as bouncy as Ally. She glanced quickly at Lydia, who hadn't seemed to find anything unusual or amusing about the pet name. *I wish the PWs could see this. They'd be rolling in the aisle.*

"He told me I didn't need to work," Ally continued without missing a beat. "That he could provide for his family, and that I should just stay home and get used to my new life. But I was getting *bored.* There's only so much shopping and Bible study a person can take. No disrespect, of course."

Lisa smiled. "None taken."

"Plus, I want to surprise him for his birthday and take him on a cruise. And I need the money to pay for it. I'll quit after that."

"Ah," Lisa said. "That sounds great."

"Waitress!" the man's voice yelled loudly.

"All right, I'm coming," she yelled back. "Gotta run! They actually expect me to work!" She giggled.

Lisa watched her glide to the next booth and hand the customer his check. "Thanks for coming," she said sweetly. "Hope to see you again soon."

It sounded as if the man said, "That'll be the day," but Lisa couldn't be sure, since she decided she needed to find something—anything—in her purse so nobody would see her chuckle.

That girl's not going to last a week. And even if she does, it would take ten years of working here to pay for that cruise. What's she thinking?

Lydia sighed and laced her hands together neatly on the table. "She didn't take our order."

Lisa laughed out loud. After all that, Ally hadn't even pulled out her order pad.

"Oh!" Lisa heard Ally's voice over the glasses that crashed onto the floor somewhere close to the kitchen.

"Ally is sort of in ever-present distress," Lisa said, trying to explain what seemed obvious. "But she really is very sweet."

"I'd heard the news about Pastor Katt's remarriage," Lydia said, watching the unfolding drama around the broken glasses. "I knew they'd said she was young, but . . ."

"Young, she is."

About five minutes later, Ally walked by and tapped on the table. "How are ya'll doing?"

"We're ready to order," Lisa said gently. *It's a good thing we're not scheduled to be someplace today.*

"I haven't done that yet? Oh, that's right. That customer kept interrupting me. Okay." She pulled out her order pad and pen. "What'll it be? Wait. Where are your menus?" She laughed as if that explained everything. "*That* must have been why I thought I'd already taken care of you two ladies!"

"We don't use the menus since we always order the same thing," Lydia said politely.

"Excellent! Okay, shoot."

They ordered their usual. Two iced teas, no lemon. Lisa asked for the tuna-salad sandwich on pumpernickel, with a side of fries and fruit.

It was Lydia's turn. "I'll have the Denver omelet, well done, with a side of salsa—"

"Excellent choice," Ally said. "That's how I eat my eggs, too. With salsa. 'Cause, you know, eggs are so slimy. I just hate that"—she pinched her fingers together, trying to come up with the word—"*slimy* quality, you know?"

"Yes," Lydia continued. "And give me the hash browns and an English muffin, no butter. I'll do that myself."

"I'm the same way," Ally said. "I think the cooks slather on the butter. It's just not good for the figure, you know? All that extra fat and stuff. Okay, anything else?"

"I think that's it," Lisa said, thoroughly enjoying this lunch date.

"All right, then." Ally waved. "Be back in two malts!"

As Ally walked away, Lydia, confused, stared at Lisa.

"I think she meant two shakes."

Lydia nodded. "So, how are things at the church?"

She definitely stuck to routine—Lisa had to give her that. They always ordered, and *then* that question was asked. Nothing was out of order or sync.

Lisa wondered why her mother insisted on this line of questioning—*especially* now, when her mother *knew* that Lisa and Joel were having major problems at the church. But Lydia always seemed to act surprised when, every week, her daughter answered that they were struggling.

Her mother acted as if she and Lisa's father had never had trouble with a church, something Lisa knew wasn't true. She remembered when she was very young, and their church had gone through a split. She never knew all the details—she'd been too little to understand or even need to know—but she knew it had been ugly. However, her parents had never mentioned it, and they never mentioned any of the troubles they surely had at Cloverdale Assembly of God, the church where her father was now pastoring.

Lisa paused, wondering how she could answer this time to ensure that her mother would genuinely listen. She knew it was always best to appear upbeat around her mom. Anything less would inevitably cause Lydia to give her a mini-sermon filled with platitudes like *You're just not trusting God enough. You need to give it up to the Lord.* True statements, which usually did, in fact, apply to every situation. But not exactly what Lisa wanted or needed to hear when coming without sympathy and discernment.

She pushed back her shoulder-length hair. Finally, she decided she'd just stick with the truth and let the cards fall where they may. That was easier than expecting something that her mother wasn't likely to give her today. *Maybe next time,* she thought sadly. *Next time she'll be different.*

"It's not going well at all, Mom. Tom and his group are spreading all kinds of rumors. It's hateful. And they're even including Callie and Ricky in their mean gossip. Those kids are innocent—why do they have to be part of this?" She'd said it before she could stop herself, and she knew exactly how her mother was going to respond.

Lydia did not disappoint. "We all make sacrifices when following our Savior, Lisa. You should know that better than most."

"But that doesn't make it right. Joel and I signed on to this vocation. Our children didn't."

"They're in God's hands."

Yes, I know that! But I'm thinking like a mommy right now. Could you just acknowledge that it's okay to want to protect my children?

"How is Callie handling it?" Lydia said, lifting her napkin from her lap and repositioning it. A year ago, Callie had been so uncontrollable with anger and rebellion that Lisa had shipped her off to Grandma's house for spring break. It had been risky—but it had paid off.

"She's still upset about the church and what Tom and the others are doing—but she's not backing away from her faith or from us, if that's what you're asking."

"You know, Lisa, she's awfully young to have to be aware of what's going on at the church."

"She's sixteen," Lisa said, defending herself. "Besides, she's not blind. She can see for herself without Joel or me saying a word. Plus, Tom is her Sunday school teacher, so she's directly involved in seeing things."

"And Ricky?"

Ricky had always been a favorite of Lydia's—as much as she had favorites. Lisa thought it was because Ricky was such a charmer—and because he genuinely loved the Lord. The kid wanted to be a missionary pilot. He'd decided that after he'd seen the movie *End of the Spear*, about five missionaries who worked with natives in South America and ended up being martyred. Ricky had thought that was so cool—to die for something you really believed in. He was a strange kid, but a good one. And Lydia adored him for it.

"He doesn't say much about it. Always seems to be in good spirits. It's as if he has this amazing discernment and can see through to the spiritual side of this whole thing. We could all learn a thing or two from that kid."

"He has his head on straight," Lydia said. "Always has."

That doesn't stop him from harassing his sister, though, Lisa thought and smiled. *He is still all boy and a pesty little brother.*

"Well, I know Joel asks your father fairly often for advice."

"And Joel really appreciates that," Lisa said. *At least Joel and my dad have a good relationship where they can really talk.*

Another waitress stopped by and delivered their iced teas. *Where's Ally?* Lisa wondered, but then decided it was better that Ally not interrupt this conversation at the moment.

Lydia picked up two packets of sugar and dropped the contents into the liquid. She then slowly stirred with her straw.

Lisa could sense her mother was ready to present her mini-sermon. Then they could move on to something that didn't involve trouble or honesty or vulnerability.

Lydia took a long sip of her tea before bringing the glass back down to her right on the table. "The truth is, Lisa, you're not unique in having to deal with a difficult church situation. Every pastor has, at some point in his vocation, dealt with an unruly church member, or members, or entire congregation. What you're experiencing isn't so special. You should take comfort in knowing that."

"But they're going after my family." Lisa could feel her face flushing.

"That's the way Satan works."

Lisa could feel it coming. It was as if she watched the platitude forming in her mother's mind and rolling down to her lips.

"You should just give it to God." And there it fell, as if it was a piece of liver flopping onto the table and her mother was telling her to "Eat up. It's good for you."

The other waitress again appeared with a large tray. "Tuna?" the woman asked, her face registering a blank, almost bored look.

Lisa raised her hand.

The waitress carelessly dropped the plate in front of her, then did the same with Lydia's omelet. "Anything else for you two?"

"Not right now, thanks," Lisa said.

"Fine. Here." She dropped the bill at the edge of the table.

"Um," Lisa started as the waitress began to walk away, "where's our first waitress?"

The woman rolled her eyes. "One of her *heels* broke. She had to leave to get it fixed."

Bless her heart, Lisa thought. She couldn't resist feeling slightly sorry for the poor girl. *A fish out of water.*

Lydia prayed over their meal, then began to pour the salsa over her omelet. After she took a bite and daintily wiped her mouth with her napkin, she asked, "Have you fasted over this?"

Lisa nodded. She felt like a whipped puppy. Why did visiting her mother always do this to her? And why did she foolishly continue to believe that somehow each visit would be kind and encouraging and *real*? Why did she keep putting herself through this?

Tears crept into Lisa's eyes. Why did her mother have to be so stoic?

"Did you and Dad ever experience anything like this?" She wanted to see if her mother would come clean on the church split from years ago.

Lydia paused mid-bite, as if contemplating her answer. Lydia would do many things, but lie wasn't one of them. She finished her bite and again dabbed at her mouth with the napkin.

"Of course we did," she said matter-of-factly. "You would have been too young to remember, but your father was pastor at a church in Dayton. It was his first pastorate."

Lisa waited to see if her mother would continue.

I've gone this far, she thought. "What happened?"

Lydia exhaled. "The church ended up splitting because they didn't like that he was bringing new people in and getting them saved and growing the church with the 'wrong' kind of people. Mostly young people. We ended up selling the church building and moving to another church."

"I remember that," Lisa said. "I would have been what—four? Five?"

"Yes." Her mother seemed unsure about Lisa's confession, but slightly . . . impressed? "You remember that?"

Lisa hadn't thought about it in years, but now it seemed very clear to her. "I don't remember much, but I remember walking through the basement when we were clearing everything out. You handed me a painting of Jesus to carry. I didn't know why we were leaving the church, but I remember feeling so sad about it. I knew it was a sad thing that was happening."

"I handed you a painting to carry?" Lydia asked, as if not hearing the pain that it was even now eliciting from her daughter. "I don't remember that. Waitress." She lifted her empty glass into the air. "When you get a moment, I'd like some more." She looked at her daughter. "Well, we survived it and continue to serve the Lord. And so will you."

Lisa sat amazed. *So will I?* Was her mother really that devoid of emotion? Had her life just been too painful? Or was she so used to not being able to share vulnerably with anyone that it had come to include her family, too?

"Be honest with me for once!" Lisa wanted to shout at her mother. "Tell me the truth! Tell me it tore you up inside to watch the church slander and wear down your husband and family. Tell me you got angry with God and questioned him and sometimes even doubted that he cared at all. Or that he was even still hanging around. That he'd forgotten about you. Tell me there were days when you loved God, but hated the church. Hated organized religion. Tell me what I'm going through isn't all right. That it *does* hurt. Give me *something* to work with here."

Lisa jabbed a fry into the puddle of ketchup on her plate. That well of eternal hope in her soul had begun to shrink.

CHAPTER

19

Jennifer

Monday, April 28

11:46 a.m.

"Good morning, Red River Community Church," Jennifer said into the phone while she popped open a yogurt. Sam was out doing hospital visits, so she was on her own for lunch. She figured she might as well work through the hour so she could take off a little early to get Carys from day care.

"Hello, is this Jennifer Shores?"

Jennifer cradled the receiver between her head and shoulder, set the yogurt cup on her desk, and opened her middle drawer to look for a plastic spoon. "Yes, it is. How may I help you?"

"I'm calling for Mr. Declan Brennan. He would like me to make an appointment for him to see you." The words were clipped, almost British in character but not quite.

Rifling through the drawer, Jennifer tried to place the name. *Declan Brennan. Declan Brennan?*

"Hmmm. I'm sorry," she replied, "but I don't believe I know a Declan Brennan. Are you sure he doesn't want to see my husband, the pastor?"

The woman cleared her throat. "No, ma'am. He wants to see you. Tomorrow, if you are able."

There it is—I knew I had a spoon in here somewhere. Jennifer closed the drawer. "As I said, I don't know who he is. Why does he want to see me? Is he selling something? Because we're all stocked up on office supplies, and we order most of our church supplies in January for the whole year."

"I'm sorry, ma'am, but I was asked just to make the appointment."

Jennifer was growing frustrated. She grabbed the phone receiver off her shoulder. "Well, unless you tell me what he wants, there is no way I will agree to see him," she said curtly.

Nice Christian attitude there, pastor's wife!

A moment of silence followed Jennifer's declaration. She was just getting ready to hang up the phone when she heard the woman say, "I believe you met our, uh, private detective?"

Jennifer froze. She had given up on the promised phone call. "Yes," she said, hesitating. "But his card didn't really say who he was, and he wouldn't tell me anything more . . . kind of like you're doing now."

The woman sounded genuinely sorry when she said, "I apologize, Mrs. Shores. It's just that Mr. Brennan wants to talk with you himself. Could you come here to the house tomorrow, say around one?"

This surely has to do with Mother's debt. What if I get there and they break my legs? Have I seen too many Mafia movies or does that really happen?

"I'm sorry . . . I didn't catch your name—"

"Belinda."

"I'm sorry, Belinda, but I can't go to someone's house without even knowing what it is about."

"Yes, I understand, Mrs. Shores. Feel free to bring anyone along. Your husband, perhaps?"

Oh, yeah, like I want Sam to hear some guy tell me my mother owes twenty thousand to a loan shark. But maybe I could find someone—

"So does tomorrow work for you then, Mrs. Shores?"

Her voice had a sense of urgency to it, as if she were trying to meet a deadline.

Jennifer looked at her calendar for the next day. *Oh, lunch with the PWs.*

"I can't do it tomorrow. Would Wednesday be okay?"

Jennifer started to backtrack, worried that putting off the meeting could cause her or her mom trouble, but Belinda's relieved voice stopped her. "Of course. Wednesday it is. Do you have e-mail? I'll send you directions."

Wow, these loan sharks are technologically advanced—and accommodating. Jennifer gave Belinda her e-mail address.

"So I will see you on Wednesday at one?" Belinda asked, as if she wanted to double-check the plan.

"Yes, I'll be there." *With my large, muscular bodyguard.*

"Good day then, Mrs. Shores."

"'Bye."

Jennifer, deep in thought, set the phone in its cradle gingerly. *Declan Brennan.* The name sounded too poetic to be some thug supporting her mother's gambling habit. But who else could he be?

She spun around to her computer desk and typed the name into a search engine. A list of Declan Brennans came up: software engineer, radio announcer, architect—it went on and on. And they all had one thing in common: they were in Ireland.

"I guess loan sharks probably don't have websites," Jennifer muttered, disappointed. Clicking on a directory, she typed in the name again, hoping to at least find an address or phone number. Nothing.

The e-mail from Belinda will tell me that, she reasoned.

Sitting back in her chair, Jennifer pondered whom she could take with her on this sordid adventure. Surely, no one from the church. One of the PWs would do it, but she needed a man—someone strong—just in case.

And then it hit her: the perfect choice, on so many levels.

CHAPTER

20

Lulu's Café

Tuesday, April 29

12:23 p.m.

The PWs sat in their usual booth at the back of Lulu's, chatting and enjoying their meals. Creatures of habit, they liked to say, they had all ordered the same things, except for Jennifer, who decided to shake things up a bit and order a Cobb salad.

Felicia noticed that Gracie seemed more open to talking about God. Lisa had presented her with a Bible—a New International Version, since they'd all decided that would be the easiest translation for her to understand. Gracie had seemed genuinely touched.

"No one's ever given me a Bible before," she'd said. "Plenty of folks have quoted things from it at me, though. Thanks. This means a lot coming from you gals. But don't think I don't know you're trying to convert me."

"Can't get nothing past you, Gracie!" Jennifer had said good-naturedly.

"You may want to start in the New Testament. Either the book of John or Mark," Lisa had said.

Gracie wrote those names down on her order pad. "Got it."

Felicia decided to take things one step further, so after Gracie arrived with the food and distributed it to the four of them, Felicia said, "I talked with my husband about contacting a pastor here in Cheeksville. So you may get a call from him soon. If that's okay. I hope you don't mind that I took that liberty."

Gracie pinched up her face as though a dentist were pulling out a tooth with a salad tong.

"He's not going to ask you for any money," Felicia was quick to add, trying not to laugh from the look on Gracie's face.

"Well, all right, but don't expect much. I'm set in my ways, remember. Now stop bothering me, I've got salt and pepper shakers I have to refill." But she winked as she turned away.

Oh, Gracie, God's got a hold of you, darlin'. It's just a matter of time, Felicia said to herself.

After Lisa blessed their food and they started to dig in, Jennifer spoke up. "For the record, I'm not crazy."

"Well, that's a relief." Mimi smoothed mayo over her hamburger bun.

"I *am* being trailed," Jennifer said and shoved a large forkful of salad into her mouth.

Felicia and the others waited for her to finish chewing.

"What's up with that, Jennifer?" Mimi whined jokingly. "You throw out a statement like that, then stuff your face so you can't give us more details?"

Jennifer almost choked. "Sorry," she said after she swallowed and took a drink. "I didn't even think about it—you know how I get around food. Okay, *so,* remember the private investigator? When I confronted him, he had told me that someone would be in touch with me. So yesterday I get a phone call from some woman who tells me I need to meet with her boss, Declan Brennan."

"Who's that?" Lisa asked. She looked scared for Jennifer.

"That's just it. I don't know. I tried checking him out online, and there's nothing. But I've decided I'm going to go."

"Oh, Jennifer," Lisa cried, "you can't. I don't have a good feeling about this. You don't know anything about these people."

"I know," said Jennifer. "But I think it's something to do with my mother. She's been spending all this money, and I accidentally saw a poker website on her computer. She claims she's not gambling, but . . ."

"Oooh." Felicia shook her head. "You think this guy is coming after you to collect?"

"Can they do that?" Lisa asked, wide-eyed.

"Loan sharks can do anything they want. Even come after family members," Felicia said.

"And you would know this how?" Mimi asked, dropping her hand to her hip.

"I watch *Law & Order,*" Felicia defended.

"I don't understand," Mimi said. "Why come after you if it's your mom's money?"

"Because if she can't pay, and they think we can . . . ," Jennifer said. "The guy already knows so much about me and my family. What can I do?"

"What does Sam say?" Mimi asked.

"Well . . ." Jennifer seemed uncomfortable.

"You haven't told him, have you?" Felicia knew that hesitation from her own times when she hadn't told her husband things.

"I don't want him to worry and—"

"Honey, that's his job! He's supposed to worry," Lisa said. "*And* protect you."

"I know. But I had an idea. I invited Pastor Scott to go with me." Jennifer seemed proud of her idea. "I told him to wear his collar."

Felicia breathed out quickly. She hadn't realized she'd been holding her breath. "That's a great idea. After all, who could hurt a priest?"

"But what if someone sees you with a priest in your car?" Mimi asked.

Jennifer smiled. "I doubt that anyone will think I'm having an affair, if that's what you're thinking. Of course Kitty did . . ."

"When are you going?" Mimi asked.

"Tomorrow."

"But that's Carys's birthday party."

How does Mimi remember all these things? Felicia wondered.

As if reading Felicia's mind, Mimi said, "I'm baking the birthday cake. Jennifer doesn't have time to do it—especially now. And it's something I can do for her."

"Please be careful, Jennifer," Lisa said, still looking fearful.

Jennifer nodded grimly. "Okay, let's take the spotlight off me. I don't want my one afternoon with my friends turning into a discussion on the number of ways some guy can break my legs."

Felicia wasn't comfortable with that image. "You know, Mimi," she said to change the subject, "if you really want to do some baking . . ."

"What's up?" Mimi looked excited all of a sudden. *That's Mimi. Loves to volunteer for anything.*

"I just found out that my family—*all of them*"—she clipped the words—"is coming from L.A. to celebrate Dave's birthday next month. And half of them aren't even speaking to one another. Ugh. And my mama wants the entire church there as well."

They all nodded in understanding.

"That's tough," Jennifer said. "It's the all or nothing. If you invite only some people from church, it could start a civil war. They label you as playing favorites—even when you don't mean it that way!"

"You constantly have to second-guess yourself to make sure you're not offending anyone. It wears on you, doesn't it?" Mimi asked. "We had that problem with a family from our church, the Taylors. They have children the same ages as ours. It just works out that we spend time together because of our kids—same school functions, same ballet recitals—but several members of our church have made veiled comments about it."

"Well, it looks like I'm going to have more than two hundred people coming and going from my house."

"Yowsa!" Jennifer cringed. "Why not just have it at the church?"

"Thought of that. I wanted this birthday to be low-key and nice for Dave—it's a milestone and he's feeling it. If it's at the church, I feel like I'll lose some of the control over it. And I'd have to deal with other people making decisions about what we'll do and have."

"Oh, honey, you're not going to need me," Mimi said. "You're going to need a therapist."

"Oh!" Lisa yelled out. "I forgot to give you something, Felicia." She pulled a card out of her purse.

What's this for? Felicia wondered, but she was touched by the gesture—whatever the gesture was. It was sealed with a small sticker. Felicia easily opened it and pulled out a bright, multicolored card with print that shouted at her: *Happy Cinco de Mayo*. As soon as Felicia opened the card, a tinny blast came out playing "La Bamba."

Felicia wasn't sure how to take the card until she heard her friend start laughing. She looked at Lisa.

"I know Cinco de Mayo's coming up," Lisa explained. "And I love those musical cards. As soon as I saw it, I had to get it."

"Where did you find this?" Felicia asked, laughing.

"At Walgreens. I was looking for a get well card for one of our church members and I saw this whole section of Cinco de Mayo cards. I knew you'd get a kick out of it."

"Walgreens has Cinco de Mayo cards?" Felicia was really laughing now. "For whom? There's one Mexican person in town. Me."

"Well, they must have found out you're thinking about adding to your family," Jennifer suggested. "You still are, aren't you?"

"Still undecided. And Dave's no help. We finally talked a little about it, and he said he was going to leave the decision up to me. But now that my family's coming next month, I think I may want to postpone the decision until June. I can only handle one crisis at a time, thank you."

"Ah, families." Mimi picked up a fry and pushed it through the sea of ketchup she had on her plate.

"Now what's happened?" Lisa asked.

Felicia hated to admit it, because she knew the situation was tragic, but Mimi's father's antics were funny. Destructive, but funny.

"The neighbors who live behind us have a garden." Mimi rolled her eyes. "He decided to help me cook supper one night. So he strolled to their garden and started picking their spinach. *All* of it. He couldn't understand why I was upset. Or why our neighbors were upset, for that matter. Is it really too much to ask for a normal father? I just want to be normal! To have a normal family."

"Oh, honey, don't we all!" Lisa said. "I wish one time my mother would really listen to me and show some sign of affection."

"I'd love to have a normal family," Jennifer piped up.

"Sometimes I'll watch some of the families in our church," Felicia admitted. "The husband sits next to his wife. And they obviously love each other. And the kids are well behaved and don't bite. Everybody gets along . . ."

"And then they get in the car to go home and the facade drops!" Mimi laughed, thinking of her own children on the way home from church every Sunday.

"It's taken me more than thirty years to figure out there is no such thing as a normal family. Those families that look perfect on the outside—they're just really good at covering things up. But if you dig a little, you'll see that they have their stuff just like everybody else."

"Yeah, but mine seems so much more"—Mimi scrunched her nose, as if she were having trouble saying it—"dysfunctional."

"And that's exactly what the enemy wants you to believe," Lisa insisted. "Because if he succeeds in that, he succeeds in isolating you and getting you into pity-party mode, which keeps you from fully serving the Lord."

"So your dad's still drinking?" Jennifer asked Mimi.

"Ha," Mimi said. "My father's body is so full of alcohol, he'd fail a sobriety test on a day when he'd drunk only water. I guess the one good thing in all of this is that my little curtain-climbing chimps have been fairly good lately. I mean—it's all relative, of course, in MJ's case—but I think because they've been watching how stressed out I am over my father, they must figure they'll give me a break. Again, something I wouldn't need to be concerned with if 'normal' were anywhere in my family's description."

"But if you were normal, you probably wouldn't want to hang around with us anymore," Jennifer said. "You'd find us too out there."

"I think you're already out there," Gracie said, stopping by with an iced tea pitcher.

"Gracie, do you think we're normal?" Felicia asked.

"Good grief, you're about as normal as a freak show in a carnival." She laughed at her own joke. "But then, who am I to judge? I just took in five cats."

CHAPTER 21

Jennifer

Wednesday, April 30

12:57 p.m.

Jennifer snaked her Corolla down the long driveway, leading to what she hoped was Declan Brennan's house. Belinda hadn't sent the e-mail with the directions until late Tuesday afternoon—so late in fact that Jennifer started again to think the whole thing was a hoax. By the time she'd received the information, she was due to pick up Carys from day care, swing by the store and get groceries, and then get back to church for a women's society meeting. Later that night, though, she had Google-mapped the place—and was really creeped out when the satellite view showed an empty lot.

"I guess this place really does exist," said Father Scott as they came to a clearing where a large house—a mansion, really—stood majestically in its Tudor glory.

"Good grief." She slowed the car and leaned forward to take in the place. "How could this big of a place get built so close to Red River and we've never heard about it?"

The house's pitched roof gave way to a dark-timbered-looking exterior filled with lighter brick in a herringbone pattern. It had large, heavily curtained windows on the bottom, with small dormers near the roofline. Several chimneys poked out from the roof at various levels. The house looked as if it was built to appear older, but Jennifer could see it was actually quite new.

Father Scott adjusted his collar. "Jen, these kinds of people do all sorts of things on the sly. It's a dark world they live in."

Jennifer felt a slight chill. Even with Father Scott along, she was still frightened about what she might encounter inside the house.

They parked in the property's circular drive, got out, and approached the door. Red and white flowers were planted along the walkway, giving the otherwise cold landscaping a bit of natural color.

Before ringing the bell, Jennifer looked at Father Scott, in full vestments, as she'd requested, for effect.

"Thank you again for doing this," she said, lightly patting his shoulder.

He smiled. "Hey, this is about the most excitement I've had as a priest in Red River since Mrs. Mueller's teeth fell out and hit the floor as I was giving her Communion."

They both laughed, dissolving some of the tension for Jennifer.

The doorbell sounded ominous, like something from out of a movie.

Clicking heels approached and the fifteen-foot door opened slowly.

"Jennifer, please come in," the woman said.

They stepped through the doorway, and the woman extended her hand. "I am Belinda, Mr. . . . Brennan's assistant. Pleased to meet you." She was dressed about as plainly as a woman could be, Jennifer thought—white, high-collared blouse, black skirt below her knees, and sensible black shoes with thick heels. Her face wore no makeup except for a touch of powder, and her dark hair was pulled back into a harsh bun.

"Hello," Jennifer said. "This is my friend, *Father* Scott McCall." She emphasized his title as if Belinda wouldn't be able to see he was a priest.

"Father, my pleasure," Belinda said, shaking his hand.

"How do you do?" Father Scott replied.

This feels like a 1930s movie. We're even talking stilted. Jennifer half expected to see Gloria Swanson from *Sunset Boulevard* walking majestically down the large staircase in front of her.

"Please come this way," Belinda said, turning and leading them down a hallway.

The house was deadly silent, as if they were the only ones there, although Jennifer sensed many people bustling around quietly. The interior of the residence was as cold and joyless as the outside. Most of the walls were covered in paneling, with large pieces of art everywhere—paintings, sculpture, and even a tapestry over the stairs.

"Here we are." Belinda pulled back a pocket door. Jennifer held her breath in anticipation of seeing Tony Soprano inside—but the room was empty, except for a museum-like display of elegant furniture, artwork, and books. A gigantic fireplace, sitting empty, was the focus of the space.

"Please make yourselves at home and I will see if Mr. Qui . . . Brennan is ready for you," Belinda said. "May I get anyone some tea?"

"Yes, please," Father Scott answered before Jennifer could pipe up. She noticed he seemed to be relishing their adventure.

After Belinda clopped away in small, fast strides, Jennifer finally felt as though she could let down her guard.

"She looks like a nun I used to know—actually, all the nuns I've *ever* known," Father Scott said dryly, causing Jennifer to cover her mouth before she laughed.

"Wonder why she keeps messing up his last name, like she's about to say something else?" Jennifer asked.

Father Scott shrugged. "Maybe she used to work for someone else. Wow, this place is really something, isn't it?"

They each spun around, taking in the room's grandeur.

"Is this how loan sharks live?" Jennifer asked quietly. "I thought they—"

Belinda interrupted her, reentering the room holding a tray with both hands. "I asked Channing to put on the kettle for you," she said, as if they knew who Channing was. "But in the meantime, here are some biscuits for you, Father. Jennifer, he is ready to see you now, I believe. He asked if you could come alone."

Jennifer, a bit startled at finding out the visit would now be a solo mission, gave Father Scott a "pray for me" glance and followed Belinda out of the room, down the hall, up the gorgeous wooden staircase (*I'd love to see Carys come down stairs like these in her wedding dress,* Jennifer mused), and down another hallway. Jennifer was dying to ask Belinda questions about the house and its contents (and its owner), but Belinda kept a fast pace ahead of her. Jennifer found herself barely able to keep up.

Finally, at the end of the hall, Belinda stopped outside a closed door. "Here we are," she said brightly.

Does she do tours as a side gig? Jennifer wondered.

Belinda turned the knob and motioned for Jennifer to follow her as she opened the door.

Lord, please help me not to do or say anything stupid that might make any of this—

Her thoughts stopped when she saw what was before her. Instead of some thug, as she'd imagined, there was an elderly man, hooked up to a breathing machine, lying in a gargantuan bed. He was propped up on pillows and covered with a gray velour bedspread. Judging from the bottles of medication on his nightstand and the pallid color of his skin, Jennifer thought the man must be very ill.

At least I don't have to worry about him breaking my legs.

"Mr. Quinn, this is Jennifer."

Quinn? I thought I heard her start to say that before.

Jennifer must have looked questioningly at Belinda, because before she could ask her what was going on, Belinda said, "Mr. Quinn will explain everything. Here, please sit down."

She pulled a wood and brocade-upholstered chair to the man's bedside. "I will leave you two alone now."

Jennifer slipped over to the chair while Belinda made her way out the door and closed it. The man removed his breathing mask. Jennifer thought she saw a tear escape from his eye. *Wow, he must really be in pain. Wonder why he can't just have someone else tell me what Mother owes?*

"Jennifer," he said weakly, in a slight Irish brogue, "I am not a man who beats around the bush. So I want to tell you why I asked you to come here."

"Me neither, Mr. Brennan or Quinn or whatever your name is," she said. She didn't want to be disrespectful to such an ailing man, but she also didn't want to spend any more time than she had to in dealing with this. "I brought my checkbook, but you should know I have only seventy-two dollars. Whatever she did, though, I can make payments or whatever to make it right. Just don't hurt us or bother us anymore." *I cannot believe I am here doing this! Again! For her!*

He looked amused. "Jennifer"—he said her name as if he knew her—"this doesn't have to do with money. Well, not exactly."

Jennifer wasn't sure if she should be relieved or even more scared. "What do you mean?"

He tried to clear his throat, which made him cough, then spoke slowly. "I asked you here because I am a dying man. I had Belinda give you a false name because I didn't want you to look me up before you arrived. I've done a lot in my life, and I've been very fortunate in many, many ways."

Yes, that's obvious with this house. And all that art!

"But perhaps the most important thing I did," he continued, "I never had the pleasure of enjoying. And that's . . . you."

Jennifer squinted. "Me? What are you talking—"

"Jennifer, I'm your father."

Perhaps for the only time in her life, Jennifer found herself speechless. Her emotions jumped from anxious to curious to shocked to ecstatic in a matter of seconds.

"You're my father? But how—"

"I think you know how. You have a baby daughter, right?" He smiled at his little joke.

Jennifer sat back in the chair and stared at this man, the one she'd dreamed of all her life, even though her mom had told her he was a drunk who'd left them before Jennifer was even born. She'd always wondered if that was true, and as a child thought maybe *she* would have left her mom, too, if she'd had the chance. She felt a strange sense of solidarity with the dad she'd never known.

And now here he was, a sick old man. Not the big strong daddy about whom she'd fantasized.

"Why did you leave us?" she asked tentatively, tears forming in her eyes. "Why didn't you come for me? Do you know what I grew up in? How my mother was?"

She saw water pooling in his blue eyes—the same shade of blue as hers. "I am so, so sorry, Jennifer." He took a deep breath, as if he wasn't sure where or how to begin. Finally he said softly, in a voice that sounded ashamed, "I was married when you were conceived. I just couldn't walk away from my wife. Know this, though"—he sounded slightly defensive—"it was a loveless marriage, and if I could have, I would have left her to be with you and your mother."

"But what about your other family—with your wife?" Jennifer asked, wondering about any half siblings she might have.

He shook his head. "Aileen never gave me any children. You're my only . . ." He seemed to drift off in thought for a moment before he said, "Jennifer, I know what I did was wrong. But I did love your mother. I still do."

The picture of Jo Jo's living room—full of bags and boxes—flashed through Jennifer's mind. "Did you buy her all of that stuff?" she said and sniffled.

He hesitated. "Do you mean Jo Jo? Did she go on a shopping spree?" He looked amused again. "Yes, well, when I knew Aileen's cancer was terminal, I started building a house here, thinking I'd move in and enjoy my retirement years, hopefully with Jo Jo. But meanwhile I was diagnosed with congestive heart failure, and by the time I got here last year, I knew I wasn't going to make it much longer. I thought about not even looking up Jo Jo, but I had to. I decided even a few months would be better than nothing. I wanted to try to make up for how I'd treated her. And you."

"Me?" Jennifer asked tersely. "You said you got here last year. Why are you just now contacting me?"

He swallowed in what looked to be a painful way. "Your mother wouldn't let me. She said it would be too confusing for you to find out all of this at your age. But now . . . I just had to see you, Jennifer."

Jennifer's mind was whirling. So Jo Jo wasn't gambling? But why hadn't she told her about her real father a long time ago? Why the lies?

As excited as she was to meet her father, Jennifer couldn't help but feel angry as well. Even if he couldn't have lived with them like a real dad, he could have at least made himself known to her. She would have kept his secret.

"So what do we do now?" Jennifer asked. "Are we going to start getting to know each other? I've missed you, you know." She choked up again.

He reached out his frail hand and she took it in hers. "I'd like that. But you should know, you'll never want for anything again. I set up a small trust for your mother, but everything else I have is yours—the money, the house, everything."

Jennifer heard what he was saying, but couldn't digest it. Instead, she was mesmerized by the feel of her dad's soft, almost translucent skin and the knowledge that she finally had a father. "You're right, I never will want for anything again . . . because you're the only thing I've ever really wanted . . . Dad." She wiped away a tear with her free hand. "Is it okay if I call you that?"

His fingers caressed her hand. "Nothing would make me happier." A coughing fit overtook him, which seemed to be like a bell calling Belinda. She burst into the room and rushed to his bedside.

"Jennifer, you'll need to go now," she said as she readjusted his oxygen mask. "Mr. Quinn needs his rest."

Jennifer backed away from the bed. "But I don't even know his real name yet," she said, feeling as if she were losing him once again. "And can I come back tomorrow to see him?"

"His real name is Finbar Quinn," Belinda called over her shoulder as she struggled to fit the mask over his face while he was coughing. "And yes, you can come back, but not tomorrow. That's his doctor's-appointment day. Friday would be best."

Jennifer looked at the bed. Even coughing and with Belinda hovering over him, she saw her father's eyes fixed on her. She gave a little wave. He raised his hand in an attempt to answer.

"I'll see you Friday, then, Dad," she said.

Most people who discovered they had a secret, wealthy father would feel as if they'd hit the jackpot—or better. But walking down that long hallway to the magnificent staircase, all Jennifer could reflect on was that she finally had a real dad, with a face and a name.

CHAPTER 22

Felicia

Wednesday, April 30

1:15 p.m.

"Mrs. Morrison?"

"Yes," Felicia said into the phone. *When am I going to learn to stop answering this thing?*

"This is Robin Flanders. Charles Flanders's daughter?"

Felicia thought for a second. "Yes, the one in Pittsburgh?"

"That's right. I'm sorry to bother you. I tried to call the church, but I got the machine and this number was on it. Is the pastor home?"

"No, he's not. May I take a message for him?"

Robin let out what sounded to Felicia like a tense breath.

Before Robin could respond, Felicia asked, "Is there something I can do to help? Is Charlie okay?"

"That's just it," said Robin. "I haven't talked to him in a few days. I called my brother Randy in Nashville and he hadn't heard from him either. Dad always speaks so highly of his pastor, I wondered if he might stop by to check on him."

Charlie Flanders was a widower in his early eighties, and a real hoot,

Felicia thought. He always said exactly what he was thinking, even when it wasn't appropriate. While everyone attributed it to his age, Felicia saw a twinkle in his eye that told her differently.

"My husband is out of town at a ministers' meeting all day today," Felicia said. Before thinking she added, "But I'd be glad to go see if Charlie is all right."

She looked at the stacks of papers and folders surrounding her. *What did you offer to do that for? Again?*

"That would be wonderful," said Robin. "Would you mind calling me back afterward? I'll give you my number."

"Of course."

Within minutes, Felicia had ended the call with Robin, located Charlie's address in the church directory, Google-mapped it (even though Red River was a small city, Felicia still got lost occasionally), grabbed her purse, and slid behind the wheel of her cobalt blue BMW Z4.

What if I get over there and he's . . . She wouldn't allow herself to think it.

Arriving at Charlie's simple but immaculate green-sided house with its white trim, she climbed out of the car and hurried to the door, anxious about what she might find. She was instantly relieved to see Charlie inside, watching TV.

They made eye contact before she knocked, and he shuffled over to let her in.

"Felicia," he said with a wide grin. "To what do I owe this special treat?"

She smiled back, genuinely relieved to have found him in one piece. "Hi, Charlie. May I come in?"

"Oh, of course, of course," he said, backing away from the door so she could enter. The house, although neat, smelled of rotted fruit.

Felicia tried not to show her surprise at the odor. "Robin called," she said, standing just inside the door. She hoped this would be a short visit so she could get back to work. "She was concerned because you hadn't been answering your phone."

Charlie leaned against the wall. Felicia thought he looked noticeably frailer since the last time she'd given him a good look at church.

"I haven't gotten any calls," he said. "The phone hasn't rung one time in days. Of course, I call all my girlfriends every night, but I never give them my number."

He winked. Felicia chuckled.

She surveyed the room. Seeing the phone next to his chair, she followed its cord with her eyes. The wall connection was behind a chair.

"Maybe it just got pulled from the wall?" she suggested.

Charlie hobbled over to the phone and yanked slightly on the cord. It came flying out.

"Well, look at that," he said, turning to face Felicia and then back to the cord. His face showed a mix of confusion and embarrassment.

Felicia didn't want to impugn the man's pride. "That happens all the time at our house," she said quickly, mentally pardoning herself for telling a white lie since it was for a good cause. "Do you think you can get it back in the wall or can I help?"

She immediately wished she hadn't added that last question. He clearly wanted to convey an image of independence, and far be it from her to tug at his resolve.

His response told her she was right to ask after all. "I can't see as well as I used to," he said, waving her over and holding out the cord. "Maybe it would be better if you reached back there so you can make sure it's in this time."

"Happy to." Felicia shimmied behind the chair and crouched down to see the phone jack. "Do you have any tape handy?" she asked, leaning backward.

Charlie dug through a plastic organizer near his chair. Finding the tape, he handed it to her. She pulled off a few pieces and used them to secure the cord in the jack.

"That should keep it from falling out again," she said, coming out from behind the chair and smoothing her pants. Charlie was standing in the middle of the living room, waiting for her. He looked as if he didn't know what to say. All the time she'd known him, she'd thought he oozed self-confidence. But now, seeing him in his lonely home, so lacking in communication that he didn't know his phone was inoperable, she saw a completely different man.

She looked at her watch. Almost two—still an hour before Nicholas was out of school.

"I've been kind of craving some ice cream," she started. "Would you be up to accompanying me over to the Baskin-Robbins?"

The look on his face almost brought tears to Felicia's eyes. "Let me get my cap," he said eagerly.

On the way out the door, Felicia knew she was with the same old Charlie when he asked, "Felicia, you said you were craving ice cream. When you ladies crave something, that usually means one thing. You pregnant?"

If only he knew, she thought, shaking her head and smiling in response.

CHAPTER

23

Jennifer

Wednesday, April 30

5:15 p.m.

Jennifer pushed Carys's high chair to its place on one side of the dining room table, then stepped back to observe the setup.

Wow, that cake really is something, she thought, admiring the pink-and-white princess confection Mimi had made for Carys's birthday party. A party hat was set at each of the three place settings and at Carys's high chair, and princess-themed paper decorations—Mimi had offered to make them, but Jennifer said the cake was already too generous and bought them at the store instead—hung from the light above.

She knew she was overdoing the celebration for a first-year birthday, but growing up she had never had parties, so she was eager to provide one for Carys. It seemed like every year on her birthday her mom would get drunk by midday, leaving Jennifer to watch TV or go to a friend's house. She never would tell her friends it was her birthday, too embarrassed to explain why she wouldn't be home having cake and ice cream.

Wonder how that might have been different if my dad had been around?

The what-ifs had been plaguing her all afternoon. She was hoping to get more answers that evening from Jo Jo, whom she had called after returning home with Carys and the cake. In the midst of her shock and confusion over meeting her father, she'd realized her assumption about Jo Jo's newfound "wealth" was incorrect, so she'd phoned her to call a truce and invite her to Carys's birthday dinner. But with picking up the cake and then Carys, getting her down for a nap, getting dinner on, and decorating, she hadn't had time to really talk to her mom besides telling her she'd met Finbar. So as much as she was looking forward to seeing Carys smash cake all over her face in the first birthday tradition, Jennifer was also eager to get details from Jo Jo about her father.

The problem was, even though she felt empathy toward Finbar, her animosity toward her mother seemed to have deepened. She kept telling herself that wasn't reasonable since *he* was the one who had left them behind, but the bitterness wouldn't go away.

"There's my birthday girl," Sam called as he walked in the back door.

Jennifer took in a deep breath. She had waited until Sam was home to tell him everything—this wasn't a conversation suited to a quickie cell phone chat.

"Hi, honey," he said as he stopped for a peck. Jennifer hugged him and held on for a moment longer than usual.

"Sam, I need to talk to you about something."

She pulled away and saw concern in his eyes. "Did something happen?"

"Yes, something pretty big happened," she said, clutching his hand and leading him through the kitchen and into the living room, where they sat together on the sofa. Carys crawled behind them, then stopped just inside the room to play with a set of blocks she'd left there earlier.

"I have some amazing news," Jennifer started.

Sam beamed. "You're not!"

Jennifer tapped her forehead with the back of her hand. "Oh, not that," she said, realizing his conclusion. "No, this is about something I found out today. But first I need to tell you what happened before that. Please don't be angry with me."

She saw his face change from joyful to hesitant, so rather than prolong the agony, she jumped right in. "For the past several weeks, I've noticed a black town car following me," she started and proceeded to tell him everything that had been going on.

"How could you do that with Carys in the car?" he responded to her playback of the confrontation in the cul-de-sac.

"Wait, there's more," she said, putting up her hand as if to stop his worrying. Next she told him about the call from Belinda and her visit to the mansion.

"Whoa, you went by yourself?"

"Not exactly," she said slowly. She didn't want to sidetrack her news about her father by having to explain her relationship with a priest, but she wasn't exactly sure how else to tell him. "I took Pastor Scott from the church across the street from ours."

He registered a blank look. "What church across from ours?"

She cocked her head and stared at him. *Really? You don't know the church?*

"There's just a Catholic church . . ." She saw the light dawn in his eyes. "How do you know the priest from that church?"

She tried to explain briefly how several years previously, when she had been struggling so much with her faith and her infertility issues, she'd gone to him for counseling. Sam seemed to take it all well—even though he did roll his eyes and grimace over the fact that she hadn't taken him with her to the mansion.

"You really should have told me about this, Jennifer."

"I know, but . . ." What could she say to not make it appear worse, or as if she were trying to discount her husband's ability to protect and advise her? "Look, let's not get hung up on that right now. The rest of my news is much bigger."

He pushed his glasses farther onto the bridge of his nose, then crossed his arms.

"The man at the mansion . . . is my dad."

"What?" Clearly startled, Sam sat up straight.

Jennifer dove into the rest of her story—telling him everything from why her father abandoned them to all the money she was going to inherit. Once she'd told him everything, she leaned back on the sofa, feeling as though she'd just run five miles (not that she really knew what that felt like!).

Sam was a person who required time to absorb news before he could respond. So she waited.

After a minute or two of looking into space, he turned to her. "How much money do you think he has?"

Jennifer gasped. "I tell you I've found my father after all these years and you wonder how much *money* he has?" she asked, incredulous.

"Sorry," Sam said sheepishly. "It's just . . . well, it is something to think about."

He reached for her and cradled her in his arms, kissing the top of her head. "I am so happy for you, honey," he said lovingly. "I know how much you've always wanted to know about your father."

Jennifer finally let loose in a good cry. Between the meeting and getting the birthday party together, she hadn't let herself be open to the emotion she'd felt. But now, in Sam's arms, she could let go.

He held her, stroking her hair, until her tears subsided.

Backing away, Jennifer sniffed a few times and dabbed her face with her sweatshirt sleeve.

"Mother is going to be here any minute," she said, snapping back into the moment. "I need to get myself together."

"Jo Jo's coming?" Sam asked in annoyed surprise.

Jennifer rose from the couch. "Well, yes, it is her granddaughter's birthday, too."

She glanced back at him on her way to the kitchen. His expression told her he was thinking the same thing she was: even on a "normal" evening, Jo Jo could be difficult with her bewildering, impulsive behavior. But with so many questions to answer, this evening could prove to be even more challenging.

Jennifer kept walking, afraid Sam might try to talk her out of having Jo Jo join them. But just before getting to the kitchen she did hear him call out, "And we need to talk about that Catholic priest thing, too."

She leaned on the kitchen counter, steadying herself before launching into the final dinner preparation. *What a day!*

8:30 p.m.

Jennifer returned to the living room after getting Carys to sleep. Bath time had been extra long that evening because Carys had managed to get cake just about everywhere on her body—even behind her ears.

Sam and Jo Jo were sipping coffee. Jennifer knew that although Sam didn't really enjoy Jo Jo's company, he was always warm to her. She wished she could be as loving toward her mom as Sam was. Then again, Sam hadn't been through what she had with her mom. His family life had always been so . . . *normal.* At least that's what it had always felt like.

"Did you finally get her down?" Sam asked as Jennifer curled a foot under her and eased onto the sofa next to him.

"Yeah. She's all snuggled up against that stuffed caterpillar you got her." She looked at Jo Jo.

"Actually, that's from Finbar," Jo Jo said quietly. "He asked me to put his name on one of the presents."

Jennifer felt Sam's hand squeeze hers.

"Mother, I need to ask you some things about all that."

"About *all what*?"

Sometimes her mom could be so literal. "About my father. About Finbar."

Jo Jo nodded and looked away. Jennifer could see a combination of trepidation and relief on her mother's face.

Jo Jo set her coffee cup on the end table. "What do you want to know?" She pulled her legs underneath her on the chair opposite them and fanned her skirt out around her.

"I'm going to let you two ladies discuss this in private," Sam said, standing.

Jennifer appreciated his sensitivity.

"Besides, I think I have some work to do." He turned to Jennifer. "I'll be in our room on the laptop."

She smiled, then watched him walk away.

"I guess I just want to know what happened with you guys," Jennifer asked once he had left the room. "How did you get together? And why all the lies?"

Jo Jo exhaled deeply. "Well, remember I told you I used to cocktail-waitress over at that Holiday Inn on 71?"

Jennifer nodded. Her mom had worked there off and on, and drank there when she wasn't working, until Jennifer was born—and then she mostly just drank.

"One night Finbar came in with a couple of guys. They were staying there on business for a few nights."

It occurred to Jennifer that she had no idea what kind of work her father did or how he had made whatever amount of money he appeared to have. She interrupted her mother's story. "What did he do to get so wealthy?"

Jo Jo shook her head in disbelief. "He started out working for a box factory in Boston, where he grew up."

Ah, that accent, Jennifer remembered.

"Eventually he worked his way into management, then bought the whole company. It really took off, so he moved it to Dallas. Then I guess he invested in oil there in the seventies and eighties, which really made him roll in the dough. But when *I* met him, he'd just gotten into that."

She paused. "I think it was about ten years ago, I was reading an article in *People* magazine about self-made millionaires and there he was. Came from Irish immigrants who had nothing, and look at him now."

"Huh, Irish," Jennifer said. "I always knew there must be a reason why I love potatoes so much."

Her mother chuckled. "And it explains your strawberry blond hair and freckles." She reached for her coffee cup again and took a drink. She clearly wasn't taking pleasure in this story, though. "They came in again their second night, and after I got off work I went back to Finbar's room with him. One thing led to another and—"

"Okay, I get that part," Jennifer said, not wanting too much information. "But how did he know about me if he was gone after that?"

Jo Jo smiled, seeming to relax as she reminisced. "Our relationship ended up being more than a one-night stand. And for the record, I didn't know when I first got involved with him that he was married."

Jennifer thought her mother said that last part in defense of her choices.

"I'm not a complete hussy, if that's what you've been thinking."

"I didn't say you were, Mother."

Jo Jo continued her story, ignoring Jennifer's statement. "Even though Finbar had to go back to Dallas the next day, he called me a lot—we were constantly talking on the phone or he'd send me little notes and presents. And then eight months later, he surprised me by showing up one Friday night at the bar. You can imagine his reaction when he saw me with a big belly—I'd never told him I was pregnant."

"What? Why?" Jennifer couldn't believe her mom would keep such a secret from him.

Jo Jo looked down for a moment and smoothed out her skirt. "Because I didn't want him to think I was trying to trap him. If he wanted to be with me, I needed it to be because he loved me, not because of a sense of duty."

Jennifer felt the back of her neck getting hot again. *What about me? Was what was best for me ever a thought?* She backed off. "So what did he say when he saw you?"

"We talked, and as I suspected, he said he wouldn't leave Aileen."

Jennifer knew, as a Christian, that the entire affair, and leaving a wife for another woman, was a sin. But even so, she had desperately wanted to be part of a real family for so long that she couldn't help but ask. "He told me he wasn't in love with her, that he loved you. So why wouldn't he leave her?"

Jo Jo smiled slightly again, clearly glad to hear he'd told someone he loved her. "That may have been true, but he felt, as a Catholic, he couldn't get divorced and that was that."

"Oh, but he could sleep with another woman and get her pregnant? Exactly how did that jibe with his faith?" *Wait till I tell Father Scott about this!*

"I don't know, Jennifer." Jo Jo seemed drained. "But it didn't sit too well with me either. I told him if he wasn't going to leave Aileen and marry me, then he couldn't have anything to do with you. A few days after he left, I received a contract from his lawyer with a check for three hundred thousand dollars. The contract said that by accepting the check, I agreed I wouldn't sue him for support, and I wouldn't tell you or anyone that he was the father. I really needed that money, so that's what I did."

Jennifer couldn't believe what she was hearing. Her mother signed away—sold—her rights to her father?

"I always wondered when I was growing up how we lived without you or Monty working much," she said, edging up on anger. Then she remembered the times she couldn't do school activities because they didn't have the money, like when she wanted to join the Girl Scouts in second grade but Jo Jo said they couldn't afford the uniform. "Wait, though. If we had all that money, why were we always so poor?"

Jo Jo chewed the inside of her mouth. Jennifer could tell her mother thought she was under attack, but she didn't care. After thirty-six years, she felt she deserved to have these questions answered. "I used some of it to buy the house," she said cautiously, "and then the rest . . . well, since I wasn't working and needed my meds and stuff still . . . and I really couldn't work, you know, when I was sick . . ."

Her voice trailed off. Jennifer knew exactly what Jo Jo wasn't saying. It wasn't her prescribed medication that ate up the money—it was the recreational drugs and the booze. While Jennifer was taking sugar-and-butter sandwiches to school for lunch, her mom was home with that loser stepdad Monty, snorting cocaine and drinking Jack Daniel's all day. Meanwhile, she thought her father had left them when instead Jo Jo had shut him off first.

She could feel Jo Jo staring at her, so she met her eyes. "I cannot believe you let me think all those years that my father left us because he couldn't handle being a dad," she said in a quiet rage, hot tears forming in her eyes. "And then you took the one thing he left to provide for me and used it for yourself. Didn't you care about me? How I felt?"

Jo Jo leaned out from her chair and reached across the coffee table to put her hand on Jennifer's, but Jennifer pulled hers away. "Don't you try to comfort me now, Mother. You should have been doing that years ago, not now."

"Jen, I was so sick, and they didn't know as much then as they do now about medicines and therapies—"

"Don't talk to me about being sick." Jennifer stood. "You've used that mental illness your whole life as a way to get out of doing things. I realize having a kid was probably a real buzz killer for you, but you should have thought of that before you had sex with him."

Jo Jo gasped as the shrapnel of Jennifer's verbal shot filled the air.

But she wasn't finished yet. Ignoring an inner voice that was telling her to stop, she pressed on. "And I'm guessing you purposely got pregnant because you knew you could get some money out of my father," she seethed.

Jo Jo let out a high-pitched cry as her hands flew to her mouth. She jumped up from her chair, grabbed her coat off the back of it, and rushed toward the front door.

"How dare you, Mother," Jennifer hissed as she ran by. "How dare you."

Jo Jo flung open the door and raced through. Jennifer followed her as far as the front porch but refused to watch her mother drive away.

She walked back in the house, shutting the door behind her. She really wanted to slam it for effect but knew it would wake Carys. As she stormed away from the door, she noticed her hands shaking. Her anger had taken over her whole body. And that inner voice was still speaking to her.

Jennifer went into the kitchen and began loading the dishwasher, scraping the remnants of chicken marsala, mashed potatoes, and birthday cake from the plates. As much as she wanted to wallow in her anger and self-pity, she couldn't get a Scripture out of her mind: "'Vengeance is mine,' says the LORD."

She realized how harsh some of her words to her mother had been and felt ashamed. Even though her mother might have deserved Jennifer's wrath, her words had been cruel and meant to cause pain.

God, I'm sorry I took things into my own hands, she prayed as she rinsed and stacked. *Please help me find a way to deal with my feelings and my mother. I want to let this anger inside me go. I give it to you.*

The prayer calmed her down, but her heart jumped into her throat again when she realized she'd have to talk with her father more about his decision to deny his daughter and stay out of her life. Suddenly that situation seemed even more dire than the one with her mother.

And please show me how to talk with my father. I've just found him, and I don't want to lose him because of misunderstanding. So show me the way, Lord. Show me the way.

CHAPTER

24

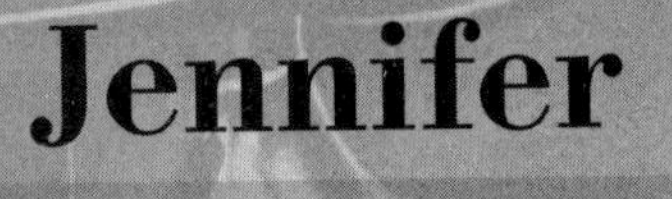

Jennifer

Friday, May 2

8:12 a.m.

Jennifer loved her family day off. She and Sam had taken off Mondays and Saturdays before, but they found there were too many loose ends to tie up on a Monday after their church's Sunday services. So now they took Fridays and Saturdays. By Friday, Sam could have his sermon written (at least that was the goal) and they had most of the week's church business handled. Plus it gave them two days off in a row.

Of course, it was rare for them even to have one day off without someone from the church needing one or both of them. But it was good in theory, at least. And this Friday was set to be busier than most, with a visit to her newly found father. She was eager to introduce him to Carys and Sam. And, of course, to get more of her questions answered. She'd even written them on a piece of paper she kept in her purse—she was up to forty-seven!

This morning, both Sam and Carys were sleeping later than usual, so Jennifer savored the quiet time. She put on a pot of coffee, then propped open the back door slightly to get fresh air. A deliciously warm sun was already pouring light into the breakfast nook.

Curling up on a dinette chair while the coffee brewed, she read her morning devotional from *My Utmost for His Highest* and said a brief prayer for the day's events. By that point her coffee was brewed, so she poured herself a cup, using her favorite, an *I Love Mommy* cup that Sam had given her last year for her first Mother's Day.

She walked back to her seat and turned her attention to that morning's paper, which she'd retrieved earlier from their front porch step. She flipped it open and started paging through the contents. World news, local news, editorials—those parts didn't interest her much. The lifestyle section featured dresses that "go from the office to happy hour"—not a real draw for a pastor's wife, she thought. Continuing to turn the pages, she ended up in the obituaries section. Since she'd lived her whole life in Red River, it wasn't unusual for her to find the parent of a former classmate—or even the classmate himself or herself—listed.

The small entry at the top right of the page caught her eye:

Quinn, Finbar, 81
Died May 1. Arrangements pending.

Jennifer let the paper fall to the table. *Dead! Already? Why didn't anyone call me? This isn't fair!*

As if on cue, the phone rang. She rose to answer it, her mind still swimming with questions.

"Hello?"

"Jen, it's Mimi. I just read about your dad. I'm so sorry."

Hearing Mimi say it made it all real for Jennifer. "Yes . . . yeah, I just read it, too."

"What? No one even called to tell you about it?"

Jennifer's throat started to tighten. "No," she managed in a small voice. *My father, I've lost my father! I just found him and now he's gone.*

The line beeped. "Mimi, let me call you back. It's the other line."

"Sure. Let me know what I can do to help, okay?"

"Okay, thanks. 'Bye."

Jennifer cleared her throat to prepare for the other call, then pressed the button.

"Hello?"

"Jennifer, this is Belinda. I'm glad I was able to reach you."

"Belinda, I just saw it in the newspaper. Why—"

She could feel Belinda's grimace through the phone. "Oh, Jennifer, I am so sorry you had to find out that way. Thursday is my day off. I got here as fast as I could, but I was in Indianapolis visiting my sister. I guess he passed in the late morning. The staff couldn't reach me, so they called the authorities to come remove the . . . body."

Belinda's voice went squeaky when she said "body," as though she were attempting to stifle a cry.

"I can't believe I just found him after all these years and he's gone already," Jennifer said, half thinking aloud and half wanting to share the grief with somebody.

Belinda seemed to regain her composure. "Yes, he purposely waited until he had just a few weeks before contacting you," she said, obviously unaware that Jennifer knew the real story. "He told me he didn't want you to feel obligated to have a relationship with him, given the circumstances of what he'd put you through in your life. So he figured two or three weeks would allow you a chance to get to know each other, if you wanted. And he also wanted to make sure you were, uh, suitable to be his heir."

The detective. "Is that why he had me followed?" One of the first questions Jennifer had been going to ask her father was why he had hired a detective instead of just calling her himself.

"Yes, well, that was really Channing, our butler," Belinda answered. Her use of "our" caught Jennifer's attention, but she didn't say anything. "When he contacted your mother after we moved here, she told him all about your life and how you were a pastor's wife. But he . . . he said he wasn't sure he could quite trust your mother, for some reason."

Oh, I know all about those reasons. "So he asked Channing to check you out."

It was a lot to absorb so early in the morning. On the one hand, Jennifer was encountering another closed door regarding her father. But on the other, she was learning more about him, which felt good even in the midst of the disappointment.

"What can I do?" Jennifer asked. "Will there be a funeral?"

"Mr. Quinn asked that we not do a funeral," Belinda replied matter-of-factly. "His body will be cremated today. His will dictates that his ashes be spread over County Clare, in Ireland. It's where his family is from."

Ireland! "Who will do that?" Jennifer asked innocently. "You . . . or another of the . . . staff?"

"I suppose as his heir and daughter, it would be your right," Belinda offered, but Jennifer detected a hint of resentment in her tone.

Jennifer had never imagined going someplace like that. "Whew, sounds expensive," she said under her breath. Then realizing that might have sounded impolite, she added, "But of course, if that's what he wanted, we will find a way."

Belinda huffed. "You do understand that you're inheriting quite a sum of money? I know you didn't get a chance to discuss it, but you *are* his sole heir."

That was one of the forty-seven questions, too, but not a huge priority for Jennifer. "Yes, he mentioned that. The house and so forth."

Belinda huffed again. "Oh, it's much more than that, Jennifer. His holdings are in the one hundred million range."

Jennifer nearly dropped the phone.

CHAPTER 25

Mimi

Monday, May 5

11:24 p.m.

Peace at the Plaisance house was short lived.

Mimi's father faithfully attended his AA meetings several nights a week, kindly escorted by Dan McCarthy. The rest of the time, he just as faithfully continued drinking. He swore he wasn't, that he'd given up the stuff. But hidden beer cans, foul-smelling breath, and odd behavior continued to follow him around like trusted companions.

Mimi grew frustrated that nothing seemed to change.

"I'm tired of feeling like a prisoner in my own house because I can't trust my own father to behave." She turned on a whirring floor fan—they both needed the background noise to sleep—and crawled into bed beside Mark, who was flipping in his Bible to where he'd last left off. It was their nightly ritual for Mark to read a passage from the Bible and then for them to pray together, thanking God for the blessings of the day. "I've had to start skipping PTA meetings, most of my volunteering, and the women's Bible study so I can stay home and be a warden."

"That isn't necessarily a bad thing," Mark said, not looking up.

"Mark, I'm serious."

"I know you are. Look, ever since I've known you, you've had a busy-ness gene in you. Since Archie's been staying with us, the situation has forced you to slow down."

"But—"

Mark held up his hand. "Maybe all for the wrong reasons, yes. But still, maybe it's also been a blessing in disguise."

"Let's stay focused on my father, shall we? We don't need this to turn into yet another of your lectures on how my life is so busy and out of control."

Mark shrugged. "I'm not. I'm just saying what I'm seeing."

"You act like you *like* having him around."

Mark laughed. "We both know that's not the truth!"

Mimi would not be appeased. "He's ruining my life. I thought he couldn't do more damage than when I was a kid. But now he's hijacked my family, my privacy, *and* my sanity."

"That's debatable." Mark smiled at her. "Your sanity was sadly lacking before Dad came on the scene."

"Ha. Ha. Ha. You get to escape to the church. But I'm left with four monkeys and my father." She was on a roll. "We draw clear boundaries, and he violates every one of them."

"I know."

"I mean, there's a *reason* no one else in my family will take him in."

"I know."

"But because I'm the good Christian, the good pastor's wife, I'm supposed to drop everything and support him and his habits. It's not fair."

"I know."

"And he doesn't even appreciate what we do for him."

"I know."

"Is that all you can say?"

Mark laid the Bible on his lap. "What do you want me to say, Mimi? You're saying it all quite well. Our complaining about it only breeds resentment, bitterness, and more anger. What does that accomplish?"

He rubbed his eyes and looked at her. Mimi noticed for the first time that Mark looked worn out. It gave her a little encouragement to see that her father's reckless behavior had been affecting him, too, even if he didn't show it too often.

"The man has no other place to go," Mark continued. "At least while he's in our home, he receives hope. At least here we can continue to show Christ's love to him. And that's ultimately what you want, isn't it? We have to keep praying for him and keep showing him love—even though we really don't feel very loving toward him."

"But for how long? How long are we supposed to put our lives on hold while he bulldozes right over us?"

"Is there a time limit on God's grace to us? Does he give up on us?"

She exhaled and leaned back against the headboard. "Ugh! There you go; being all Mr. Pastor on me again."

"Sorry, hon. I don't mean to. I'm trying to work through this whole mess myself. I question what God would have us do, too."

"Do you really?"

"All the time."

That made her feel better.

"But when I pray about your dad, I don't get a sense of release from our responsibilities."

He was right. Again. She'd felt the same way—and that was what was making her so agitated. Every day she prayed for something to give, for her father to change, for her to accept the situation. And every day she felt the same answer from God: *Don't quit on him yet.* Frankly, she wasn't too happy with God right at the moment.

But she knew Mark was right. She could get so caught up in the daily things Archie seemed to do to annoy her that she lost sight of the eternal issues on which she really needed to focus: her father *needed* Jesus in his life. Period.

Mimi felt Mark's hand touch hers. His hands were so strong, his nails neat and trimmed and clean. Completely unlike her father's rough, calloused hands with the long, yellowed fingernails.

Mark caressed her fingers. "Maybe you should confront your dad. Tell him all the things that you've felt about your childhood and about the pain he's causing you now. Get it off your chest so you can move forward with your life and forgive him."

"I've forgiven him," Mimi said defensively. "It's not my fault he keeps turning around and doing something else that tries my patience."

Mark raised his eyebrows, making her shift uncomfortably. This was territory she was not interested in traveling. "Anyway, that would go over like a lead balloon. You know my father. Nothing's ever his fault. It's never his responsibility."

"What if we looked at his life from the outside? Not as your father, but as a man who has messed up his life. Have you ever wondered what experiences may have shaped your dad?"

Mimi half laughed. "He's a selfish, unloving person, Mark. He's always been like that."

"Always?" Mark moved the Bible and turned toward her. Mimi felt as if he'd gone into mentoring mode. He was trying to get at something. She didn't mind that excitement Mark exhibited when he was turning it toward someone in the church. But she sure didn't want it turned on her. At least not about her father.

"Doesn't he drive you crazy?" Mimi said, trying to take the focus off her own complaints.

"Sure, he does. But let's stay on the topic."

"I am," she said, crossing her arms. "The topic of my father ruining our home and lives."

"No, the topic of what influenced your father to become the man he is."

The bedroom door creaked open and MJ stood in the doorway, his hair smashed against his head and his pajamas looking crinkled from too much tossing and turning.

"MJ," Mark said, "what have Mom and I told you about knocking before entering our bedroom?"

MJ stood for a moment, then slowly lifted a fist and knocked softly on the door. Mimi rolled her eyes. Normally, she would have taken his movement as being insolent, but something about his look made her pause.

"What's up, kiddo?" she asked.

"Grandpa's at it again," he said simply.

"At what?" Mark asked.

"He's mowing the lawn."

Mimi glanced at the bedside alarm clock: 11:36.

CHAPTER 26

Mimi

Tuesday, May 6

7:10 a.m.

Mimi lay quietly, listening to the rustling wind outside their bedroom window. Amazingly, everyone was still asleep. Even Milo hadn't awakened and demanded his breakfast.

The previous night's events came flooding back to her mind. Her father was out mowing their lawn at almost midnight!

It's a wonder he didn't run over his own foot. She rolled her eyes, then closed them. Why can't every morning start off like this? Simple. Quiet. Peaceful. Everything that she wasn't feeling on the inside.

Good morning, God, her mind prayed. *It's another day; a fresh start. Help me to honor you today. Better than I did yesterday. Help me to love my family better today. Help me to have patience toward my father today. Help me to keep sight of what's truly important to you.*

She rolled over and looked at her husband. His face was scrunched up, as though he was smelling rotten eggs. One arm was flung off the side of the bed, while the other was pinned behind his back. He certainly didn't look like a great spiritual leader this morning. A desire to touch him came over her, but she didn't want to chance waking him. After all, he'd stayed up half the night trying to talk some sense into her father.

Thank you for my husband, she continued to pray. *Bless him today. Give him a good, peaceful, restful day.*

He deserved it. He'd put up with a lot over the last year. Okay, really over the course of their marriage. He'd put up with her and her need for perfection and order. And she very rarely saw him lose his temper or even raise his voice. He balanced her so perfectly. But sometimes he seemed a little too perfect. Not in a bad way—it was more of a spiritual maturity he exhibited. And he always made her want to be better.

Although she did chuckle as she thought about his Wednesday afternoons: he'd sit in the living room in his overstuffed recliner and "study for his sermon." That always meant holding his Bible and concordance in his lap and within ten minutes dozing off.

Okay, so he wasn't completely perfect.

Her bladder nudged her to get up. Quietly, she shifted to move out from under the covers, but the shift must have awakened Mark, for he groaned and rolled toward her. One eye peeked open.

"Ugh," he muttered.

"Good morning." Mimi kissed his forehead.

"Where you going?"

"To the bathroom. I'll be right back. Go back to sleep. You need your rest."

Sighing, he rubbed his face and then stretched. "I have to get up. Who knows the condition of our backyard."

When Mimi came out of the bathroom, Mark was gone. *He's probably in MJ's room,* she figured. She tiptoed down the hallway, carefully avoiding the squeaky floorboard directly in front of Milo's room. She could just see Mark's back at the window. His shoulders were slumped.

Gazing around him she looked down at the yard.

"In all its glory," Mark whispered.

The scene of the crime looked as if the lawn mower had been attached to a bottle rocket. No rhyme or reason to the method of mowing. And certainly no straight lines. Not even close. It almost resembled one of those symbols created in cornfields—like the ones left by aliens in the movie *Signs*.

"You know, if this were someone else's house, it would be funny," Mark whispered again and motioned for her to follow him out of MJ's room. Fortunately, MJ didn't stir.

Poor kid, she thought. *Couldn't get any sleep because Grandpa was making so much racket. Now he has to get up and go to school.*

As soon as they stepped out of MJ's room, Mark said, "I bet we get a thank-you note from that kid's teacher today."

"Why?"

"He's probably going to sleep through her class. That will be the best behaved MJ's ever been."

Mimi grabbed Mark's arm and jerked him back. "Watch the step there," she said, pointing down to the squeaky floorboard. "We don't want to wake Milo any sooner than we have to."

"Hey, I have an idea," Mark said, seeming to brighten. Stepping ahead of her, he motioned for her to follow him back into their bedroom. As soon as she was inside the door, he closed it and clicked the lock they'd had installed. Then he turned and gave her a come-hither look.

"Now?" she asked incredulously. They could be on a sinking ship, and he'd want to make love.

"Everybody's asleep. We haven't had a moment to ourselves in weeks."

"Weeks? Mark, last week is hardly weeks."

"Well, it feels like it. And I did a manly thing last night and took care of your father."

"Are we one-upping now?"

His grin told her he thought he'd won.

She spied herself in the dresser mirror. *I look terrible!* Her blue eyes had dark rings around them. *I could be from the raccoon family.* Her blond hair desperately needed a root job. And it looked like a small pimple was forming just above her lip.

"Come on, Mims. I've been a good boy."

She sifted through her mental to-do list. With all the kids still asleep, she could knock off half a dozen chores. "I need to brush my teeth. And I should take a shower first."

"Then it will be too late."

She really wasn't in the mood for intimacy. But the words she'd just prayed came back to her. *Bless him today.*

Well, she mused, *he'd definitely consider that a blessing.*

"Okay," she said, walking toward the bed. "But under two conditions. You don't get me pregnant. I'm not having any more oopsy babies. And two, it's got to be quick, before those kids wake up. Milo will be yelling any minute."

10:27 a.m.

"Well, well, look who decided to get up." Mimi was going through the kitchen pantry and making a grocery list. She'd already tackled cleaning the kitchen—it had been cleaned the day before, but with four kids and two messy men, in Mimi's opinion it was never clean enough.

Her father was dressed in the same clothes as the night before. She noticed he had a grass stain on his left knee. He must have fallen while mowing, she figured.

His grunt was his only response.

"Want some coffee or something to eat? I can fry you up an egg."

"Nah. I'm not hungry."

"Dad, I wish you'd eat something. You're getting skinnier and skinnier."

"You sound like your mother. She was always nagging me."

"Sorry. I just assumed you'd want to eat." *I'm not going to let you ruin my day today. It's been really nice so far.* She thought of herself and Mark earlier. She hadn't been in the mood, but she'd enjoyed it once they'd gotten started.

He opened the refrigerator and grabbed the butter and a loaf of bread.

"Do you want it toasted?" she offered. "I can do that for you."

"I'm not completely useless!" he spat from out of nowhere. "I can butter my own bread. Just leave me alone. You treat me like I'm inept." Then under his breath she heard him finish, "You and everybody else. Worthless."

Mimi swallowed hard. "I . . . didn't mean anything by it, Dad. I just wanted to take care of you. I—"

"Well, don't." He slammed a butter knife onto the counter and stormed out of the kitchen.

CHAPTER

27

Lisa

Thursday, May 8

8:37 p.m.

Lisa sat on her dark green "slightly used" couch, knitting an afghan and half listening to *Are You Smarter than a 5th Grader?* Ricky and Callie were lying in the middle of the floor, homework strewn—and untouched—around them. Thursday nights were one of their favorite TV-watching evenings as a family.

Spending time together had always been important to Lisa and Joel, but it was even more so now that the kids were teenagers. In the blink of an eye, Lisa knew, the kids would turn into adults and be out of their house.

Fortunately, Thursday was also one of the only times Lisa could be assured that Callie wouldn't have her ear attached to their phone talking to Theresa, her best friend. But in the last year, it wasn't only Theresa who was calling. Callie had developed more as a young lady and now had "gentleman callers," as Joel teasingly called them.

As a fourteen-year-old, Ricky still wasn't all that interested in girls, preferring the company of his best friend, Steve Markins, and his video games and drum set.

Tonight, though, it was just the three of them. Joel was at church for an emergency business meeting. *More like an ambush,* Lisa had thought when Joel informed her as he was leaving right after supper.

Lisa knew that dealing with unruly, dissatisfied church members was part of the job description for a senior pastor and his family. After all, she remembered none too fondly her days growing up as a pastor's kid. But even with the messiness of church life, she and Joel still believed in the importance and power of the local church and believed deeply they'd been called to minister there. That didn't make the difficult days any easier, but their fervent belief in their calling did help them see the bigger picture. Usually.

More than a year of mutiny in their church, however, was making her lose sight of that picture—especially as she had to stand by and helplessly watch her husband get skewered at every turn.

Not enough tithes coming in? Joel's fault.

The youth group not growing? Joel's fault.

The aging, slightly senile organist losing her place during the worship service? Yep, that was Joel's fault, too.

One church member had even been so upset about updating the Bible translation from the King James to the New International Version that he had written Joel a scathing letter about it, then quit attending services. His letter had said: *If the King James version was good enough for Jesus and the apostles, it should be good enough for this church.*

The church had already cut Joel's salary in half, forcing him to take a part-time job at the hardware store. *If everybody in the church tithed, we wouldn't have financial issues,* Lisa knew. But what could they do—other than get up in the pulpit and start reading off the names of those members who didn't tithe? Hardly likely—or appropriate. But it always seemed those were the same folks who yelled the loudest about the church.

The youth program isn't as big and flashy as the church's down the street.

The hymn books are outdated.

The ladies' restroom needs a fresh coat of paint.

Meanwhile, her children had to accept hand-me-downs, and she and her husband hadn't had a date night in more than a year. *And* she and Joel tithed!

Lisa glanced up at the clock during one of the commercial breaks. Joel had been gone two and a half hours. She didn't even know what the meeting was about! It was all so secretive.

Absentmindedly, she began to knit faster, making her lose count. When she finally realized what she'd done, she'd knitted right through the white section with green yarn.

"Oh!" she said, looking down and seeing her mistake.

Callie rolled over on her back. "Worried about Dad?"

For a teenager, she was surprisingly attuned to what was going on outside her own little world. Lisa supposed much of that had to do with the fact that Callie had always been aware—and a little bitter—about the church's goings-on. In fact, it had caused Callie almost to lose her faith completely because of the way the church had handled their family.

For a moment, Lisa considered denying it. But she knew that would do no good. Callie was already aware of what was going on. To lie about it wouldn't help the situation and could cause Callie's trust in her to waver.

She smiled and shrugged, hoping it looked genuine and nonchalant. "I'm just wondering how it's going."

"You mean, you're hoping they're not ganging up on him."

"Well," Lisa said, "that, too."

"You don't think they're going to fire him?" Ricky now sat up and turned his attention to the conversation.

"No, sweetie." Lisa continued her knitting. "They're not going to fire your dad." *Yet,* she mentally added. But anything was possible. "Now, hush, the program's back on."

Ricky turned back toward the television to see what question Jeff

Foxworthy was getting ready to ask, but Callie continued to look at her mom.

"Everything's going to be okay, Callie," Lisa said, hoping to reassure her daughter.

A half hour later Joel walked through the front door and threw his keys onto the side table next to Lisa.

"Dad!" Ricky said, sitting up again.

"How did it go?" Lisa asked, laying her handiwork to her side.

Joel let out a heavy sigh and shook his head.

"Kids," Lisa said, "maybe you should head up to your bedrooms while your dad and I talk. You can tackle that homework that should have been done earlier."

"Come on!" Callie and Ricky whined, almost in unison.

Always the outspoken one, Callie said, "It's not like we don't know what's going on."

"Yeah," Ricky chimed in.

Lisa looked into Joel's brown eyes. They were one of her favorite things about him. Usually warm and twinkling, tonight they seemed dull. Almost a little deadened.

He shrugged.

"Okay," she said.

"Well," Joel said, "it was definitely an ambush. They called for my resignation."

"What?" Callie jumped up.

"Who did? Who was there?" Lisa asked.

"The usual bunch. Chuck Abrahams, Richard Malloy . . ."

"On what grounds?" Callie asked.

"My poor leadership skills, my poor preaching skills, my decision to remove Tom from teaching Sunday school, you name it."

"Your poor preaching skills," Ricky repeated. "Who said that?"

"Chuck."

Callie snorted. "As if he'd know. The man has narcolepsy."

"Callie," Lisa reprimanded gently.

"It's true!"

"It was all very mean-spirited," Joel announced, sitting on the edge of the couch and removing his shoes.

"Ya *think*?"

Lisa could tell Callie was revving her engines for a fight. She also knew that to engage her would only make it worse. "So," Lisa said, "how was it left?"

"They want me to back down on pulling Tom from teaching."

"They're issuing ultimatums?" Ricky asked, astonished. "That's rich!"

"But you can't do that," Lisa said. "The man has a—" She quickly stopped herself. She was okay with the kids hearing their conversation up to a point. But giving them damning information about a member of their church wasn't acceptable.

"I know," Joel said, as if reading her mind. "I asked him if he was willing to repent."

"He was *there*?" Lisa was continually amazed by how easily people could wallow in their sins and expect you to accept them as upstanding Christians.

"Oh, yeah."

Lisa could hear laughter from the television audience in the background. "Mute that, will you, Ricky?"

Ricky grabbed the remote and hit the mute button, causing the television abruptly to go silent.

And I'm sure he fell to his knees in repentance—begging the Lord to forgive him and vowing to set his life straight, Lisa thought. "So they've taken the church hostage?"

"It appears so." He swept his hand through his black hair.

He has so much gray, she thought, as if just noticing his hair for the first time. Before this mess with the church started, Joel just had the beginnings of gray sprinkled around his temples. Now more and more of it seemed to be popping up throughout his hair. *It's the stress.*

Lisa gazed down at her hands. They were shaking. "You didn't give in, right?"

"No. But I'm getting tired of not having any of *my* supporters showing up and defending me. It's as if this church *wants* a fight."

Lisa rose, walked to Joel, and touched his cheek. Then she gently gave him a soft kiss on the lips and whispered, "Then I guess we have to be prepared to give them what they want."

CHAPTER 28

Lulu's Café

Tuesday, May 13

12:37 p.m.

The PWs had their bimonthly lunch routine down to such a science that they had often finished eating by twelve-thirty and could just relax with refills on their drinks. Some days, like today, they even indulged in a little dessert.

With all of Jennifer's news about finding her father, the meal had gone especially quickly since Jennifer was doing the talking and the other three could eat. As Gracie brought a vanilla ice-cream sundae with four spoons, Jennifer was taking the last bite of her chef's salad and finishing her story.

Mimi, Felicia, and Lisa had all talked to Jennifer by phone the week Finbar died. When Jennifer had picked up Carys's birthday cake from Mimi, she'd told Mimi all about meeting her father earlier that day. So when Mimi saw in the newspaper that Finbar had died, she first called Jennifer but then she called Felicia and Lisa to fill them in, since she knew, as she told Lisa, that they'd want to extend their condolences, too.

What none of them had grasped, though, was the extent of Finbar's riches. So when Jennifer revealed at lunch that she was the sole heir to a hundred-million-dollar fortune, they'd decided it was a perfect day to celebrate with ice cream, a pastor's wife's equivalent to a champagne toast.

As they dug into their treat, the women were full of questions.

"Didn't you think to Google him before the will was read to find out what his business was and how much money he had?" Felicia asked.

Jennifer nodded. "Sam did while I was having those terrible words with Mother." Lisa saw Jennifer cringe and knew she regretted what she'd said to her mother. "He told me later that his holdings were in the millions, but I just assumed he would have donated to charities. I never dreamed I'd be the *only* one in the will besides Mother and her trust."

"What will you do with the money?" Mimi said incredulously. "And that house. You know, I do think I remember seeing something in the Cincinnati paper about the house when they were building it."

"I guess we'll just sell it." Jennifer shrugged. "As for the money, we don't know yet. Invest it, I guess. It's not like we're giving up the ministry and moving to Hawaii or anything. Not that I didn't think of that."

They all laughed.

"I'd like to see inside that house before you put it on the market," Mimi said. "Decorating ideas, you know."

Jennifer shook her head. "Oh, goodness, you won't be getting any ideas there. Unless you like heavy velvet draperies and dark wood. It's straight out of a haunted-house movie. But I guess Dad liked that look for some reason."

All that money and *a mansion*, Lisa thought, trying not to be envious. She didn't want the money for herself but for the church. She knew extra resources would make all the difference in the church's situation and perhaps Joel could relax for once.

They all sat quietly for a minute as they munched the sundae. Jennifer's explanation was a lot to take in—she finds her father, loses her father, gets in a terrible fight with her mother, and ends up a multimillionaire. *Whew.*

"Are you planning a memorial service?" Felicia finally said.

Jennifer set down her spoon, the dessert reduced to a puddle of melted ice cream. "He wanted his ashes spread in Ireland, so that's what we're going to do, me and Sam. We're hoping we can go later this summer and have his parents keep Carys for us. Sort of a second honeymoon."

A second honeymoon. How romantic. Okay, now I am jealous. Not because I don't want Jennifer to have it. I just want to go, too!

Lisa pondered her feelings. *No, what I really want is just for things to be normal again. Routine. No interfering parishioners threatening us for trying to lead the ministry the way we feel God is calling us.*

"Enough of this Danielle Steele novel." Mimi winked at Jennifer across the table. "You guys have to hear what *my* dad did."

She told them about the late-night lawn mowing and Mark's insistence that she be forgiving and care for her father regardless of his alcohol abuse and questionable antics.

"So I'd just started to work toward that, slowly, mind you," she said, "when Mother's Day rolled around Sunday. It started out nice. The kids came in with a tray filled with half-burned food for me to choke down."

Lisa laughed. "I remember those days. Wait till they're teenagers—you'll be lucky if they even remember they *have* a mother, let alone fix her breakfast."

"Yeah, the food stunk, but it was still fun just to have them around me, cuddling while I ate. So we went to church and that was nice. We did our usual Mother's Day thing at church with the flowers for the mothers and all, like you probably did." The others nodded. "Afterward we went with the Taylors out to eat. And then . . . we got home."

Lisa leaned forward and put her chin in her hands. Mimi was clearly building to something.

"When we walked in, there was Dad on the sofa, a beer can in his hand and a cigar in his mouth. He jumped up and came swaggering over to me. I tried to get the kids out of the room, but I didn't have a chance. He got right up in my face, pointed his finger, and said, 'You know what you are? You're nothing but a tramp, like your mother. Your whole life you've been Miss Perfect and always in control. Well, I'm here to tell you, you aren't perfect, girl. You've got nothing on those street-walkers down on Metro Boulevard.'"

Lisa sat stunned; she could tell Jennifer and Felicia were, too.

"Where was Mark in all this?" Felicia asked.

Mimi sat back and crossed her arms. "It happened so fast and we were all so shocked, we just stood there. The weird thing was, when he was done with his speech, he just went back over to the couch and started looking at the TV again like nothing had happened. Meanwhile, the six of us were still standing in the doorway, and Mark hadn't even set Milo down yet."

"Alcohol makes people do weird things," Jennifer said. Lisa knew that with Jennifer's mom's history, Jennifer was used to the kinds of behavior Lisa's dad was displaying. "Don't take it personally."

"It's difficult not to," Mimi responded, a few tears in her eyes.

"The adult-child relationship with a parent is a strange one," Lisa added, hoping to build Jennifer's case for not dwelling on the confrontation. "My mother can cut me with one sentence, like no one else. Thank the Lord I have my father to lean on. He's always been like a rock."

"Just wait till my crazy family gets out here in a few weeks," Felicia said. Lisa could tell everyone was going into "comfort mode," as they often did when one of them was in a crisis. And that's what made this foursome so special—when one hurt, the others commiserated. "I'm sure someone's going to have words and someone's going to get his or her feathers ruffled."

"Yes, but this is deeper than that," Mimi said. "I think my dad has some issues that go beyond the drinking. He's just using that for now to mask his pain. But I'm not sure where his pain comes from."

Gracie appeared with their check and handed it to Jennifer. The others protested.

"Are you kidding?" Gracie said, her hands on her hips. "You should be letting Mrs. Trump here buy your lunch every time. Yeah, and I'd be changing locations out of this dump, too. A steak place maybe."

They all chuckled. "I told her to give me the check when I came in today," said Jennifer, "but I won't do it every time. I know we all have our pride."

"'But the one who is rich should take pride in his low position, because he will pass away like a wild flower,'" Gracie recited. Without waiting for a reaction from the women, she turned and walked away.

Lisa looked across at Mimi, whose mouth was agape. "Was she just quoting James to us?" Lisa asked.

"I think so," Mimi said cautiously. She watched Gracie amble toward the kitchen, as if she might learn something by looking at her longer.

"Guess that Bible we gave her is paying off!" Felicia said, shaking her head and chuckling.

CHAPTER 29

Jennifer

Wednesday, May 14

4:35 p.m.

Jennifer walked into the house to find Sam's parents, Dale and Patty, sprawled on the floor with Carys, watching her build a tower of blocks.

"Mama!" Carys said. She toddled over to Jennifer, knocking down the tower in the process.

"Hi, peanut," Jennifer said, reaching down and lifting her onto her hip.

"How did it go this afternoon?" she asked Dale and Patty. They had driven up from West Virginia that morning and stopped by the church before picking up Carys at day care to spend some time with her.

"Fine, of course," Patty said, standing and smoothing Carys's hair. "She's our little angel."

"Ah, you haven't seen her when she doesn't get her way," Jennifer joked, kissing Carys on the cheek and depositing her on the floor, where she made her way back to the blocks. "Well, I'd better get dinner going."

"Let me help," Patty offered, following her.

"Sure," Jennifer said. Normally she didn't like extra people in the kitchen when she was cooking, but Patty was different. She felt calmer with her around—the exact opposite of what she felt around her own mother. In fact, early in her marriage she had taken to calling Patty "Mom." She wouldn't even call her own mother Mom, instead calling Jo Jo "Mother."

"How was your Mother's Day?" Patty asked.

Jennifer pulled a package of pork chops from the refrigerator and set them on the counter, then leaned down to inspect the produce drawer. "It's nice to actually be able to go and enjoy church that day now," she said. She pulled out several plastic bags. "All those years before Carys, I dreaded church on Mother's Day."

She looked at Patty, who was nodding sympathetically. Patty took the cucumber and green pepper she handed her, then turned to the sink to rinse them. "You know, seeing what you and Sam went through trying to conceive has made me so much more sensitive to people in our congregation who might be going through that." Dale and Patty attended a small nondenominational church in West Virginia.

Those frustrating feelings of failure because of infertility seem so long ago, Jennifer thought. *So much has happened since then.*

As if reading her mind, Patty, who was now chopping the pepper, asked, "Have you been able to find any of your father's family?"

Jennifer popped open the plastic around the pork chops. "No. I've done every Google search I can think of. Even the staff at his house didn't know about anyone. And that Belinda, she took off like a rocket as soon as she'd made sure her job was done. She didn't even tell me she was leaving. I stopped by the house and one of the housekeepers there said she had called a taxi the night before. No note, no call, nothing."

Patty scraped the chopped pepper into a large bowl. "Why do you suppose she did that?"

Jennifer shook her head as she walked to the sink to wash her hands, the chops now frying away in the pan. "I don't know, except she did act really weird at the reading of the will. I think she . . . maybe expected something from my father."

Patty joined her at the sink to peel the cucumber. "You mean she thought he would leave her money?"

Jennifer dried her hands. "That was my sense. But even the little contact I had with her, I always thought she was too involved in his life, a little too dedicated. You know what I mean?"

"Maybe she had feelings for your father. It sounds like she was with him for a long time."

Jennifer thought about that for a moment. "That's possible. And I could see how difficult, then, that would be for her to know that he never felt the same about her."

Patty nodded. "Unrequited love."

Jennifer felt sorry for Belinda. In fact, she had planned to give Belinda a generous sum to help her get established elsewhere, but now that she was gone, with no contact information, she wasn't sure she'd be able to find her.

"It's like I've been playing a long game of hide-and-seek these last few months," Jennifer said, seasoning the chops. "First that detective, then my father, and now Belinda and my father's family. Even though I've found some things, I seem to be seeking more."

"Maybe your mother could help," Patty suggested. "Surely your father mentioned some names to her over the years—a brother or sister of his perhaps? I mean, with the Internet, you'd only need a few leads to find them."

Mother. Jennifer hadn't talked to her since Carys's birthday. Although she knew it wasn't right to blame her for her father's death, she couldn't help but wonder how things could have been different if she had at least known who her father was all those years. Just having the assurance that her father did want her could have made all the difference in the world to her self-identity, she thought. That her mother denied her that opportunity and instead spent the money intended for her, leaving her to flounder in a sea of turmoil and disadvantage, was not something she could just forgive and forget. She justified her decision to the Lord by saying she wasn't taking vengeance into her own hands as the Bible rebukes. She was just staying away from the toxic person with the problems.

She pulled three plum tomatoes from a plastic bag and started slicing them.

Patty stepped over to the stove. "We'd better turn these," she said gently and picked up the spatula next to the pan.

After flipping the meat, Patty moved back to the counter where she had been chopping the cucumber.

Now tearing lettuce in her hands and dropping it into the bowl, Jennifer said, "I've pretty much cut off communication with Mother. I couldn't take being around her after I found out what she'd done."

Patty laid down the paring knife and wiped her hands on a dish towel. She turned to Jennifer, who kept her eyes on the bowl. "Jen, your mom did the best she could with what she had. No, she shouldn't have spent that money the way she did"—Jennifer had told her the whole story over the phone—"but she chose to give you life when clearly she could have done something different."

Jennifer thought about that. Abortion wasn't legal then, but from what she'd read and heard, it was still possible to get one. Knowing her mom's lack of morals, at least at the time, it was surprising she *hadn't* terminated the pregnancy.

She looked at Patty. "I guess you're right there. But I wish she'd just put me up for adoption. Maybe I could have had a better chance—"

"I think you did all right," Patty assured her. "Look where you are now! God knew what he was doing. His hand was on your little life from the beginning."

God? Jennifer thought. She wouldn't believe that he had anything to do with her mom's decision-making process then. If he had, she wouldn't have been conceived to begin with. But she did believe he was in charge, even if her mom didn't acquiesce to his leading all the time.

"I still wish I could have been adopted," she said defiantly. Good reason didn't always break through her tough emotional layer. "I think if my mother really cared about me, she would have given me the chance at a better life."

She thought about Jessica and how she had let them adopt Carys to them. *Oh!* she thought. With all the hubbub over her father, Jennifer had forgotten to mail Jessica a photograph of Carys. She made a mental note to do that and to remind Sam that Jessica had not tried to make further contact with them, as they'd both worried when they'd received her letter a few months earlier.

"That's difficult to know, Jen," Patty said quietly, putting the veggies into the salad bowl. "And who knows what kind of person you might have been had you been raised elsewhere? Having to care for your mother and go through what you did has made you who you are today. Think of the ministry opportunities you've had because of that."

Jennifer tossed the salad with a pair of tongs. Though she knew what Patty meant, she wasn't ready yet to relinquish her disgust over her mother's behavior. She wasn't going to confront her about it anymore, she just wasn't going to deal with it—or her—at all. After all, she didn't want to take vengeance into her own hands.

CHAPTER

30

Lisa

Thursday, May 15

2:35 p.m.

"Thank you for seeing me on such short notice," Lisa said, twisting the glass of lemonade in front of her.

The elderly woman chuckled. "We seem to have these important afternoon teas and chats about once a year, don't we? But there's no need for you to be so nervous."

Lisa smiled. Bonnie Bentz was one of Lisa's favorite people at the church—a true spiritual giant. When Lisa and Joel had had marital problems a few years earlier, it was Bonnie who invited Lisa to her house for tea and a chat. The widow had given her excellent advice, encouragement, and prayer support. Then last year, when Callie had started to act out her rebellion, Bonnie was the person to whom Lisa turned.

Now, once again, Lisa sat in Bonnie's sunroom that overlooked her flower-covered backyard, having tea, lemonade, sandwiches, and conversation. Lisa noticed the garden looked as if it had had a slight revival since the last time she'd visited.

Bonnie slowly settled herself into a chair across from Lisa and lightly patted her pure white, wispy hair. "My granddaughter visited a few weeks ago and insisted on fixing up my backyard," she said, obviously noticing Lisa's gaze. "My Charlie and I used to love working out there. Ah." She sighed. "Those days are long gone. I'm ninety-two this year, you know. I can't believe the Lord has been so gracious to allow me this long on the earth. And to keep my mind sharp . . . He is good, is he not?"

"He is," Lisa agreed.

"But he does seem silent right about now, doesn't he?"

Lisa nodded.

Bonnie lifted a plate of dainty finger sandwiches and passed them to Lisa.

"Charlie and I were some of the founding members of this church way back in the Stone Age." She winked. "One of the things that concerned Charlie and me—and still does concern me—is the number of pastors we've gone through and the pattern by which those pastors have left. We've had good pastors, very good ones. Godly men who loved the Lord and his work. We've had not-so-good pastors. We don't need to worry ourselves over them, though. The longest pastor we had was our second one. He stayed for twelve years, if I recall correctly. The others moved in and out all in about the span of five years or so. Now, I don't claim to be an expert in these things, but that certainly doesn't seem to be coincidence, does it?"

Lisa shook her head and nibbled on her ham-salad sandwich triangle.

"And now here you are. Pastor's been here a little more than five years, and surprise, we're having trouble. But!"—Bonnie lifted an arthritic, crooked finger in the air—"Pastor is fighting back. He's a good man, your husband. I believe God has brought him to this church to break the cycle of what's been happening here. But the fight is costly." She narrowed her eyes at Lisa and grimly nodded. "Yes. And you and your family are paying a heavy price."

Surprisingly, Lisa started to tear up. She knew Bonnie understood.

"Oh, my dear," Bonnie said and reached across the table to a tray that held a box of tissues. She held the box out for Lisa to take one. "I know this doesn't feel too comforting right now, but there are plenty of good people in our church who are praying for you and your family and for our church's very survival."

"But why is nobody standing up against this?" Lisa blurted out. "I appreciate the prayer support, but where is the action? My husband feels like he's being filleted."

Bonnie simply nodded. "You're right. And he's right to feel that way."

"Then why isn't anybody *doing* anything about it?"

Bonnie nodded again. "They should be. But I think they don't know how. To some degree, they're afraid. And those who aren't are like me . . . we're considered old, past our prime." She held up her hand when Lisa started to protest. "I'm not saying *I* believe I'm past my prime. I'm saying that's how I'm treated. An old woman who speaks her mind, but who too often gets pushed to the side because of my age. I get humored, but not listened to. And I do think I have a little bit of life experience and wisdom."

Lisa smiled sadly. She felt sorry for Bonnie because she knew it was all true. A ninety-something saint had a wealth of wisdom and knowledge, but nobody in the church ever seemed to want to hear it. They were more interested in listening to big talkers who hadn't lived through the fires of life.

"Charlie and I used to speak out against Tom and the others," Bonnie said. "It's been very frustrating."

"Why didn't you leave the church?"

"My dear, do you up and quit when things in your life aren't exactly the way you want them? No. Neither do you leave your church when things go wrong. Besides, if we left, who would be there to continue the fight?"

"If he's been such a problem, why *hasn't* somebody kicked him out—or at least stood up to him?"

Bonnie smiled grimly and passed Lisa the lemonade pitcher. "Because . . . he's a bully. Everybody is afraid of him. They *should* have kicked him out long ago. But the elders always made excuses, saying we shouldn't judge, that we should accept people, including Tom and his bullying, sinful behaviors. What do they call it nowadays? Tolerance? I call it cheap grace."

"Joel has talked to Tom on several occasions and called him to repentance."

"Good, good."

"He's tried to follow the calling of Jesus in Matthew 18—to talk to him first in private, then along with some others as witnesses. And . . ." Lisa trailed off.

"The truth is, your husband has a difficult decision to make. He knows what needs to be done. He also knows the reality of the consequences to that. He's run out of options, hasn't he?"

Lisa swallowed hard. She could feel her breathing becoming shallow and her shoulders tensing at the thought.

"Well then, I was right. Your husband is the man God sent to do the job. The man we've been praying for, for years." Bonnie leaned forward until her sagging breasts pushed against the table edge. "Stand true, Lisa. Place a spiritual hedge around your family, because this is serious business. This is a fight. And the consequences can be eternal. But stay focused on the spiritual things. God is in control and he *will* right the wrongs."

"I've watched my husband go through this," Lisa said. "He doesn't want to pursue this drastic measure—not because he's afraid, but because he's burdened over Tom's soul."

"Yes, yes. Tom's heart is so hardened, I fear for him, too. But this church needs a new beginning. And, Lord willing, I'm planning to stick around long enough to see it happen. I believe God wants to do mighty things through our church, but he needs to clear the way first."

Lisa agreed. But the anxiety was still overwhelming. Why did it have to be Joel to carry this out? Why couldn't it have been the previous pastor? Or even the next one? She thought back to a saying she'd heard before: Sometimes there's only one way to peace. It's not to back away from a challenge. It's not to go around it, trying to avoid it. It's to go directly through it.

"God grant us the strength, courage, and grace to walk through this," Lisa whispered, not realizing she'd said it aloud.

"Amen," Bonnie whispered back. "May it be so."

CHAPTER
31
Felicia

Friday, May 23
6:30 p.m.

Felicia's parents and her sister Maria's family took separate flights that arrived exactly two hours apart. With no car large enough to carry the whole clan, Felicia had gone first to pick up her parents and bring them to Red River. Dave was now on the road, headed to the airport to get Maria, Javier, and Estella.

"If it's my birthday, why am I doing all the work?" Dave had asked when Felicia informed him he'd need to help with the airport runs. Although she knew he didn't really mind, she still felt bad that he had the hassle of her family on his birthday weekend.

Wait till he finds out no one's talking to one another, she thought, wiping down the kitchen counter after serving her parents dinner. They were both ensconced in front of the TV with Nicholas, who was showing his grandpa a video game.

When Felicia had picked them up at the airport, there had been the usual hugs and smiles common to their greeting. But once they were in the car, Felicia got a foreboding sense of dread from what her mother informed her.

"Javier and I are not talking," she'd said from the backseat.

I can't believe she'd think Maria wouldn't have told me about it.

"And your papa is supporting me in this," her mother continued.

Felicia sneaked a glance at her father, in the passenger seat. He didn't look too committed to the idea.

"Mama"—Felicia tried to keep an even tone—"maybe you two can just, I don't know, agree to disagree. I mean, you're still talking to Gina, right? So why hold Javier accountable?"

Although she knew Dave's logic wouldn't work on her mother, she had decided to give it a shot anyway.

"Gina has nothing to do with this," her mother said.

Felicia caught a slight snicker from her father.

Felicia sighed. She did not want the next five days in her home to be full of acrimony, especially with Dave's big birthday party the next night. While she knew it was silly, she still felt a little out of place as a Hispanic in a mostly white town. The last thing she needed was for people to see her family caught up in some kind of mama/macho drama.

She bit her lip and drove. It wasn't in Felicia's nature to tell her mother what to do. So rather than pursue it, she changed the subject.

But now, with Javier and family on their way to Red River, Felicia wondered how things would shake out. Would her mother shun Javier? Would Javier just ignore her?

She didn't have long to think about it because, as soon as she'd finished rinsing the kitchen sponge, she heard Dave's car pull in the driveway.

"They're here! They're here!" Nicholas screamed, jumping up and down and racing around the family room.

"Okay, Nicholas, calm down," Felicia said quietly, walking toward the back door. She felt as excited as he was, though, to have her sister's family there.

Estella came bouncing in first, clutching a doll that had seen better days, with an eye missing and an arm dangling from its socket. Maria followed, a shopping bag hanging from her arm. Javier and Dave brought up the rear, each with two pieces of luggage in hand.

"Estella! Maria!" Felicia called, doling out hugs.

Nicholas wasted no time. "Hey, Estella, wanna go to my room and play?"

Felicia wanted to tell him to wait a few minutes, until they got settled, but with all the hubbub, the two escaped without instruction.

"That'll probably be the last we see of them until they get hungry," Maria said, setting the shopping bag on the breakfast nook table. "I brought tortillas from the place."

Felicia squealed. She knew "the place" meant Lavequeria Tortilla factory, home of what the Lopez family thought were the most delicious tortillas of anywhere in L.A. The company's name was such a mouthful they'd shortened it to "the place" years ago.

Felicia's parents came over to greet the new arrivals. *Oh, here we go.*

"Hi, Papa," Maria said casually, offering him a hug. She then did the same for her mother.

Felicia saw her dad start to offer a handshake to Javier but her mom pulled back his arm.

"Josef," Javier said solemnly. "Lupita."

They both nodded at him in recognition.

Felicia felt Dave prod her in the small of her back. "Let's get this luggage to your room," she burst out, hoping to stomp out any buds of anger building between her parents and brother-in-law. "And I bet you're starving. I made Mama and Papa some sloppy joes—we can heat them up."

"Sounds like a plan," she heard Dave mutter from behind. He led the way as he and Javier hauled the luggage toward the Morrisons' third bedroom. Felicia made a mental note to stop in that room—her office with a futon—to make sure she'd cleaned up the papers on her desk. She'd worked right up until it was time to head for the airport that afternoon.

"I see you haven't been able to talk some sense into your husband," Lupita said to Maria.

"Ah, Lupi," said Josef, waving off his wife and returning to the sofa.

"Mama, I tried," Maria said meekly. "But he says it's for you to apologize."

Lupita shook her head. "For me? After the disrespect he showed me?"

Maria looked at Felicia as if she thought Felicia might have an idea about what to do.

Felicia grasped the shopping bag and darted for the kitchen. "Let's get some dinner heated up for you guys," she said, hoping again to change the subject. *Wonder how many times I'll have to do this over the next few days?*

What she really wished was that Gina was there. Even though Gina was aggressive-bordering-on-disrespectful, she knew how to cut through the niceties to get to the meat of a situation, sometimes painfully so. Felicia didn't have that kind of resolve when it came to family. It was as though she used up whatever assertiveness she possessed in her job, leaving none for these kinds of circumstances.

But unfortunately, Gina and Li's flight was arriving so late that night that they would just stay in Cincinnati and take a bus to Red River for the party. Felicia hoped (and prayed) that having all the church people in the house would quell any potential for a battle between her mother and Javier, giving them plenty of space to be apart. If they wanted to argue or give each other the cold shoulder the rest of their stay, that was fine with her, sort of, but she wished they would avoid each other at the party and deal with their differences another time. She didn't need the whole church to witness a tongue-lashing between the two.

Deep down, though, she knew peace was about as likely as Lavequeria Tortilla opening a branch in Red River.

CHAPTER 32

Lisa

Friday, May 23

10:57p.m.

Joel sat on the edge of their bed and wearily removed his shoes. Lisa had just changed into her nightgown and finished her nighttime routine of brushing her teeth, washing her face, and combing her hair. And now she walked toward the bed, hoping she'd get a good night's sleep.

As she looked at how worn out her husband appeared, she realized he needed that rest even more than she did. Neither of them had been able to sleep much over the last several weeks as the situation at the church seemed to worsen. Tom had refused to back down and give up his Sunday school teaching position. He had every member of his group write letters to the paper, the mayor, and the town council, claiming Pastor Barton was a hypocrite and a troublemaker.

And the sweet spirit Lisa used to enjoy during worship times now seemed to be gone. Coldness was taking its place.

Lisa reached out for her husband and rested his head against her chest as she massaged his neck and ran her fingertips through his hair.

"Oh, honey, I know the kind of toll this is taking on you. And I'm worried about you. I'm worried *for* you."

His arms went around her waist and tightened. She could feel his body shaking.

They held each other quietly as she listened to the wind blow softly through the tree outside their bedroom window.

Joel's body continued to shake, jerking every few moments.

"Joel?" she said finally. That was all she knew to say. What comfort could she give her husband? What words could she possibly say that would bring a sense of peace to what they both felt God was calling him to do?

"Joel," she said again and leaned down to kiss the top of his head.

"Why won't he repent, Lisa?" His face looked anguished. Frown lines had appeared where youthful skin once lay. "Why? Why is he going down this road to destruction? And taking others with him?"

"I don't know, baby."

"And why am I the person called to make this right? I know I should feel honored that God has chosen me. Your dad told me I was the man for such a time as this. But why me? Why?"

Lisa knew she'd be thinking the same thing if she were in his place.

"I'm not perfect, Lisa. I mean, *you* know that better than anybody. I've made a lot of mistakes. Like two years ago when I almost lost you and our marriage! I haven't handled every church decision well. I've failed too many times. I've messed up. I've blown it. Over and over and over." He dropped his head back against her.

"We all have, Joel. But I know you've done the best you could. You've always tried to put God and the church first. You've—"

"But what if I'm making a mistake? What if I'm making a terrible mistake, and I'm leading these good people down the wrong path?"

"Look at me, Joel," she said sternly. "Aside from your fear right now, do you know that what Tom is doing is wrong?"

"Yes."

"And it's hurting the church—whether you're the pastor or not?"

"Yes."

"And haven't you asked a group of strong spiritual believers to pray and fast about this decision?"

Joel nodded.

"Well, then, don't you think God is going to answer your prayers and give you wisdom?" She spoke more boldly than she really felt.

He looked at her, unsure. "How can I lead these people when I have so many doubts myself?"

"You and every leader in the Bible. And yet, every time in the Bible, God showed up and provided abundant amounts of grace. Joel, he's going to do that for you, too. I believe that." *Oh, Lord, I believe. Help my unbelief.*

CHAPTER 33

Felicia

Saturday, May 24

6:13 p.m.

Felicia stood between the living and family rooms and looked back and forth. She was surprised by how calm she felt, considering her house was ready to burst at the seams with her family and many of the church members milling around at once. But as she circulated among them, picking up empty plates and glasses and stopping to chat along the way, she was pleased to see everyone was enjoying themselves, especially Dave.

Thank you, Lord, she thought, dropping a handful of icing-smeared cake plates in a trash barrel next to the door that led from the kitchen to the garage. *I couldn't have done this without you.*

Even the morning had been fairly pleasant. Her mom and Javier weren't talking, but with eight people in the house—plus Gina and Li when they arrived with Felicia, who had picked them up at the bus station—there was no shortage of conversation. The only time Felicia's enthusiasm waned was when Lupita proposed, in front of the whole family, that it was Dave and Felicia's "turn" to have the next baby, her third grandchild. Fortunately the oven timer rang—saved by the bell!—and Felicia was able to slip away to retrieve the breakfast casserole she'd baked.

The afternoon had been filled—the women got the food ready and the men played golf. Li hadn't gone with the guys, saying he wanted to "wander" in downtown Red River, which Felicia found amusing. Dave had offered to help him learn the game—like he had helped Josef and Javier years ago in L.A.—but Li politely declined.

Felicia had been concerned about Josef and Javier being together, but when they'd gotten back and Felicia had had a chance to corner Dave, he'd said everything was fine. "We all carried on like nothing was happening," he'd told her.

Now hearing Dave laugh from across the room, Felicia was so pleased her family had come from California to join them. She felt a sense of validation having them see where she lived and meet people from the church. And she could tell the church folks were just as eager to meet her family. Especially Charlie, who had cornered her father, next to her.

"So you live in Los Angeles?" she heard Charlie ask Josef. When he answered yes, Charlie said, "How do you deal with all those weirdo actor liberals out there?"

Felicia cringed, but her dad handled it smoothly. "We turn them into Republicans and elect them as governor," he said, patting Charlie on the back and chuckling. *Perfect answer.*

But Charlie wasn't finished yet. "I always figured the Lord was waiting for one more liberal to get out there and then he'd just break off California and send it out to be an island," he said a little too loudly and a little too seriously.

Felicia saw a few church members look at Charlie disapprovingly—they were used to his antics—but no one grabbed him by the hand and drew him away, as Felicia had hoped. Her dad wasn't used to those kinds of jabs, she thought.

Or maybe he was. "Ocean-front property in Nevada!" Josef said excitedly. "We'd better be getting our down payments ready!"

Charlie's disposition seemed to lighten at Josef's response. *I guess he passed the test.*

Just when the two had started to talk Reds and Dodgers baseball, Charlie stopped and sniffed the air. "Is that something burning, Felicia?" he asked in a less intrusive voice than before.

She had been so intent on monitoring their conversation that she hadn't noticed there was indeed the tiniest hint of smoke in the air. Spinning around, she looked at the oven and top of the stove. Nothing. Following her nose, she opened the garage door to a waft of smoke, then, realizing what it was, closed it again quickly. But not fast enough.

"Is that marijuana I smell?" Charlie practically bellowed.

Felicia stood with her back against the door. She could feel her face turning hot as everyone near them stopped talking and stared at her. A few faces even peeked around the wall from the dining room.

"My Robin used to smoke that junk in her bedroom when she was a teenager, before I caught her," he said accusingly.

"Uh, no . . . no, that's just my sister and her boyfriend smoking a cigarette out there," Felicia said. She thought she might melt into the floor.

"Smoking!?" Lupita appeared, seemingly from nowhere, eyes blazing like an inferno and hands on her hips. She marched up to the door where Felicia was pasted like the Swiss guard at the Vatican.

Felicia nodded quickly but didn't move. "Mama, please," she whispered when Lupita got close enough. "Let's not make a scene."

Dave had disappeared from Felicia's line of vision, and there was no way she was leaving that door to go find him for help. Just when she thought her mother was going to peel her away, Javier strode in.

"What's going on?" he asked, his eyes going from Felicia to Lupita.

"Nothing," Felicia said through gritted teeth. She felt the knob turn on the door, so she reached down and secured the lock. A pounding came through the door and into her back.

"Eh, your mother-in-law just found out she's got grown kids," Charlie said sarcastically. "And one of them smokes."

"Smokes? Gina smokes?" Lupita asked, searching Felicia's eyes.

Felicia felt a fleeting sense of sorrow for her mother at this revelation, but it was no time to be offering an understanding shoulder.

Charlie scratched his head and crunched up his face, as if in thought. "Smells like Marlboros to me," he said, changing his tune. Then a sheepish mask came over him. "From my army days, I mean."

Felicia eyed him appreciatively—he had just saved her family from *Red River Chronicle*'s headline news.

The few church people who were nearby—most had dispersed, clearly sensing a "private" moment—snickered knowingly. Felicia saw their sympathetic expressions about her situation.

"Hey, Mama, Estella was asking if you'd help her sing a song to Dave for his birthday," Javier said, giving Felicia the "I'm trying to help here" look. "Why don't we go see which one she wants?"

Lupita eyed Javier suspiciously, then walked away, but not before giving Felicia the "this is not over" glance.

Everyone returned to their eating, drinking, and chitchat, allowing Felicia to take a breath.

"I think I'll go see what this song is all about, too," Josef said, seizing the opportunity.

After he was out of earshot, Charlie leaned in to Felicia. "Well, that was a close one," he said conspiratorially, seeming to miss the fact that he had caused the scene in the first place.

Felicia nodded and Charlie hobbled off to his next victim. She took a quick glance to see if anyone was nearby, then unlocked the door and opened it just far enough to slide into the garage.

Gina and Li were gone. The only thing that remained was a haze of pot smoke. And a pack of matches from Lou's Tavern in downtown Red River.

CHAPTER

34

Felicia

Sunday, May 25

11:15 a.m.

Felicia was having a difficult time concentrating on Dave's sermon. After the little "incident" at the party the day before, she'd gone from contented to crazed, doing everything she could to make sure no one got near the garage. At one point she'd seen Becky, trying to be helpful even though she was a guest and not on duty, start to duck into the garage for a new trash bag. Felicia yelled, "No!" a little too forcefully from twenty feet away, following up with a meeker, "There are some under the sink, Becky."

After the party, she'd thought her family would get into it again. But with everyone worried about Gina and Li, and how they had left without a good-bye and now weren't answering their cell phones, even Javier and Lupita seemed to put an end to their Cold Shoulder War. They weren't hugging, but they were at least talking.

I guess we can be thankful for something, Felicia thought. She was still worried about Gina and Li, though. *Why wouldn't they at least talk to me?*

No one but Dave (and maybe Charlie, but she wasn't sure what was in his head and she wasn't asking) knew the truth about what Gina and Li had been smoking in the garage. When she'd told him, as they were finally in the family room alone on the sofa bed—the house quiet and everyone sequestered in their rooms—Felicia was astonished when Dave laughed after she revealed it to him.

"Dave!" she said in a stage whisper, rolling over and lightly punching him. "It's not funny!"

"I know, I know," he said, catching himself. "It's not funny that they're using drugs, and of course we need to get them some help, and it's completely disrespectful of you and our family. But it did happen, and you have to admit it's pretty entertaining that someone is smoking marijuana in a pastor's garage when practically all of his church is inside gorging themselves on birthday cake and ice cream."

Felicia didn't see the humor at first—she was still trying to strip away the layers of mortification she'd felt. But she had to admit, from that vantage point, it *was* humorous—or at least she hoped in several years she'd think so.

Now, listening to Dave wrap up his sermon, she wondered what the church people would think if they knew their pastor had laughed about his sister-in-law smoking pot in his garage. For some reason, that thought brought a smile. Dave seemed to catch her gaze and smiled slightly back at her.

After the sermon, the music leader asked the congregation to stand and sing "Just As I Am." During the second verse, Felicia sneaked a peek at her family lined up in the pew next to her—Maria, Javier, Mama, and Papa (Nicholas and Estella were in children's church). That's when she saw her mother, who had the world's tiniest bladder, signal her father that she wanted to slip out.

But rather than go out the back, as Felicia thought her mother would, she turned toward the front of the church. When she got to the altar, she knelt for prayer.

Felicia looked up and caught Dave's eye. He motioned for her to join her mother.

"Mama, can I pray with you?" Felicia asked, crouching next to her on the carpeted bench. She could see her mother was crying.

"*Sí,*" she whimpered. She had a tendency to revert to Spanish when she was emotional.

"Do you want to share with me why you felt led to come forward?" Felicia rarely had seen her mother at the altar, although she knew she read her Bible, prayed, and attended church faithfully. It was her example that had helped Felicia form her own good "quiet time" habits as a teenager.

"*Soy una madre terrible* (I am a terrible mother)," she whispered between sobs.

Maria joined them on their mother's other side just in time to hear her mom's declaration.

"Oh, Mama, no, you are not," Maria said, hugging her sideways. "We all love you. Even Gina. She's just lost her way right now."

Felicia was touched that her mother felt like a failure because Gina was smoking. *If she only knew,* she thought. Then it occurred to her that maybe she did—a mother's intuition is an incredible force.

"Let's pray for Gina," Felicia suggested, wanting to take her sister to the Lord in prayer, too.

"Okay," her mom said. "And Li, too."

Felicia shot Maria a raised eyebrow, then bowed her head. "Dear God, we bring our sister—and daughter—before you," she prayed. "We know she knows you as her Father, Lord, but like the son who wandered . . ."

Saying the word caused Felicia to reflect momentarily on Li saying he wanted to "wander" in downtown Red River. *Wow, how symbolic.*

"She is lost in the world. We know you see her, even from afar, and are waiting to take her back in your arms again. Heavenly Father, we ask that you show us how to guide her back to you. And God, we pray for Li, that he might come to know you as his personal Savior and give his life to you. We know without you, Lord, we are all lost. Draw us into your presence, God, and remind us that it is your will that should be done, not ours. We love you, Father. In Jesus' name we pray, amen."

At "amen," the three women, still on their knees, rose from their kneeling prayer position. The congregation had finished singing and was sitting patiently while the organ played softly in the background. Felicia spied a box of tissues and reached around the altar rail to get it.

"I need to be a better example," her mother said quietly, dabbing her eyes with the tissue Felicia handed her. "How can I expect Gina to want to return to the church when I am holding a silly grudge against her brother-in-law?" She shook her head in disapproval of her own behavior. Felicia rubbed her back gently.

"We are human, Mama. But that's why the Lord is there to help us."

Felicia grasped her mother's forearm and helped her stand so they could move back to the front pew, as was the practice at that church after praying at the altar. Someone else was still kneeling at the altar, with Dave joining him, so the music continued for a few more minutes. When they had finished, the praying man moved to a pew and Dave bounded up to the pulpit.

"Let's all rise for the recessional," he said.

Hearing her mom's and sister's voice with hers as they sang "Blessed Be the Tie That Binds," Felicia felt a deep sense of loss over Gina. She'd never cared too much that she and her sister didn't have a relationship to speak of, but knowing what she did now, she longed to make that connection, and she felt convicted for not reaching out to her sooner.

Felicia raised her voice at the song lyrics, "'We shall still be joined in heart, and hope to meet again.'"

I'm really going to try to keep in touch with Gina, she vowed. *Maybe if I call her more often, I can show her I do care, and she'll open up to me.*

CHAPTER 35

Mimi

Sunday, May 25

9:50 p.m.

The knock came at the back door. Mimi glanced at the rooster clock hanging above the kitchen sink. *Ten till ten.* She shook her head and finished washing the strawberries she was preparing for the kids' school lunches for the next day. For a moment she thought about not answering.

It would serve him right.

But she knew that would do no good. After all, they would be able to see her through the lacy light blue curtains hanging over the door window. Since she was standing less than ten feet away in a brightly lit kitchen, it was a little difficult to hide or run to another room and pretend she wasn't home.

Ugh. At least they're coming to the back door now. That's something. They used to come to the front door where all the neighbors could see. And at least they no longer arrive in a police car. It's now an unmarked one. That's something to be thankful for, right?

But still, that didn't mean she had to *rush* to answer.

She finished with the last strawberry, then slowly wiped her hands on a kitchen towel before she opened the door.

There stood Officer Dan McCarthy in his street clothes. And next to him was her father, swaying slightly.

Mimi knew Dan didn't work on Sundays, so this was an unusual drop-off. He had taken care of her father on multiple occasions, quietly delivering him to Mimi's door on the many nights when her father had gone out and gotten falling-down drunk and disorderly. Dan had never written a ticket or thrown her father in jail—something he rightly should have done.

"A buddy of mine picked him up and called me," Dan said in explanation to Mimi's confused look. "I said I'd drop him off."

With a heavy sigh, Mimi opened the screen door wide enough for both of them to enter.

This has to stop, Mimi thought. *Why does he keep acting like this?* Mimi turned back toward them and crossed her arms. "Dad, I need to talk with Officer McCarthy for a moment."

Her dad lifted his arms and, in the process, almost fell over. "Be my guest! I'm not stopping you."

"Privately, Dad. That means you leave the room."

"Well, I'm not ready to leave the room. I'm hungry." He swaggered to the refrigerator.

In a flash, Mimi blocked his way. "I'll fix you something and bring it to you," she said through clenched teeth. "Now, *please* go to the living room."

He jutted his chin out and narrowed his eyes but otherwise didn't move. She could tell he had gone into stubborn mode—he had no intention of giving in to her request. For years she'd excused away his stubbornness by blaming it on the alcohol. But he'd been an alcoholic for so long, she didn't know what was the beer and what was her father's actual character and personality. *I'm not going to back down, Dad, so you'd better give in.*

The back door creaked and Mimi heard Mark step through. He'd stayed on at the church after the evening service for a special music rehearsal and then to take care of a few business items.

"Officer McCarthy," Mark said gravely. They made a point of never calling him Dan in front of her father.

Not moving her eyes from her dad, Mimi said, "I've asked Dad to leave the room so I can talk to Officer McCarthy, but he doesn't seem to want to go." She hated this! She hated that her greeting to her husband wasn't a kiss and sweet words. No, it had boiled down to a reprimanding tone and an announcement about yet another incident.

Mark gently took Archie's arm. "Let's go get you a shower and ready for bed."

"I want something to eat," her father said belligerently, his eyes piercing Mimi's.

"I'm sure Mimi will make something for you after she's finished her talk. Okay?"

Her father shook his head. "They're going to talk about me—and I have a right to know what they're saying."

As if you couldn't guess.

"I'm sure you'll find out soon enough," Mark continued. "Come on, let's—"

"I'm not worthless, if that's what you two are going to talk about! I have rights. That's just like her," he spat. "Little Miss Perfect. Thinking she's so much better than everybody else. Well, you're not!" He pointed a crooked, arthritic finger—thick and yellowed from decades of smoking—at Mimi. "You're nothing! You hear me? Nothing!"

"All right, that's enough," Mark said, forcefully pushing him out through the doorway and into the dining room. Her father's hateful monologue continued from different rooms of the house as he was obviously being dragged upstairs.

Mimi stood frozen, every nerve in her body shaking from what had just happened. It seemed to be getting worse. There was the verbal lashing on Mother's Day—her favorite day of the year, and he'd ruined it, right in front of her children. Now he was bashing her in her own house. In front of a police officer, who also happened to be a member of their congregation. And he was headed upstairs, where he'd inevitably continue his tirade and wake up her children with his hateful words about their mother. She knew her kids wouldn't believe what their grandfather said. But a little part of her still feared his words would rub off on them.

She felt eight years old again. Helpless. Broken. In desperate need of a daddy who loved her.

"Mimi"—Officer McCarthy's gentle voice broke through her thoughts—"I'm sorry."

"It's okay," she said, making sure she didn't turn to face him. She didn't think she could handle seeing his look of sympathy. She knew she couldn't.

"Maybe tonight isn't a good time for us to talk about this," he said quietly. "Give me a call later this week . . . when you're ready."

Mimi opened her mouth to speak but couldn't find the words. Her mind had shut down. She bit her lip and tried to simply nod.

"Okay. I'll . . . talk to you later then." The door closed behind her.

Slowly, Mimi walked to the counter where she'd left her kitchen towel. She lifted it to her face and began to sob.

God, she prayed. *Why is this happening? Why don't you stop it? Why don't you answer me? Where are you? How much more of this do you expect me to take?*

CHAPTER 36

Felicia

Wednesday, May 28

1:21 p.m.

"Did everyone make it back to L.A. okay?"

Felicia recognized the voice on the phone as Gina's.

"Gina! What happened to you two? I've been trying to call. Why didn't you answer or call me back?"

Gina sounded remorseful. "I knew Mama and Maria and them were all leaving today. I didn't want to have to face them."

Felicia pushed away from her desk. She really wanted to lay into her sister about smoking pot. At her house. Upsetting her mother. Instead, she figured this wasn't the time. "You're going to see them at home anyway," Felicia said.

A moment of silence passed before Gina said, "No, I'm not."

"You're never going to see Mama and Papa again?" *First Mama and Javier, and now this?*

"No, well, yes, I will see them at some point. But it won't be easy. We decided to move here."

Felicia was growing impatient. "Move where? What is going on with you?" The image of her sister and Li smoking pot popped into her head. Were they into drugs worse than she even thought?

"We're here, Feef . . . in Cincinnati."

Cincinnati? Their flight was supposed to leave yesterday. "What do you mean, Cincinnati?"

"Li and I bought one-way tickets when we came out. We decided we needed a change of pace. So we packed what we could and brought it with us."

"Oh." Felicia wasn't sure what to say. She'd never had a warm, sisterly relationship with Gina, so having her near didn't feel like much of an advantage. If she were honest with herself, it seemed like a negative. A big neg.

She tried to recover quickly. "Uh, wow. That's a big surprise. Did you find a place to live? Where will you work?"

"We rented a studio apartment yesterday. It's in the city, on the bus route. We figured we'd need that since we don't have a car. And as for jobs . . . it's not like we're looking for some big-time career like you would be." Felicia heard a critical note in Gina's voice. "I'll probably just waitress, and he can get on bartending or tattooing or something. But for now, we have some extra cash from selling my car, so we have time."

"You sold the car Papa helped you with?" Felicia didn't mean to sound so accusatory, but her father had spent hours on evenings and weekends rehabbing an old Cutlass for Gina. Felicia had predicted Gina wouldn't know how to appreciate it. *Typical Gina.*

Gina sighed. "Listen, Feef, I didn't call to get you to analyze our decision. I just thought . . . you might like to know we're here. But I'm not looking for you to support us or anything. It's not like you have to have us over for dinner."

Felicia felt the jab. "Aw, Geen, I didn't mean to get all on my high horse. It's just, moving is a big decision. Especially across the country. What if you guys don't like it here?"

"We'll just move on," Gina said matter-of-factly.

As much as Felicia wished she could have Gina's lackadaisical attitude about such a huge life change—about anything, really—she couldn't help but dread the inevitable. Over the years, she'd helped Gina find jobs, places to live, and clothing. She had even given her cash a few times. No matter what Felicia said and did to try to help Gina get her life on track, Gina always ended up back at the "needing" stage again. Felicia wondered if Gina's decision to come to Cincinnati was just random or if she knew being near Felicia would provide her with a fallback plan. Felicia was pretty sure it was the latter.

"Let me bring you some things," Felicia heard herself saying. The turn-the-other-cheek Christian and the don't-let-yourself-be-used sister were doing battle inside her. "I need more room in my office, so we have to get rid of this futon," she said, kicking it as if Gina could see it through the phone. "And I bought new dishes a while back, and the old ones are boxed up in the garage. But, Gina," Felicia said hesitating, "there is one thing. What you guys were doing out in the garage . . . that's really bad, Gina. Not to mention illegal."

Felicia heard a deep sigh, like a bull getting ready to strike, before Gina exploded with a string of expletives directed at her and the family. "And I really don't care what you or anyone else thinks about what I do," Gina spat out in conclusion. "Me and Li, we're just fine with each other."

Opening her mouth to respond, Felicia realized quickly she didn't need to; a click was followed by the dial tone.

She didn't even give me her address.

CHAPTER

37

Lisa

Friday, May 30

7:30 p.m.

The church seemed chilly inside the sanctuary as Lisa, Joel, and seven elders and spiritual leaders sat on the platform in a circle. They had come together at Joel's request to spend some serious time praying over the church's situation and the battle that was ahead of them. They had also spent the past week fasting for direction and discernment over God's leading.

"Thank you all for coming," Joel said, sitting next to Lisa. "Obviously, we understand the serious nature of what we have set out to do, and we desperately need to hear from God that this is the direction of his leading. Are we all in agreement?"

Lisa looked around the circle and saw everyone nod solemnly.

"So tonight, in a sense, we need to hear from God. We know the path we're about to walk down, but like Gideon before he led the Israelites against the Midianites, we need to lay down our fleece and hear from God."

Joel opened his worn, cracked, dog-eared Bible and flipped to the

Old Testament book of Judges. "I'd like to read from Judges 6." He took a deep breath and began slowly. "'Gideon said to God, "If you will save Israel by my hand as you have promised—look, I will place a wool fleece on the threshing floor. If there is dew only on the fleece and all the ground is dry, then I will know that you will save Israel by my hand, as you said." And that is what happened. Gideon rose early the next day; he squeezed the fleece and wrung out the dew—a bowlful of water. Then Gideon said to God, "Do not be angry with me. Let me make just one more request. Allow me one more test with the fleece. This time make the fleece dry and the ground covered with dew." That night God did so. Only the fleece was dry; all the ground was covered with dew.'"

Joel closed his Bible and placed it underneath his chair. "We need to call on God and ask him to let us know clearly and beyond any shadow of a doubt that this is what he wills for us as a church to do."

They began to pray. Each one took a turn, going around the circle, starting with Bonnie Bentz, who sat at Joel's right. Joel would close out their prayer time. Her prayer was powerful, and Lisa immediately felt chills run down her arms and neck as Bonnie called upon the Lord. The prayer time seemed to grow in fervency as they prayed longer and harder than Lisa could remember ever having prayed before.

As one of the last in the circle, sixty-seven-year-old Don Angle, sitting to Lisa's left, began to pray, Lisa heard the door at the back of the sanctuary creak open and closed.

I wonder who's here? She fought the urge to open her eyes, instead wanting to refocus on Don's prayer. She heard no other movement, so thought maybe she'd imagined hearing the noise. But within seconds, she felt a pair of large hands rest upon her left and right shoulders. The touch was light, but definitely there. *Who is that?*

But somehow, it didn't feel as if she would have been able to turn around to see who owned those hands—or why they were on her shoulders.

There was silence for a moment as Lisa realized it was her turn to pray. "Father," she began, and choked up as she felt the hands squeeze her very lightly, "you are such a good God . . ."

As Lisa finished her prayer and Joel began his, there was one last slight bit of pressure from the hands. Then, just as suddenly as they had come, they disappeared.

Joel finally ended the prayer time with an "amen" and Lisa's head immediately shot up to look around. No one was there. And she was absolutely sure whoever it was had not used the door at the back of the sanctuary to exit, because there had been no creak. All of a sudden she noticed that the others in the group, wide-eyed, had turned toward the back of the sanctuary as though they were looking for someone—or something?—too.

"Did anybody else feel hands—," Joel started.

"On my shoulders. Yes!" Don Angle said.

"Me, too," the others echoed.

"And the door," Lisa said. "While Don was praying, the back door—"

"Yes, yes!" everyone said.

Joel and Lisa looked at each other.

"Did you hear the door for them to leave?" Lisa asked Joel.

He slowly shook his head, looking awed.

"That door didn't open but for that one time!" Bonnie Bentz said. "I may be ninety-two years old, but my hearing is still sharp as can be!" Tears glistened on her cheeks.

They had received visitors. God had shown up.

CHAPTER 38

Felicia

Thursday, June 5

11:16 a.m.

Felicia pulled into Becky's driveway. She saw Becky come out the front door and rush to the car.

"Felicia, I can't tell you how much I appreciate this," she said as she opened the passenger door and climbed in. "I didn't want to ask Eli to come home and take me. He's hourly, you know, and they dock his pay when he's gone."

Felicia looked in her rearview mirror as she backed out. She knew Eli, a former rabbi, worked hard at the tool-and-die plant. She felt sorry that his congregation had gone so sour he'd had to take a tough job with his brother to survive.

"After all you've done for me, Becky, I'm more than happy to help," Felicia responded.

Becky had called Felicia that morning in a panic. She had gone out to start her car, and it was dead. Normally that wouldn't have mattered, but she had a doctor's appointment at eleven-thirty. When Becky called her, Felicia didn't inquire about the appointment because she knew how private Becky was. If she wanted her to know, she'd tell her.

They rode in silence for a few minutes.

"Whew, that air-conditioning feels good," Becky said, fanning herself.

Felicia glanced over at her. "Are you doing okay, Becky? This doctor's appointment . . ."

Becky put her hands in her lap. "Yes, I'm fine. Just a few . . . issues."

Wanting to avoid an obvious pause at Becky's veiled response, Felicia changed the subject. "So you said the doctor's office is over on Surrey Lane, right?"

"Yes, the building in back."

"I know just where you mean, I think," Felicia said. "My gynecologist is in that building, too."

"Dr. Hizer?"

Felicia smiled. "That's the one! But I wish sometimes she didn't do OB, too. I always feel like such a loser when I go in there and see those mothers with two or three kids plus a big belly, another one on the way. And meanwhile, I'm struggling to raise one. How do they do it?"

Becky chuckled. "I have no idea. When we had Aaron, our first, I thought the mommy thing was pretty easy. But then when Silas came along . . . oh, boy. Everyone says having two kids is workable because you have two hands—that it's three kids where you get in trouble—but I thought I'd bit off more than I could chew with two. Just between us, there were times, with Eli's work at the temple and everything, that I really wished I'd stuck to one. Not that we didn't love Silas, of course—"

"I know just what you mean," Felicia said a little too exuberantly. *Finally, someone who gets it!* She calmed her voice. "But I'm afraid if we don't have another one, I'll always wonder. On the other hand, if we have just Nicholas, he might become one of those spoiled only children."

"Oh, I didn't know you were considering having another baby."

Felicia hit the brake at the stoplight a little too forcefully. She wasn't sure how to take that comment. The spark of surprise in Becky's tone sounded as though she thought their having a second child would be a mistake.

"Do *you* think we should?" Felicia asked. She knew there was no way Becky could make that decision for her, but she was tired of mulling over the ramifications by herself.

"Is Dave excited about it?" *The million-dollar question.*

Felicia was a little embarrassed to answer. "He said it's my decision—that he's happy either way."

"Huh," Becky said. "With men, that usually means they do have an opinion, but they don't want the responsibility of admitting it."

Exactly! "I don't know if that's true with Dave," Felicia said, wanting to protect his integrity, "but it really has been a burden. I see both sides: the blessing of another child, and—"

"The intrusion?" Becky said.

Felicia was a tad uncomfortable discussing this with Becky. It always seemed as if she was the one on display, while Becky didn't share much at all from her life. But she had always trusted and appreciated her advice, especially with Nicholas.

She pulled the car into a parking space. "Do you think it's wrong not to have another baby when we could easily afford one and provide a good life for it? Do you think I'll regret it?" She tilted her head back against the seat. "I feel so guilty!"

Becky yanked her purse from the floor into her lap and unbuckled her seat belt. "There's no reason to feel guilty, Felicia. There really is no right or wrong answer to these things. You can either throw caution to the wind and go for it, or you can say you got it right the first time and be happy with Nicholas."

Felicia smiled at her "got it right" description. When Nicholas was going through his biting stage a few years ago, she wouldn't necessarily have said that; but at five he was a genuine pleasure.

Becky opened the door. "You coming in with me?"

"You know, I think I'll just wait out here. Listen to some music or something."

"All those babies inside?" Becky smiled.

Felicia laughed. "Yeah, too much pressure!"

After Becky got out, Felicia rolled down the car windows and flipped on the radio to a smooth jazz station. She thought again about what Becky had said: no right or wrong answer.

But how can that be? Isn't there always a correct way to do something, or at least a more *correct way?*

She tapped her fingers on the steering wheel. Throughout her life, choices had been fairly black and white for her. Get good grades to get into college on a scholarship. Do well in school to get a lucrative job. Fall in love and get married. Have a baby to experience motherhood. Her life's formula was: to get Z, you just do X and Y.

Now she was at a crossroads where either path could be beneficial or detrimental. There were no Xs and Ys—just Qs, for questions.

If God wanted me to have another baby, wouldn't he give me that desire instead of this carousel of contemplation? Or maybe he is *trying to give me that desire and I'm fighting it! Am I telling God what to do?*

She laid her forehead against the steering wheel and closed her eyes. "Lord, I'm giving this to you. I ask you to work through Dave and me to lay out the plan you have for our family. Help me know what I should do. Speak to Dave so he will tell me how he really feels. Give us a sign of your will."

When she lifted her head, she saw a happy young mother with a ponytail emerging from the medical building, pushing a large blue stroller in front of her, a toddler inside it.

Is that my sign? Felicia thought. Then the woman turned to walk down the sidewalk and Felicia saw what was behind the stroller: a second-trimester bump. *Or is* that *my sign?*

"Ah, real funny, God," she said aloud. "Good one."

CHAPTER 39

Jennifer

Thursday, June 5

11:55 a.m.

Jennifer climbed the few steps to Father Scott's office. He'd called her twice, asking her to bring Carys by for the birthday present he had for her. When he'd called a third time, earlier that day, she'd told him she would run over and get the gift and then perhaps bring Carys by another time.

"I do need to talk with you," she'd said.

Now, as she entered the waiting area, she wished she hadn't told him that. Her life was going well without her mother, and she knew telling him about the situation would inevitably require her to make contact.

"Hey, Jen," he said, opening the hallway door to let her through. "Come on back. I was hoping you might bring Sam."

"Well, I did tell him I was coming over, but he had a lunch meeting to go to," she said. "But we want to have you over for dinner sometime, okay?"

He turned to her. "I'd love that," he said, sounding genuinely touched.

When they got to his office, he handed her a package wrapped in newspaper comics.

"That's how we used to do it when we were kids," he said sheepishly.

Jennifer turned the rectangular box in her hands. "I think it's a great idea!" *Wonder if Mimi's ever thought of this?*

He must have seen her looking at it curiously because he added, "It's a rosary wrapped around a crucifix."

She shot him a questioning look, trying not to appear too alarmed.

"Just kidding," he said. "It's a jewelry box that plays music. I put a little bracelet in there for her. She's such a little lady, I thought she needed some bling."

Jennifer wasn't sure what amused her more—his fondness for her little girl or his use of the word *bling*. She smiled. "She . . . we . . . will cherish it forever."

"You said you wanted to talk, right?" he said, moving toward the sitting area of his office.

She nodded. As usual, he sat in his burgundy leather chair and she eased onto the small sofa. She set her purse and the gift next to her.

They looked at each other, both silent for a moment.

"I'm guessing this has something to do with your father," Father Scott said, breaking the ice. "You've had a pretty big couple of months. I've been praying for you."

She wasn't sure whether it was hearing him say he was praying for her, or being back in the office where she had done so much work on her faith a few years ago, but she felt a weight lift from her shoulders as she admitted, "Actually, it's about my mother."

"Ah." He nodded and sat back. "How has she been handling all this?"

It suddenly occurred to Jennifer that in the swirl of her own emotion over finding and losing her father, she hadn't even thought about the effect of his death on her mother.

"I don't know," she said pensively.

"What do you mean?"

"I haven't spoken to her since Carys's birthday, which was a day or two before my father died. So . . . I don't know how she is, or how she's dealing with him dying."

Even though she was still angry, the thought of her mother feeling anguish over her father passing away made the ice around her heart melt a little.

"I take it you had words over your mother's decision not to allow your father to have contact with you," said Father Scott.

"Yes, something like that. I have to admit, I really wanted to lay into her, but I just said a few things." *A few very bad things. Very bad.*

"And what held you back? If you knew you were going to cut her off anyway, why didn't you just let loose with what you had to say?"

"I didn't want to do the Lord's job and take vengeance on her." As soon as the words hit the air, she knew how ridiculous they sounded.

Father Scott smiled and sat forward. "But isn't not talking to her or seeing her a kind of vengeance?"

She nodded reluctantly, crossing and recrossing her legs. Subconsciously she'd known for weeks that that was exactly what she'd been doing, but not admitting it to herself somehow kept it from becoming reality.

Father Scott must have seen the guilt seeping out of her because he said, "Well, sometimes it can be good to step back from a difficult situation and take time to sort it through before you say anything hurtful."

Jennifer sighed. "I'm afraid I already did that. I was just so angry with her. All these years she could have told me the truth instead of letting me think something awful. And like I told my mother-in-law, why didn't she just have me adopted by someone who could have raised me right?"

"She could have aborted you," Father Scott said.

"Yeah, my mother-in-law said that. I'm surprised she didn't, knowing how she was."

"Why do you suppose she didn't?"

"Probably to get the money from my father," she fumed. Then she remembered something her mom had said to her once when she was in a drunken rage. "Although . . . she did tell me when I was about ten that I should appreciate her because she went nine months without a drink and with no medication while she was pregnant."

Father Scott raised his eyebrows. He didn't say anything right away, as was his nature. "What a beautiful example of Christ," he said finally.

"Huh?" Jennifer was sure she hadn't heard him correctly.

"Your mother, her suffering for you, is such a terrific model of Christ's suffering. She gave up so much to give you life. He gave his life to give us ours."

Jennifer was stunned. Her mother was the last person she ever thought to look to as a model of Jesus' love. And she'd never considered her mother as "suffering," although she'd seen her hold her head in her hands many times, saying, "It just spins and spins and won't stop." She had been so caught up in "doing" for her mother that she'd lost sight of really reaching out to her and loving her just as she was—crazy or not.

"I guess I should see how she's doing," she started, not wanting him to see how truly convicted she felt. "I've lost my father. I should try to make it work with my mother."

Father Scott reached across his desk and grabbed his cordless phone. "No time like the present," he said, handing it to her.

"No," she said, not taking the phone from him. "I'm not ready." As much as Father Scott had helped her thinking, she knew she needed more time to process everything rather than risk another angry encounter. Even though she felt justified in her anger, she knew she was wronging her mother, and ultimately God.

As she rose to leave, Father Scott stayed seated. He reached over to his desk calendar and flipped a page.

"I'm making a note here to call you in a month," he said. Then he looked up at her. "Don't let this thing drag on, Jennifer. She's your mom."

No, she's my mother, Jennifer thought, then paused. *But maybe, just maybe, there is a mom in there somewhere.*

CHAPTER

40

New Life Church

Middletown, Ohio
Saturday, June 7
9:12 a.m.

The usual chatter at this pastors' wives' fellowship was subdued, almost like talk at a funeral, and Lisa knew why. The day before, the *Dayton Daily News* had carried a story about a pastor's wife, Ruth Mannington, who had gone to a ministry conference in Indianapolis the previous weekend—and never returned. Even CNN picked up the story. When Lisa saw on Friday's evening news that Ruth's husband pastored a Baptist church, she'd called Felicia to see if she knew anything about it.

"I think I met her at the last wives' fellowship," Felicia had told her. "And Dave has talked with her husband a few times. But we don't really know them."

Small groups of women were gathered, pretending to nibble on Danishes and sip coffee, but as Lisa milled around to make sure everything was set up correctly for their meeting, she picked up on the content of their hushed tones.

"Do you think she was kidnapped?" one woman in a yellow sundress asked the two with her.

"From what I heard, she told her friend at the conference's final service that she was going to the restroom and never came back," said another. "All she had on her was her purse. Her luggage was in her friend's car, and it was still there later."

"Can you imagine what that must have been like for her friend, looking for her after the service and she's just gone?"

"What about her husband? That poor man. Well, at least she didn't shoot him like that other one did."

Lisa saw the three shake their heads in disbelief.

She scooted over to Etta, New Life's senior pastor's wife and host of the meetings, who had just come in a side door. "I think we should get started as soon as possible," Lisa told her. "And let's open with a prayer for Ruth."

Etta nodded grimly. "Ladies," she said in a loud voice, "good morning. Let's take our seats."

Lisa followed suit, taking a chair in the second row.

After everyone was settled, Etta came to the front, her flip-flops slapping as she walked. She was wearing chambray pedal pushers and a gauzy blouse with a rose-colored T-shirt underneath. A paper coffee cup occupied one of her hands.

She paused and looked at the floor before raising her eyes to the group. "I think we need to open today with a special prayer for our fellow pastor's wife, Ruth. Who would like to lead today?"

After their first meeting last year, Etta had asked different women to pray as a way of getting more people involved in the sessions. But as Lisa and the PWs had discussed, even the prayers felt staged and shallow, which especially discouraged Lisa, who really wanted the pastors' wives' fellowship to have depth.

Not one woman raised her hand in response to Etta's request. Lisa wanted to, but with all that was going on in her church, she was spiritually drained and felt inadequate to stand before her sisters that day.

"But what would we pray for?" a voice from the back asked. Lisa turned to see a fiftyish African-American woman. "We don't even know what's going on."

"Yeah," another woman called out. "Was she taken against her will? If so, how come there's not one piece of evidence?"

Silence fell over the room.

"Maybe she did it on purpose," an older lady near Lisa said in a soft voice. "Maybe she just couldn't take . . . the pressures . . . anymore."

Lisa found that difficult to believe. How could a woman walk away from her husband and children? Although the impact she had felt from her church's dissension was pretty severe, she'd never leave Joel and the kids because of it. Never.

The others were of the same mind-set.

"No way would she disappear and leave those little ones and her husband to fend for themselves," a younger lady said. "I mean, how bad could it have been?"

As Lisa turned to see the woman who'd spoken up, she saw a few of the more senior wives shoot one another knowing glances.

"She could've, like, just needed a little shopping therapy," Ally offered, seemingly unaware of the seriousness of the situation. "Maybe she, like, got lost on her way to the mall. I do that all the time—"

"Let's not jump to conclusions," Etta cautioned from the front, a successful attempt at saving Ally from herself. "We don't want to convict Ruth of anything."

Her request for prudence fell on deaf ears, however. The more the women speculated about Ruth, the more they began to open up about their own experiences.

"If she did it because her husband wasn't paying attention to her anymore, I get that," a woman in a gray pantsuit said. "Ralph and I went round and round a few years ago when I accused him of 'giving it all at the office' and leaving none for our family. It was a horrible time in our marriage, but we got through it."

Others started to chime in with similar stories—all based on Ruth's probable motives, which appeared to make the women feel safer about sharing. Soon the chairs moved from rows to a giant circle as the group naturally shifted into a passionate discussion.

Felicia reached into her purse and pulled out a slip of paper. "Can I share some statistics I found online with you?" she asked rhetorically. Lisa saw the women give her their keen attention. "A few Christian organizations did some studies and this is what they discovered. 'Eighty percent of pastors' wives feel left out and unappreciated by church members. Seventy percent do not have someone they consider a close friend.'"

Cleared throats, shifting in chairs, and nervous sighs were signs to Lisa that these results were not atypical to the fifty-plus women gathered at New Life that day.

"'Fifteen hundred pastors leave the ministry each month due to moral failure, spiritual burnout, or contention in their churches,'" Felicia continued slowly. "'Fifty percent of pastors are so discouraged that they would leave the ministry if they could, but have no other way of making a living.'"

Felicia stopped and looked around the room. Lisa was nearly holding her breath at what Felicia was saying. She even saw a few women so overcome that they were dabbing their eyes with tissues.

"Girls, this is the one that really gets me," Felicia said, her voice cracking. She returned to the paper in her hand. "'According to one survey, a majority of pastors' wives said the most destructive event that has occurred in their marriage and family was the day their husbands entered the ministry.'"

If the floor hadn't been carpeted and someone had dropped a pin, it would have sounded like a boulder crashing. No one said a word, although Lisa noticed some of the wives impulsively clutching the hands of those next to them.

Even though the depth of pain in the room was palpable, Lisa felt a strange sense of relief bordering on happiness. *Finally,* she thought, *these women are becoming vulnerable to one another. Even in their silence, they are admitting their hurt and disappointment.* She noticed that Ally's demeanor had changed as well, her thoughtful expression a sign to Lisa that she was absorbing the enormity of what it meant to be a pastor's wife who often was overused and underloved—a willing partner in ministry but a pawn in the hands of church congregations who did not always appreciate the servanthood to which these women had committed themselves.

Lisa saw Etta swallow hard as she made her way to the center of the haphazard circle. *Wow, even a superstar pastor's wife can relate to this.* "Ladies, I think we know where we need to be in prayer now," she said quietly. "Not only are we praying for Ruth, that she might be safe and return to her family, but we need prayer for ourselves and for each sister here. We're all struggling"—she choked a bit on *struggling*—"but our God is greater than any problems we might face."

Etta sat on the floor and crossed her legs. "I don't think any of us probably feels like leading a prayer right now," she said, getting nods from some. "So why don't we join hands and just go around the circle, and anyone who wants to talk to the Lord aloud can do so. If you don't feel led, just squeeze the hand of the next person. I'll close. Mimi, why don't you start?"

Mimi nodded her acceptance, but Lisa figured she probably wasn't too eager to jump in since her heart was so heavy over the situation with her dad.

"Let's bow our heads," Mimi encouraged. Lisa heard her take a labored breath. "Lord, we come to you today as your daughters who need you. We *need* you, Lord." The emphasis Mimi gave to *need* brought quiet sobs and sniffling from some. "This path on which you've placed us isn't always easy. We are honored to be in ministry for you, but the challenges can be overwhelming sometimes. Lord, we think of our sister Ruth and her family. We don't know what the true story is there, but we know you do, God. We ask that your will be done in her life . . . and in ours. Keep blessing us, Lord, as we press forward."

As the next woman expressed her petitions, Lisa felt a weight lift from her shoulders. She had prayed many times over Joel and their ministry, and she'd felt the connection with the PWs who shared that calling, but there was something special about this room full of pastors' wives, raising their voices to God that he might strengthen them to fulfill his plan.

And in a strange way, she felt Kitty, the pastor's wife who most could have benefited from humility and candidness, was there with them in spirit. Because Lisa was sure the Lord had taught Kitty a thing or two in heaven by now. That thought—even in the midst of the pain these earthly souls were pouring out to God—brought a smile to her face.

CHAPTER

41

Mimi

Saturday, June 7

12:15 p.m.

Mimi pulled into her driveway and turned off her worship CD. The pastors' wives' get-together had gone really well. She felt as if the women truly were starting to trust one another and become transparent about the challenges and struggles of serving God while tolerating the church. She was still humming "How Great Is Our God" when she noticed Mark's car was missing. Normally, she wouldn't have given it much thought, but since her father had taken up residence in their home, she'd learned not to take anything for granted. Just like when she'd been a child in her mother and father's home.

Okay, don't panic, she told herself. *Mark must have taken the kids with him. But why didn't he call?*

She rifled through her purse until she found her cell phone. Sure enough, the screen said there was a missed call. *I must have had the music playing too loudly and didn't hear the ring.* She checked her messages.

"Mimi." Mark's voice sounded strained. "I got a call from Anne Payton. She had to rush Bill to the emergency room. He's had another heart attack. I tried calling Gladys to see if she could watch the kids, but nobody answered. So—don't panic—I left the kids with your dad. He was sober and seemed willing to babysit—"

"Oh, great," Mimi said, grabbing her purse and jumping out of the car. "What were you thinking, Mark Plaisance? You know my father as well as I do!" She'd barely closed the door before she was running into the house.

"Kids? Dad?" she yelled as soon as she was through the front door. Silence. *Don't panic. Don't panic.* "Michaela? Dad, where are you?"

As she raced into the kitchen, she noticed the back door standing wide open. Laughter was filtering in from the yard. Condiments for burgers were sitting on the kitchen counter, and a large pot was on the stove, covered. She was just getting ready to move outside when she spied something that made her blood boil.

A tall can of generic-brand beer was lying in the kitchen sink, crumpled. Another can was sitting on the counter next to the sink.

"Are you kidding me?" she said aloud. "This is *so* not happening. Enough!"

She dropped her purse on the counter, all thoughts of the PWs and praise music locked out of her head, and burst through the screen door.

MJ, Michaela, and Megan were playing dodgeball.

And at the grill was her father. In one hand was a large spatula. In the other arm was baby Milo, gurgling and laughing. Her father was bouncing Milo up and down and singing, "*'Jesus loves me this I know, for the Bible tells me so . . .* '"

The smoke from the grill was wafting up toward the baby, but her dad didn't seem to notice. He was laughing and flipping the burgers.

MJ had just lobbed the ball toward Michaela when he whirled around and caught sight of his mother. "Hi, Mom!"

Michaela looked over. "Hi!" she said as she grabbed the ball and threw it back at MJ.

Megan was squealing and running around, delighting in the play.

Mimi no longer cared that her children could hear or see what she was about to do. She was no longer concerned about keeping her cool. She became like a mama bear attacking a predator who was threatening her cubs.

"Get your things and get out," she told Archie as she marched up to him. "I'm tired of you stomping all over our rules and disrespecting my home and my family."

Immediately, the kids fell quiet, the ball bouncing once and coming to rest at MJ's feet. The singing stopped and Mimi's father turned, a surprised look covering his face. He started to speak, but Mimi stopped him. She didn't want to hear any more excuses.

"How many times have we told you? You will not drink around my children. You will not bring alcohol into my house. What is wrong with you?" She didn't wait for him to answer, instead seizing Milo from his arms. "I'm finished. I mean it."

"I wasn't drinking—" he started to say.

"I don't want to hear it, Dad. There are beer cans all over the kitchen. Do you think I don't see those things? You couldn't even hide them! Or did you think you had time to clean up the mess?"

"Mom—" MJ said, trying to interrupt.

"Get inside, kids. Go to your rooms."

"But—"

"I said go inside. Now."

Normally not one to question her mother, Michaela quietly walked over to Mimi's side. "But, Mom, Grandpa—"

"What did I just say?"

Michaela swallowed hard, tears welling in her eyes, then looked up at her grandfather.

"Go ahead, sweetheart," he said to her gruffly, his voice shaky, as though he were getting ready to cry, too.

Mimi waited until the kids walked—at a snail's pace—into the house before turning back to her father. "We give you a house, we feed you, we take care of you, and we ask so little in return. And how do you repay us?

You drink, you make the police become your taxi service—by the way, if it weren't for Officer McCarthy, you would have been in jail more times than you could possibly count. And then you're completely rude to me."

Half expecting him to start spouting off, she paused. But he didn't utter a word. He didn't even open his mouth.

Still fuming, she threw caution to the wind. "You're always going off on how everybody thinks you're worthless. You already blame me for thinking that—so, fine. You want me to call you worthless? Fine. I'll go ahead and say it. You're a drunk. You're a no-good father who can't even keep a commitment to his family."

Like a javelin, she could see her words pierce right to his heart. His face drained of color.

She'd done what she'd set out to do—confront him. She'd gotten years of pain off her chest with those brief, biting words.

Now she wanted to take them all back as she watched her words slam into him. Mentally, she grasped for them, trying to pull them back into her head, to keep them sheltered there. But it was too late. So she crossed her arms, figuring she was already committed. "I think you'd better go."

He put down the spatula next to the grill; the burgers were now burning, the charred scent rising to her nostrils.

"And don't go through the house. The kids have been tainted enough."

She watched her father, head bowed, shoulders sagging, walk around the side of the house and disappear. She didn't know where he was going. Part of her wanted to say she didn't care, but she knew that wasn't the truth. She'd made a terrible mistake.

1:00 p.m.

After the confrontation, Mimi had walked into the house and called Mark. She didn't really know what she could tell him to make it sound not as bad as she knew it really was. Not surprisingly, he wasn't as supportive of what she'd done as she'd somehow hoped he would be.

"Let's talk about this when I get home, okay?" he'd said.

"Well," she half whined, "when will you be home?"

Mark sounded exasperated. "I don't know, Mims. Bill isn't doing too well. He's in intensive care, and his family really needs me here with them. I can't just up and leave because you had a run-in with your dad."

"Well . . . fine. I'll just fix lunch for the kids." She'd started to get snippy with him. He wasn't giving her *any* sympathy.

Selfishly she got off the phone and internally railed about how, once again, he couldn't be home for his family because somebody in the church needed him. *Like we don't ever need him,* she thought bitterly. *Like we come in second to the needs of the church. Always.*

A small voice inside her head tried to talk reason to her, but she wasn't interested in listening. *Don't even try to convict me on this one, God. I don't want to hear it.*

A dull thud was starting in her temples.

Bill might not make it, the voice in her head reminded her. She headed to the living room and sat in Mark's recliner, putting her head in her hands.

"I'm sorry, God," she whispered. "I know Mark needs to be at the hospital right now. I know Bill's in intensive care. I . . . Please be with Bill and the doctors. Please be with Anne and her family. Comfort them. Please . . ."

She couldn't think clearly. How could she pray for somebody else and think that God would hear her when this huge dark cloud was hanging over her, reminding her of her own sin? She thought of Jesus' words when he told his followers that if they were at the altar and remembered that they held something over somebody, they should leave the altar and go and make peace. Then return to the altar.

How do I do that? Do I just become a doormat and allow my father to walk all over me and my family?

No, came the gentle voice whispering in her ear. She glanced over at Mark's worn Bible sitting on the end table next to her. It was frayed from so much use; the binding had gone out of it long ago.

She picked it up and let it flip open on her lap. First Corinthians. *Figures,* she thought, knowing it contained the love chapter. She remembered the sermon Mark had recently preached from that chapter. He'd asked his congregation to replace the word *love* with *I*.

Turning the pages to chapter 13, she moved her finger down to the fourth verse and started to read.

> *I am patient. I am kind. . . . I am not rude, I am not self-seeking, I am not easily angered, I keep no record of wrongs. I do not delight in evil but rejoice with the truth. I always protect, always trust, always hope, always persevere. I never fail.*

It felt as if someone had pressed an anvil against her chest. *I keep no record of wrongs . . . I always hope . . . I always persevere . . . I never fail.*

She closed the Bible and returned it to its place on the table just as Buster walked over and placed his black, fluffy head on her knee. Big dark eyes looked up at her.

"Don't you make me feel guilty, too," she said, patting his head.

Slowly she stood and started toward the kitchen. Normally when she felt bothered about something, she'd clean. There were days when she'd scrub the kitchen floor three or four times in a row. But this time she just didn't want to. She remembered the kids hadn't eaten yet. They were probably hungry.

In the kitchen, the large stockpot sitting on the stove attracted her attention. Lifting the lid, she saw it was filled with chili.

Memories flooded over her. She was six years old, and she sat at the kitchen table watching her father frying hamburger for his famous chili. He'd always let her have a taste and ask her what it needed.

It never needed anything. "It's perfect, Daddy," she'd tell him. And he'd laugh and pat her head and say, "That's what I like to hear, my little princess."

She'd forgotten about her dad's chili. When he'd make chili while she was growing up, that meant he was in a good mood and he was sober. He and her mom would get along and not fight. Her mother would laugh and be affectionate with him. It was the one time when she could count on everybody being happy.

Dad's super chili, they'd called it. It was his own secret recipe—and it called for beer.

Mimi's head shot up. The beer can in the sink and the one on the counter were still there.

What have I done?

"Kids!" she yelled as she grabbed her purse and ran to the bottom of the stairs. "Let's go. We have to find Grandpa!"

10:32 p.m.

No sign of him.

Mimi and the kids had spent several hours driving around, trying to find her father. She'd called Mark, who had told her to call Dan. Dan had told her he'd start looking in all the bars in the area and call if he found out anything. But he hadn't called.

Megan had complained enough about being hungry that Mimi had finally given in and stopped at the Clucker House to get them something to eat—but also to see if Peggy was working and might have seen her dad. No luck there either.

The kids had been surprisingly quiet during the whole ride—she assumed they knew something was wrong.

"You know I said some things to Grandpa that weren't very nice, don't you?" she'd asked.

No one spoke.

"I was really stressed and I made some assumptions I shouldn't have made. I shouldn't have said those things to your grandpa."

"He wasn't drinking," MJ said quietly.

"I know," Mimi said.

"He was just making chili," Michaela offered. "He made us stand in the kitchen with him while he poured the beer into the chili, then he had MJ pour the leftover down the sink. We all watched."

"He said he wanted us to surprise you 'cause he knew you really liked his chili," MJ said.

"I know. Well, let's concentrate on finding him, and then I can apologize."

But they hadn't found him.

Now it was late Saturday night. The kids were in bed. Mark was home and going over some last-minute details for church the next morning, as well as calling the prayer chain to update them on Bill's stabilized condition.

Meanwhile, Mimi had emptied the kitchen cabinets and scrubbed them and was now giving an overhaul to the pantry.

Apparently knowing Mimi would feel better if she was able to clean uninterrupted, Mark had left her alone to her thoughts and soapsuds.

She looked at the rooster clock. It was a little past 10:30.

Come on, Dad. Come home.

She'd finished the pantry and had decided to start on the refrigerator when there was a knock on the back door.

Finally! She dropped the sudsy bucket on the floor, allowing water to splash over its sides.

"Thank God you're home!" Mimi threw open the door. "I was worried sick . . ."

"Mimi." Dan was standing in front of her, nervously fidgeting with his hat.

She leaned out the door and looked off to the side of the house. "Where's Dad?"

"Uh, Mimi," he began.

"Did you find him?"

He nodded. "He's been in an accident."

She stared at him, confused. "An accident? What do you mean? He doesn't even have a car. You impounded it months ago."

"He was riding with someone."

"Is he okay?" She watched him look down at his hat.

"No. He's—"

"He's not dead?" Panic was rising in her voice. "He's not dead, is he?"

"No. He's in a coma."

CHAPTER

42

Lisa

Sunday, June 8

10:48 a.m.

A *Celebration* hymnal flew past Lisa, missing her nose by inches.

Joel had just informed the church that Tom Graves was being removed from fellowship and would no longer be allowed to attend there.

For a split second the sanctuary went silent before Tom jumped to his feet and yelled, "Oh, no, you don't! This is BS. You're kicking me out of this church? *My* church? The church I helped to found and build and rebuild?"

"You don't have the authority to do that!" Chuck Abrahams yelled, then reached to the back of his pew, grabbed a hymnal, and flung it across the room.

The sanctuary erupted in anger, accusations, and flying objects. Hymnals, praise chorus booklets, purses, a shoe, and even a Bible became weapons of destruction as other church members got in on the act.

"Barton has ruined this church!" one man yelled before lobbing a chorus book, narrowly missing a man across the aisle, who stepped out of his pew, fists clenched and ready to punch.

What is going on? Lisa wondered in shock as she glanced toward the front where Joel stood at the pulpit in amazement. Several times Joel raised his hands to calm the crowd, but ended up using them as shields.

"He's a dictator!"

"He's the best thing this church has ever seen."

"Has anyone checked to see what he's doing with all our money?"

"He doesn't have anything to do with the church's money. That's Anita's job!" Another man pointed toward the church's treasurer. "Why not ask *her*?"

Anita's husband, Jason, stood, fists clenched. "Don't you make accusations about my wife!"

"And what about our youth? Now that Joel's kicked Tom out, who will they look to?"

"Yeah! What a stupid decision. And as usual, he acted alone!"

The voices became more and more frenetic as everyone continued to yell.

"Friends!" Joel tried to speak into the microphone.

But George, the soundman, quickly turned it off, causing a harsh, tinny squeal before the microphone went dead.

"Calm down!" Joel yelled out, walking to the front of the platform. "Everyone get hold of yourselves. What are you doing?"

Edna Abrahams picked up her cane, slowly walked to the front, and smacked Joel across his legs. "I've had enough of you. You call yourself a pastor."

Lisa started toward her husband, but Joel caught her eye and shook his head. *What am I supposed to do? Sit here and helplessly watch some old woman cane my husband?*

"Enough!" Don Angle said. Walking slowly to the front of the church and looking as if he weighed roughly the same as an SUV, he was a big enough man that everybody slowly quieted themselves. "Is this what Christians do?" He pointed at one young man standing in the middle of the center aisle holding a chorus book he obviously was getting ready to hurl.

"Who made *you* our leader?" Alma Watson yelled out. She was a tiny woman, but a spitfire all the same. She had her hands on her hips, waiting for a response. When nobody answered, she stepped into the left side aisle and pointed threateningly. "I'll tell you who made you a so-called leader. That man who calls himself 'pastor.' He appointed you without so much as a please or thank you."

"Now, Alma," Joel started, "you know that isn't true. Just because you weren't at that meeting—"

"I've been attending this church for twenty years and we've never experienced the mess that you've gotten us into."

That's because you kicked out every pastor when he started to make changes, Lisa thought. Almost like clockwork, around the five-year mark, every senior pastor had left Red River Assembly—left or been kicked out. Now, five years into Joel's tenure, it was his turn. The only difference was, Joel didn't seem interested in leaving. He just kept trying to lead the church—even though half or more of them didn't want to be led.

"Well, *Pastor* Barton, is this how you lead?" Tom laughed. "And you want to kick me out? You should be ashamed."

"Tom, this is no longer up for discussion—"

"Shut up!" Tom yelled.

Chaos erupted again, but this time someone threw a punch.

That's it, Lisa thought. *I know Joel really didn't want to have to bring in the police, but this is shameful.*

Earlier that week, Joel had contacted the police department and had explained the situation, asking for two officers to be there that morning. But he had also asked them to remain in the parking lot and not enter the church unless things got out of hand.

Well, Lisa decided, things were out of hand. She quickly moved to the back of the sanctuary, dodging attendance booklets and the little pencils that were kept in the back of each pew.

In the parking lot, she waved her arms to get the police officers' attention. "Please come," she shouted. "Hurry."

The two uniformed officers stepped from their squad car and half walked, half ran toward Lisa. They passed by her and entered the sanctuary with her quickly following behind.

The officers walked down the center aisle toward Joel, who was still trying to calm the crowd.

Tom laughed harshly. "Oh, so this is what the pastor does? Calls in the cops to help him take care of business?"

As if Tom had a bull's-eye on him, one of the officers stepped over and placed a hand on his arm. "You're going to need to leave."

"Get your hand off me! I'll leave because *I* say I go. And I won't have some police officer who's following the orders of this joke of a pastor escort me out." He pushed his shoulders back and turned to exit. Most of the crowd had quieted to watch Tom leave. At the back door, Tom turned and lifted his hand in the air, as if he were swearing in a court of law. "You haven't heard the last of me, Barton. You can count on that."

The other police officer walked to the front and stood off to the side, staring at the audience.

Joel stepped back over to the pulpit. "Would you turn the mike back on, please?" Lisa was wondering if his request would be answered when she heard a tinny sound again.

"Obviously, there are others in this congregation who do not hold to the highest interests of what's best for the church. If you stay after today, I will consider that you are loyal to this church and the work God is doing here. And that I can count on you to pray for and support me as your leader. If not, and a majority of you are against what I'm trying to do, then I will resign."

Lisa inhaled sharply. She wasn't expecting that announcement.

She could hear hymnals thud as they hit the floor, and several of Tom's supporters walked out.

Joel leaned over to the police officer and said something. The officer nodded and began to walk up a side aisle, to the door.

Lisa looked around. The sanctuary—this house of God—was in a shambles. And for a moment, she thought the congregation was, too. But she looked again at the people remaining. Except for a few she assumed were still there to report to Tom—his moles—the rest were loyal, good people.

Well, that's over. She and a few others stepped back out of their pews and began to pick up some of the mess.

"Leave it," Joel told them. "I want us to spend the next moment or two looking at what can happen when we lose focus on the things of God, the things that honor him. This is exactly what our enemy wants."

Everyone in the room either sat or stood silently, glancing around. She noticed Bonnie wiping her eyes with her handkerchief and shaking her head.

"We will carry on," Joel said, walking off the platform. "And we will be stronger. Let's gather in a circle and sing some praises to our Father. I was going to preach, but today, I think we need to worship."

Lisa knew this would ultimately prove to be a good thing, but it sure didn't feel like it right then. She'd never witnessed the kind of behavior among adults—so-called Christians!—that she'd seen today. And she certainly never wanted to see it—or even hear about it—again.

God, I know you've removed the cancer from our midst, but now the difficult part really begins.

The healing.

Don't leave us in this mess.

She remembered the strong hands on her shoulders the night the spiritual leaders prayed. If not for the assurance that they were a sign from God, she doubted that she'd be able to handle all of this, or that she and Joel would be able to stay in the ministry at all. But she knew things were going to get better. At least she hoped so.

CHAPTER 43

Mimi

Tuesday, June 10

8:12 a.m.

Mimi stepped into the intensive care room where her father was lying. Wires attached to him led to monitors beeping all around the head of his bed. There was one to help him breathe; one to monitor his heart rate—she knew those. But there were so many others, she couldn't keep track of which ones were doing what.

His eyes were closed and black. His face was still swollen and bruised. But he was beginning to look a little more like himself. Three days previously, she could hardly recognize him.

"Good morning, Dad." She stepped over to the windowsill and rearranged the photos and drawings from her kids. "Megan drew you another picture. It's a tree with a bird in it. It looks like Big Bird, actually. Those branches must be really strong." She tried to laugh lightly. "I'll just put it here by the rest of your pictures."

She pulled a visitor's chair to the side of his bed. "The kids all send their love. This is their last week of school, so they're really excited about that. Of course, I can't get MJ to focus on his schoolwork—not that that's anything new." She paused to see if anything she was saying registered.

"I can't believe Megan's gone through her first year of school. It goes so quickly, doesn't it? I remember when I was her age and you'd make . . ." The words caught in her throat. Why was it so hard to say, "I'm sorry"? Even to a man who was in a coma?

"Dad." Mimi placed her hand tentatively on her father's. He felt chilly. "Daddy," she said softly. She couldn't remember the last time she'd touched her father kindly. Her touches had been to move him somewhere or to get him out of the way; they weren't kind, gentle, loving touches. She didn't hug him or kiss him—she hadn't for years.

"I'm so sorry," she finally whispered. She blinked to keep tears from running down her cheeks. "I've failed you as a daughter. I'm sorry I said those hurtful things to you. I'm sorry that I never tried to understand you. I judged you. I . . . I wanted something from you that you just weren't able to give and I held that against you."

She glanced up to see if the nurses were around or if anybody was listening. She could see through the glass that a nurse was standing across the hall caring for another patient.

"Dad," she whispered close to his ear, "if you can hear me, I love you."

In the movies, her father would have squeezed her hand and opened his eyes for a miraculous recovery. He would have smiled and said, "I love you, too. I've always loved you. I'm sorry for how I ruined your life, but I vow I'm going to spend the rest of my days making it up to you."

Mimi looked into her father's face, waiting—hoping—for that magical moment to happen. Instead, all she heard was the cacophony of the monitors' beeping rhythms. Slowly, she straightened back into her chair and sat still, wondering what she was supposed to do now. She hated the feeling of helplessness, and briefly considered cleaning his room. When a nurse walked in to change his IV bag, Mimi decided it was time to go.

Again, she placed her hand over his. It felt odd to touch him. Her hand squeezed his lightly, then let go.

"Thanks for taking care of him," she murmured to the nurse before exiting his room.

CHAPTER 44

Lulu's Café

Tuesday, June 10

12:12 a.m.

Jennifer pulled up to Lulu's in her new deep red SUV, the one she'd had her eyes on for months. She'd taken Sam to see it not long after they adopted Carys, lobbying him, telling him that she needed a bigger car than her Corolla for a baby. But ever practical, Sam told her a baby didn't take up that much space and would fit quite nicely in any car, including a Corolla.

With the money they'd received from her father, though, buying the SUV, even with the satellite radio and leather seats, was no problem. In fact, Sam had suggested it when he and Jennifer had discussed how they wanted to allocate the money.

"I'd feel safer knowing you're in a larger vehicle," he'd said. But she knew that was just his way of justifying his buying a motorcycle, something he'd wanted since he was a kid.

Aside from the vehicles and a few other purchases, though, they'd kept spending to a minimum so their church wouldn't see them any differently. Sam really feared parishioners becoming complacent about tithing as they found out about Jennifer's windfall through the grapevine, and as he had said, "Their giving isn't really about what the church needs, it's about what *they* need spiritually. Tithing is a biblical mandate." Jennifer had even taken joy in tithing from her father's funds.

She slid out of the driver's seat just as Mimi pulled in.

"Hey, nice wheels," Mimi called out the side window when Jennifer walked around to greet her.

"My new toy," Jennifer said. She looked more closely at Mimi as she got out of her van and saw she appeared exhausted and drawn. "You doing okay?"

Mimi shut the van door. "Not really. I'll tell you the whole thing when we get inside."

Air-conditioning poured out of Lulu's when they opened the glass door to enter. It might have been early June in Ohio, but it was as hot and humid as August already.

"Hi" and "How are you?" floated between the four as Mimi and Jennifer slid onto either side of Lisa and Felicia.

"Mimi, I don't mean to be rude, but you look like you've seen better days," Felicia said hesitantly as they got settled in the booth.

"I have," Mimi sighed.

Lisa leaned over and placed an arm around her for a hug. "What's going on, hon? Your dad say some more mean things to you?"

Jennifer saw Mimi open her mouth to explain just as Gracie approached the table.

"All right, here's the deal," Gracie said, as if she were answering a question though none of them had asked one. She put a small plastic glass of water in front of each of them. "That pastor friend of yours called." *She must mean the one Felicia was going to ask Dave to contact for Gracie.* "I've darkened the doors of that church a few times, but if that pastor asks one blasted time for money, I'm outta there." Then without a segue she added, "And I already put in your orders, so just hang tight and I'll be back with your drinks."

As so many times before, she darted away before any of the PWs could respond to her.

Jennifer looked across at Mimi and Lisa, then quickly turned to Felicia, next to her, seeking some sort of nonverbal reaction to Gracie's news. They seemingly were as dumbfounded as she.

"She's going to church?" were the words Felicia finally uttered. "Wow. I knew when Dave asked the pastor at Cheeksville Baptist to go see her, he would, but I was kind of afraid to ask her about it. I didn't want her to think I was being pushy because, you know, that never works if someone doesn't really want to go."

"I know!" said Lisa. "I guess everything she's been through with her sister has softened her heart a bit to what the Lord has for her. Praise him!"

God, you are amazing.

Once their surprise dissipated, the women returned to Mimi.

"So, Mimi," Lisa repeated, "what's going on?"

Mimi told them about the misunderstanding, her father with the beer in the chili and the backyard barbecue. "For the first time since he's come back into my life, my dad stepped up to do the right thing and I quashed it right in front of him," said Mimi. "And, even worse, in front of the kids. So I had to apologize to them."

"I hope you sought some forgiveness from him, too," Jennifer asked. *Well, aren't you just the pot calling the kettle black?*

Jennifer saw tears suddenly rolling down Mimi's face. "Mimi, what's wrong? What could be worse than that?"

Just then Gracie arrived with their drinks. She clearly saw the intensity of their conversation and silently placed their glasses on the table then slipped away.

Mimi sniffled, reaching down into her purse for a tissue. Felicia handed her one from across the table.

"He was in a car accident Saturday night," Mimi finally said. "He's in a coma."

Felicia, Lisa, and Jennifer gasped.

"Mimi, why didn't you call one of us?" Lisa asked. "We could have been praying!"

Mimi shook her head. "I know I should have. I've just been . . . paralyzed over it. I spent all Sunday at the hospital and most of yesterday. But last night the doctor told me they didn't know when or if he would come out of it, and they would call me if he did. So I went home but I was there again this morning."

"No change?" Felicia asked gently.

Mimi shook her head again and looked down.

"Was it a DUI?" Jennifer asked. *Please say no.*

"Yes, well, not for Dad, but for the guy he was with. He died, though. Tragic," Mimi said. "But for me the worst part is the last thing I told him: that he was a 'no-good father.' And that's just not true. He's created in the image of God! He's just messed up. And now . . . I don't know if I'll ever get a chance to tell him face-to-face that I love him."

"I'm going to pray that he rises off that bed," Lisa said forcefully. "So you be planning your speech for your dad." She gave Mimi another one-armed hug.

Mimi swiped her eyes with the tissue and blew her nose. "Okay, let's not focus on this. Part of why I came today was to get a little bit of normalcy. So let's talk about something else to take my mind off my dad." She looked across at Jennifer. "Like how you're spending your greenbacks."

Although Jennifer knew she was kidding, the money thing was already making her uncomfortable. Who knew being a millionaire, hitting easy street—something so many dream about—would be a burden? "Eh, we just bought a few things."

"Like that shiny new SUV?" Felicia nudged Jennifer and smiled.

Jennifer changed the subject. "Wasn't that amazing Saturday at the wives' meeting? The transparency in those prayers!"

The other three nodded in agreement.

"I feel like we're finally making some headway," said Lisa, "in getting that thing turned around from Kitty's fake fest to something we can really cherish. Even Ally seemed to be into it."

Felicia sighed. "I saw her in the parking lot afterward, though, and she asked me what one of the women meant when she prayed, 'Satisfy our ministry.'"

"Who prayed that?" Mimi asked with a furrowed brow.

"No one." Felicia chuckled. "What the woman prayed was, 'Sanctify our ministry.' Evidently Ally had never heard that word before."

"Presbyterians," Lisa said, shaking her head in mock disapproval.

Felicia continued. "She said 'Normy' told her she needed to take a couple of theology classes down at the Bible college in Cincinnati."

The thought of Ally in her miniskirts and five-inch heels traipsing around a Bible-college campus made Jennifer erupt in giggles. "I hate to be mean, but can't you just see Ally sidling up to those stodgy professors with her questions about sanctification?"

They all laughed until Felicia waved them to quiet down so she could speak. "Yeah, well, she didn't seem to think she could hack Bible college either. She asked if the four of us could help her. For some reason she sees us as role models."

The mirth died down as the women considered what that meant. *A role model? Me?*

"Now don't shoot me, but maybe we should help Ally," Lisa, always the peacemaker, said. "I've been thinking about a mentoring program for our wives' group. The more experienced PWs would be mentors and the younger ones would be apprentices. Wouldn't it have been nice when we were starting out to have an older PW to help us along?"

The others considered her statement before nodding.

"What would you call this mentorship?" Felicia asked. "Have you thought of a name for it?"

Jennifer couldn't help what popped into her head. "With Ally as our first apprentice, I think 'Bringing Up Baby' is appropriate."

They all broke into laughter again.

CHAPTER 45

Mimi

Sunday, June 15
10:41 p.m.

Father's Day. "The official day to honor the man who sired, reared, and trained you." At least that's how that morning's church bulletin had put it.

How do I honor a man who is in a coma thanks to me? Mimi had wondered all day. Since her father had come to live with them, Father's Day had not been a particularly joyous day for Mimi. For years before, she was able to avoid giving much thought to her own father because she focused solely on helping her children honor and celebrate their dad, her husband. That had been an occasion into which she could dive heartily and thoroughly, making banners and cupcakes and his favorite meal.

But now there was no avoiding thinking about her dad on Father's Day. She'd decided to overcompensate for it by staying up late into the night on Saturday, baking cupcakes and cookies to take to everybody at church. Then she decorated the living room with WE LOVE OUR DADDY banners and signs. She knew Mark would appreciate that.

But all that work had taken its toll. She had begun to feel it during the morning worship service. The problem wasn't so much that she was falling asleep, it was more a lack of control over her emotions.

The service was geared specifically toward fathers—each receiving a boutonniere and a ballpoint pen. And the oldest father received a gift certificate to none other than the Clucker House. Needless to say, Mimi had not been included in deciding on the presents for the fathers this year.

But as each father stood, Mimi slid farther into her seat and picked apart the overly used tissue she was grasping in her hand. She bit the inside of her cheek, blinked a lot, pretended that she was having trouble with something in her eye—anything to keep her from crying and to keep people from *thinking* she was crying.

Finally, blessedly, it came to prayer time. After singing "Turn Your Eyes Upon Jesus," and allowing the congregation to offer up any prayer requests, Mark stood at the pulpit and began to pray. And that's when Mimi allowed herself to cry silently. She wiped and wiped her eyes and nose and prayed that Mark's prayer would be long and drawn out. After prayer time came fellowship time, and Mimi planned to quickly walk out of the sanctuary to find her own sanctuary in a stall in the ladies' restroom.

But instead of waiting for Mark's prayer to end, she decided to leave now. If she could move silently enough, no one would notice she'd gone. She really just wanted to go home and disappear, but there was no way that could happen. First, she had too many children who would squawk over her being gone, not to mention making enemies out of the nursery workers for leaving them too long with Mighty Mouth Milo, the kid who seemingly never shut up during church. Second, they'd all driven together, so how would Mark and the kids get home? Third, the whole church would start talking about her—more so than, she was sure, they already did.

Opting for the bathroom, she sneaked out of her pew and, keeping her head down and her eyes pasted to the blue carpet, quickly moved toward the back of the sanctuary. She opened the door at the back of the sanctuary just as Mark said, "Amen."

Not looking around her, Mimi walked straight down the hall and turned to the right, pushing through the ladies' room door. It was silent inside. She reached the last stall, stepped in, and locked the door behind her. At last, letting her emotions overwhelm her, she grabbed the toilet paper—pulling off two long strands to cover the toilet seat—sat, and began to sob.

2:31 p.m.

Mimi survived the rest of the service and lunch afterward. She'd made Mark his favorite dish, lasagna, and an angel food cake for dessert.

"That was a great meal, as usual," Mark said, helping her clean off the table and carry the dishes into the kitchen.

Mimi smiled. "I hate to ask you to do this, especially on your special day, but would you mind taking the kids for a while? I'd like to be alone."

"You going to see your dad?"

"No, not right away . . . I think I want to go back to the church."

He pulled out a set of keys from his pants pocket and placed them on the counter. "I think that's a good idea. Take your time. The kids and I will be fine."

"Thanks."

"As a matter of fact, why don't you go now? I'll get MJ and Michaela to help me clean up."

Mimi paused. She could only imagine what kind of mess MJ would make in his effort to clean.

"Don't worry about it," he said, as if reading her mind. "I'll keep a close eye on him."

"I love you," she said and picked up the keys.

At the church, she stood at the back of the sanctuary and stared at the front. A cross with a red cloth draped over it hung there. A ray of sunlight broke through one of the windows and splashed across the middle of the cross, making the cloth a deep, bright red. *The color of blood,* she thought.

The sanctuary seemed so quiet and peaceful. She didn't bother to turn on the lights, preferring to stay in the dark.

She walked down the center aisle and over to the piano, sitting on the right side of the room. She touched it lightly. She'd never particularly cared for playing the piano—her dream had been to play the bagpipes. But she'd taken piano lessons when she started dating Mark, since that was the "appropriate thing to do" as a potential pastor's wife.

Now she felt a deep need to play. She used to play during every service until two years ago when she finally admitted to Mark that she hated it. Thankfully, he understood and encouraged her to quit. There were two other pianists in the congregation who genuinely enjoyed playing.

She ran her fingers over the black and white keys and slowly began to play the first thing that came to mind: "Amazing Grace." It was a song she'd hated growing up, but it had come to be precious to her as she matured and became an adult.

Amazing grace, how sweet the sound that saved a wretch like me . . .

She needed a dose of that grace right about now.

"God, I need you," she said, her fingers still on the piano but no longer playing. Her tears splashed onto the keys. Wiping them off, she headed toward the altar.

They didn't use it much anymore, which she thought was a real shame. Sometimes the most wonderful place to be, the safest and most welcoming place, was on your knees at the foot of the cross, with a tissue in hand. Somehow she felt closer to God when she was in that position. She couldn't explain it and knew that she could pray anywhere—and did. But at that altar, right then, was exactly where she needed to be.

And right there was where she poured out her heart, praying to a

God whom she knew in her head was listening to her, but wondering in her heart if there was enough grace for her one more time.

"I feel like I abuse your grace, God. I feel like you keep tabs and on some clipboard you've written, 'No more handouts for Mimi Plaisance. She doesn't learn well, and she doesn't practice my teachings.'"

She wiped her eyes and grabbed another tissue from the box sitting behind the altar.

"I know I don't deserve this, but would you forgive me . . . again? Would you help me start fresh with my dad?" Her voice choked up. "Would you give me another opportunity with him?"

Her eyes caught sight of the cross, lit by the lone sunbeam. Then she lay on her side next to the altar and cried herself to sleep.

■

4:35 p.m.

Mimi awoke, feeling stiff in the shoulder and hip she'd been lying on. Moving her neck around and massaging it with her hand, she slowly pushed up on her knees and looked again at the cross. The light had shifted and now a shadow of the cross fell across the platform.

"Mims?" Mark's voice floated up to her from the back of the sanctuary.

"Hi," she said weakly, watching him walk toward her.

"Hey, I tried calling your cell, but you must have left it in the car."

She nodded.

"The hospital called. Your dad's out of the coma. You must have done *some* praying."

CHAPTER 46

Jennifer

Monday, June 16

5:07 p.m.

Jennifer drove toward her mom's house, deep in thought about the previous day's service. Father's Day. All she'd been able to think about during the music and even the sermon was what it could have been like to know her father. Would they have laughed together over the same things? Did he have the same idiosyncrasies as she?

Last year I didn't know anything about my father. This year I don't know much more, except who he is, she thought.

But it was the service's final prayer, led by the church's newest dad, as was their tradition, that really got to her. After acknowledging the need for God's guidance in parenting, he'd said, "Lord, not all of us had great examples of how to be good parents. But help us not to dwell on their mistakes, and instead focus on what they did right and make that a part of how we raise our children."

After her visit to Father Scott and with the PWs' encouragement, Jennifer had been unknotting the resentment she felt toward her mom.

The prayer, though, made her realize she *was* dwelling, as she had a tendency to do. It was time to do something about it.

She pulled into her mom's driveway, remembering how hesitant Jo Jo had sounded on the phone when Jennifer called her earlier.

"I don't need you to yell at me anymore," she'd told Jennifer. "So if you're coming over here to do that, don't bother."

I deserved that, Jennifer thought as she walked to the door. Her mom was waiting and opened it before she got there.

"I made some iced tea for us," she said, hustling out with two glasses. "I thought we could sit out here and enjoy the late-afternoon air. It's been so humid this week."

Jennifer caught a glimpse inside the house, which looked to be in as much disarray as it was last time she'd visited. She had hoped to see an improvement since the medication would have kicked in by now.

Jo Jo handed her a sweaty glass of tea, and then they each chose a lawn chair from the four propped against the side of the house. Settling in on the grass, they both took off their shoes.

Jennifer took a sip of tea. Her mom always did make the best iced tea. "So how are you, Mother?"

Jo Jo swirled the top of her tea with the tip of her finger. "I'm doing okay, I guess. Still sleeping too much. This new medicine the doctor has me on doesn't seem to be doing the trick." She looked distressed, which Jennifer took as a positive sign. It was when her mother didn't recognize she needed the medication that got her worried.

They sat quietly while Jennifer planned what she wanted to say.

"Mother, I owe you an apology," she said, turning to look at her.

Jo Jo stared down at her tea.

"I . . . I was wrong to get angry with you over all this. You know, about my father and what happened between the two of you."

Jo Jo looked at her. "Jen, you didn't do anything wrong. I was a total idiot, spending that money and not telling you about your father. I know it probably sounds hollow, but I thought I was doing the right thing by keeping you from him. I thought if you found out who he was and he denied you, it would hurt more than not ever knowing who he was."

Jennifer nodded and glanced away. It wasn't what she wished had happened, but it made sense. She wasn't too excited about the day she'd have to tell Carys about *her* parents.

"I know in your own way you did what was best," Jennifer admitted. "I just wish . . ." Her voice trailed off. She wished a lot of things could have been different. But was now the time to bring up all of that?

"I know you do, Jen. So do I," Jo Jo said, seemingly understanding what Jennifer hadn't been able to say.

A car drove by and honked. The passenger, Mrs. Delaney from down the street, waved. Jo Jo and Jennifer waved back.

Jennifer glided her feet along the top of the grass, enjoying the summer silkiness of it. She wasn't sure what to say next. Had her apology been sufficient?

"You know, you looked so much like him when you were a baby, it was kinda scary," Jo Jo said, smiling. "His round face, blue eyes, and that curly reddish hair. I know it's lightened a lot over the years, but your hair was fire engine red when you were born."

Jennifer reached up to feel her head, as if she could touch the color. "I always just assumed I got that color from you."

Jo Jo tucked her legs underneath her. "No, I've always dyed mine."

"What do you mean? I've never seen you dye it—it's always been red."

"I know," Jo Jo said matter-of-factly. "I started doing it right after you were born because I didn't want you to look any less mine than you already did. And then I kept it up. Didn't you notice in our old photos that I didn't have red hair before you came along?"

Jennifer thought about the pictures. She hadn't looked at them since before she left home, when she was eighteen, but she had loved poring over them when she was younger and desperate to feel a family connection. People were always so happy in photographs, unlike real life. Or at least the life she'd known. "I guess I thought the ones where you were blond you were wearing a wig or something," Jennifer said. *I can't believe she went to all that trouble for me, even when she was sick.*

"It was like looking at a picture of Finbar every day when you'd come toddling into the room," Jo Jo recalled. "Then at about five you started favoring me more. But by then, the damage had been done."

"Dam—" Jennifer had started to ask what she meant when the realization of it all dawned on her. The escalating drinking and drugs were a reaction to her mother's broken heart over being denied by Finbar, and the stress of having his child.

"You really loved him, didn't you?" Jennifer asked gently.

Jo Jo's eyes filled with tears as she turned away. "Yes," she whispered. She cleared her throat uncomfortably and turned back to Jennifer. "I know that probably sounds dumb, considering the little time we spent together, but I felt like he was my soul mate. And I his."

Now Jennifer was the one with tears in her eyes. Finally, she had a sense of family. It was all weird and dysfunctional and splintered and based on everything unholy, but it was what it was. And it was hers. And in that moment, it felt to Jennifer that God had taken what was meant for evil and had somehow turned it into good. She didn't understand it completely, but she felt that God's grace was floating around her.

She set her nearly empty glass on the ground and rose from her chair. Going over to her mother, she leaned down. They had never been a very huggy family, but at that moment it was all Jennifer wanted.

"Mom," she said.

It felt so foreign to her to give her mother that title. But at that moment, it felt right. She wrapped her arms around her mother and held on tightly. Her mother's arms immediately did the same to Jennifer.

"Thank you, Mom. Thank you for doing what you did to give me a chance. I love you."

A small gasp escaped from Jo Jo and her body jerked lightly. "I love you, too," Jo Jo whispered through sobs. Their hug was awkward, but heartfelt.

Jennifer pulled away and wiped her eyes, reaching into her pocket for a tissue. She tore off half for Jo Jo.

"Well, isn't this something?" Jo Jo said, wiping her eyes.

Jennifer went back to her chair and took the last swallow from her tea. She was as drained as the glass. But she had something else she needed to tell her mom.

"Listen, Mother"—it was going to take a while to use the more loving "Mom" all the time—"you know I have all this money now."

"Do tell!" Jo Jo said in a friendly, mocking way.

Jennifer chuckled. "If you're willing," she hesitated, "I'd like to take you to a clinic, a place where you can stay and they can figure out the best medication and care for you. I've been researching it online, and there are places you can go where they can monitor you while they try different medicines to see which is best."

She looked over at Jo Jo to see if she was receptive. She had a faraway look in her eyes.

"Mom?" she inquired. "Does that sound like something you'd be interested in? I know it's difficult—"

"That's the exact thing your father said to me the last time I talked to him on the phone before he died," Jo Jo said. "He was convinced they could do something for me at one of those places."

Jennifer wasn't sure what excited her more: her mother's openness to the clinic or the thought that her father and she had shared the same idea.

"Good," Jennifer said. "So it's settled then?"

Jo Jo nodded with a slightly expectant look, as if she were encouraged at the thought of feeling better.

"Oh, and Mom," Jennifer added, "don't worry about trying to go back to work when you get out of the clinic. Sam and I want to provide for you with the money my father left me."

Jo Jo turned to her. Gratefulness spread across her face.

"But try to curb the shopping sprees, okay?" Jennifer asked, grinning. "We really need to leave some items in the store for other people to buy, too."

They both laughed—the kind of easy, knowing joy only family members can share. For not only had Jennifer found her father, she now had found her mother, too.

CHAPTER 47

Felicia

Wednesday, June 18
10:08 a.m.

Getting a call from her mother in the middle of her workday was not a surprise to Felicia. But how she had opened the conversation—"Li called to tell me Gina is pregnant"—was a shocker on many levels.

"What do you mean, Li called you?" Felicia asked, confused. "And Gina . . . is pregnant?"

Lupita could hardly contain herself, she was so overwrought with excitement. "Li said he asked if he could call us to, you know, set things right between us. And then Gina got on the phone. She is very happy, that girl. The happiest I've heard her in a long time."

Felicia's head was whirling with the news. "Mama, they aren't married. I'm really surprised you're so—"

"Oh, Fifi, they will marry. They have to with a baby on the way."

Ah, now I understand. "Mama," Felicia said gently, "did they say they were planning to get married, or are you just assuming they will because there is a baby?"

Her mother was silent. Then she said tersely, "Fifi, even your sister would not bring an illegitimate child into this world. I didn't think it was necessary even to ask if they were getting married. Of course they are."

Felicia wasn't sure whether to feel indignant about her mother's theory or feel sorry for her abundant trust in her oldest child. She decided that avoiding an opinion would be best. "Did she at least leave you a phone number? After she hung up on me that time, I tried to call her back but her L.A. cell phone had been disconnected."

"Yes. Oh, someone just came in the store."

Over the phone, Felicia heard bells jingle and her mother breathlessly greeting a customer at the bakery.

A minute later she gave Felicia the number, then said, "I've got to go. Call her and we'll talk later."

After Lupita hung up, Felicia fingered the slip of paper on which she had written Gina's phone number. Could she call and not sound judgmental? Clearly she was not good at hiding how she felt, judging from her last conversation with Gina.

I have to try. She is my sister, after all, and I'm the only relative she has between here and the West Coast.

But just as she was ready to dial, panic set in.

What kind of parents will they be? she wondered. *Are they still on drugs? What will that do to the baby? Can they provide for a child? Do they even recognize the life change parents undergo?*

Even more curious to Felicia was the whole idea of it. Just a year or so ago, her sister and Li had ridiculed the idea of marriage and children. Now they were embarking on at least part of the equation.

Was this baby a mistake or planned?

She immediately felt bad for thinking it. No baby was ever a "mistake," she knew.

She dialed the number. After four rings, an answering machine kicked on. Following the beep, Felicia said cautiously (she suspected Gina was there and not picking up), "Hey, Gina and Li, I hear congratulations are in order." *That sounded about as fake as Joan Rivers's face.* "Give me a call so we can talk about the . . . news. I tried to call you a few weeks ago, but your cell number was disconnected. Gina, I'm sorry we had words. But I do want to be there for you guys, so call me. 'Bye."

Putting down the receiver, a thought occurred to Felicia. *I suppose the pressure will be off me now that everyone's focus will be on Gina.*

She wasn't sure if she was happy about that or not.

CHAPTER

48

Jennifer

Monday, June 23

1:12 p.m.

"Are you sure that's what you want to do?" said Stella Morgan, director of the Fortress, where Jennifer volunteered. They were sitting in Stella's tiny office on the bottom floor of the women's shelter.

Jennifer nodded exuberantly. "We can't live in a place like that," she said, "and it's just perfect space for what we've been needing here."

Jennifer remembered her conversation with Sam about her father's house. At first they thought they'd live in it, figuring they could hold church events there, but the more they discussed it, the more they realized it could cause a rift in the church.

"Can you imagine me, during a sermon, asking people to commit to tithing when I'm living in that mansion?" Sam had asked.

Then they had thought the obvious choice would be to sell it, but after talking to a real estate agent they realized that trying to get what the place was worth in a market of mostly three-bedroom, two-bath modest family homes at an average price of two to three hundred thousand wasn't going to happen. That's when the lightbulb went on in Jennifer's head.

"Hey!" she'd said. "Why not give it to the shelter? Think of the number of women they could house there, and the downstairs would be great for offices and meetings. Plus it's gated, so it would be secure."

She hadn't allowed the real estate agent's sullen face over the lost sale (she sent her a giant fruit basket later that week with a thank-you note) to prevail over her excitement. And Sam had seemed relieved to have this "problem" solved.

So here she was now, revealing her plan to Stella, who although very together and Jennifer's role model for calm and collected, got moist eyes when she heard Jennifer's proposal.

"You are *sure* this is what you want to do?" Stella asked again, seemingly not believing Jennifer's decision.

"Yes, Stella." Jennifer grabbed Stella's forearm, then let it go. "Sam and I have given this a lot of thought and prayer, and we really believe this is what God is leading us to do."

"Praise the Lord," Stella said quietly. Then she leaned back in her chair, punched her fists in the air, and said a little louder, "Praise the Lord."

Another volunteer, Corinne, stuck her head in the office, causing Stella to temper her celebration. "Stella? We have an intake."

Stella looked at Jennifer. "My head is spinning from all this. Could you handle it?"

Jennifer nodded and stood. "I'll take you out to the house tomorrow. It's going to need some renovation to work as a shelter. But Sam and I will pay for that, too, of course. Oh, and I asked the staff who were still there to stay on. They already know the house and the grounds, so I thought they would be nice to have around."

Stella looked as though she had just been told Santa Claus was real. "I can't believe this."

As Jennifer turned to leave, she saw Stella drop her head into her hands. It made her feel better to see Stella show some emotion—she'd always wondered how the director remained so steady, something Jennifer couldn't even attempt.

Reaching back to tighten her ponytail, she sauntered into the waiting room to find a petite young woman with a stylish suede purse on her lap looking around nervously. She walked up to her.

"Hi, I'm Jennifer Shores," she said.

"Tabitha Cramer." When she stood and set the suitcase on the floor, Jennifer could see she was pregnant. She was so small, though, it was difficult to tell how far along she was.

"Come on back," Jennifer said, taking her bag and putting an arm around her lightly to guide her to the conference room.

"So what brings you to the Fortress?" Jennifer asked, as she had many times over the last several years. Often, the women's stories, some so close to her own abuse history, were at the same time both moving and grim. But she had a strange feeling about this one, especially since she didn't see any obvious signs of abuse and Tabitha looked to be in good spirits—absolutely not typical of the devastating situations most of their clients were in.

"I need to tell you upfront that I am not being abused," she said assertively. Jennifer noticed her diction was purposeful, as if she were on the stage. "I am a student at UC . . ."

Ah, a University of Cincinnati girl. So she is as young as I thought.

"And, as you can see, I'm pregnant. Everyone said I should get an abortion, but as a feminist I find the idea of abortion to be, well, exploitative of women."

Jennifer found herself nodding, but she had no idea what Tabitha meant. In her book, abortion was just plain wrong because it was murder. She'd never heard a pro-life approach from a feminist.

Tabitha continued. "But as this pregnancy has developed—"

"And how far along are you?" Jennifer interrupted.

"Twenty weeks. As I was saying, as this pregnancy has developed . . ."

Jennifer couldn't help but be amused by this college girl's clearly practiced presentation.

" . . . I've come to understand, I do not have the tools to be a parent at this stage in my life. I'm pre-engineering, which takes a lot of studying, and I'm also involved in student government. It's just not prudent for me to rear a child now."

Tabitha ran her hand through her shoulder-length, wavy, strawberry blond hair, then crossed her hands and looked at Jennifer intensely.

"Our hair is about the same color," Jennifer said absentmindedly, which brought a confused look from Tabitha.

"I'm not here to discuss beauty tips," Tabitha said through pursed lips before Jennifer could continue.

Whew, we've got a live one here. She doesn't seem to need much comforting—just a plan of action.

Jennifer snapped into her business tone. "Well, Tabitha, we are not an adoption agency—"

Tabitha looked frustrated. "But a girl at school said her sister came here and you handled it for her," she said with a huff.

"You didn't let me finish." This girl clearly wasn't ready for a child—she was still a bit bratty herself. "We do not handle adoptions in-house, but we can connect you with a trustworthy agency that will do it for you from this location."

Tabitha appeared relieved. "How soon can I meet with them?"

"You have plenty of time. You said you are only—"

"Yes, I know I'm only halfway through the pregnancy. But I want to get all of this sorted out so I can get on . . . with my life."

Jennifer thought she saw a wave of regret pass through Tabitha's eyes. "Are you sure this is what you want to do?" she asked her gently. "Just like we can connect you with the adoption folks, we can also assist you with resources to care for your child and go to school. It is possible, you know."

Tabitha rolled her eyes. "Yes, I see those 'older' students walking around campus, pushing a stroller with one hand and hauling a book bag with the other. That's not me."

Jennifer wasn't sure she had ever met such a decisive birth mother. Although she found Tabitha's abrasive personality wearisome, she was impressed with her firm stance.

"I'll go call the adoption agency now and see if someone is available to meet with you today so you don't have to make the trip back from Cincinnati," she said, standing.

"Thank you." Tabitha sighed as she pulled a lip-gloss tube out of her purse.

Jennifer was starting out the door to the office when a thought occurred to her. "Hey," she said, coming back into the room and circling over to where she had been sitting. Tabitha was swabbing her lips with her ring finger, turning them soft pink with the gloss.

"My husband and I are adoptive parents, and we were considering adding to our family," she said, leaning down onto the table. "Maybe we would be a good fit for you."

Tabitha shrugged. "I'm not one of those women who's going to do hours of interviews. I just want the agency to tell me they have a solid family who can rear this child to be a good citizen. If you are those people, then fine."

"We do have the same hair color." Jennifer winked at her.

"You don't have to sell yourself to me," Tabitha said, seemingly unimpressed. "I don't care if you're blue, as long as I'm assured you will be responsible parents."

Feeling admonished—and kind of like the child in the room—Jennifer started out again.

"Oh, one more thing," she said, coming back around the table.

She caught Tabitha rolling her eyes again.

"The father," Jennifer said. "What about him?"

"Oh, please," Tabitha said, shaking her head and nearly laughing. "Hearing this baby is being adopted will be the best news he's had this year."

"What do you mean?"

Tabitha smirked. "He's my physics prof. Married, with kids . . . and not ready for another one. Especially with me. Kwan's just in it for the ego boost."

Normally Jennifer would have been sickened to hear about an affair between a college student and her teacher, but something else in Tabitha's explanation caught her attention.

"Kwan?" Jennifer asked.

"Yes, his name is Kwan. He's Korean. Been over here about fifteen years." She suddenly looked alarmed. "You don't know him, do you?"

Jennifer shook her head. "No. No, I don't know him."

As she walked to the office, she couldn't help but be disheartened. She and Sam were possibly going to adopt another biracial child?

Then she remembered Carys, the light of her life. She'd forgotten her race about two seconds after she'd held her for the first time. Why would it be any different with this one?

Eh, just call us Brad and Angelina, she thought. Then she picked up the phone and dialed.

CHAPTER 49

Lulu's Café

Tuesday, June 24
12:42 p.m.

"We're really getting kind of bad about this dessert thing," Mimi said, her spoon hovering between two bowls of pudding in the middle of the table. They hadn't been able to decide between butterscotch and chocolate, so they'd gotten them both.

Felicia allowed the spoon to slide smoothly from her mouth, depositing the flavorful custard inside. "I think between your dad coming out of his coma and Jen making up with her mom, we have lots to celebrate," she said between bites. "Besides, working at home has given me more time to get to the gym, so why not indulge a little?"

Lisa set down her spoon on a napkin. "How's that going anyway?" she asked Felicia. "You know, with people bugging you while you're trying to work."

"Funny you would ask that," Felicia answered, glad to talk about her newfound insight. "I used to think those calls were an intrusion. But having a flexible schedule has made me realize how I can help people. I feel like I'm really living up to people's expectations now for what their pastor's wife should be. And that's one reason I guess I wasn't too excited about having another baby—it would limit my time again."

"Ohhhh, yeahhhh," Mimi said, dipping her spoon in the butterscotch. "There's nothing like a little one to throw a big wrench into your plans. Especially one with a mouth like Milo's. I'm signing that kid up for voice lessons as soon as he's old enough. Maybe he'll be the next Pavarotti."

Lisa turned to Jennifer. "Any luck selling your dad's house yet? I know the market is off."

"I meant to tell you guys about that earlier," Jennifer said. "Sam and I decided this weekend that we're going to donate the house to the Fortress. We talked with a real estate agent and she said it would be very, very difficult to sell. We'd need an almost perfect buyer. And we certainly couldn't live there and continue pastoring with Sam giving sermons on tithing. So it just seemed logical to give it to the shelter. We're even keeping on most of the staff to help run the home and keep up the maintenance. It's going to be a posh place to live for those women trying to get on their feet again, but why not? Many of them have been through so much, a little luxury is warranted."

"That is so great, Jen," Mimi said. "What a way to honor your father, too."

Felicia looked at Jennifer. Something about her had changed, but she wasn't quite sure what. She knew Jennifer had dropped a couple of pounds, because she had mentioned how much work it had been, but there was an additional, intangible improvement about her that she couldn't put her finger on. Whatever it was, it made Felicia smile to see it.

"What?" Jennifer asked, catching her eye.

"Nothing," Felicia said. "I just think you're fantastic . . . and not only because you're buying lunch today."

"Wait," Lisa said, "I thought we said you wouldn't do that every time."

"Not every time," Jennifer explained, "just when the spirit moves me."

"Move, spirit, move," Mimi said with a giggle.

"That reminds me," Felicia said to Jennifer, "whatever became of that woman, the kind of spooky one who worked for your father?"

Jennifer sat back from the empty pudding bowls. "Yes—Belinda. It was really strange," she said. "When we had the reading of the will, she was there. I could tell she was really upset that my dad hadn't left her anything, and I felt bad about that because I knew she had been a good employee of his. I just figured it was an oversight. So I wrote a check to her myself to help her get started in a new place. But when I went over to drop it off, the staff said she had left town already with no forwarding address or phone number."

This thing with Jen's dad really is like a novel. "Why do you suppose she did that?" Felicia asked.

"I'll bet I know," said Mimi.

Jennifer looked at her and grinned. "Okay, Miss Smartypants. What happened?"

"She was in love with your dad," Mimi said confidently. "And I'm guessing it was unrequited love, too. He probably never knew."

Jennifer gasped. "How did you come up with that?"

"Am I right?" Mimi asked.

"Yes!" Jennifer exclaimed. "I asked Channing, my dad's butler—the one who was following me—what the deal was with her. He's a really nice guy, so he made us coffee and we sat at the gigantic dining room table while he told me. He said Belinda had a secret passion for my dad and truly believed they would be together one day. She even worked on many of her days off because she was sort of deluded and thought she was the lady of the house after my dad's wife died."

"That's kind of creepy," Lisa said, then lowered her voice. "Do you think your dad led her on about it? I don't mean any disrespect to your dad or anything."

"None taken," Jennifer assured her. "I had the same thought. But Channing said he never saw my dad do anything that Belinda could have taken to mean she was more than just an assistant to him. He said my dad frequently mentioned my mother to Belinda, and on more than one occasion he saw Belinda roll her eyes."

Poor woman. "So where do you think she went?" Felicia asked.

"Off to run some other rich person's house," Mimi answered as if she knew for certain. "Just like in the movies. These ladies go from house to house looking for some rich man to make a Cinderella out of them."

"Speaking of disappearing women," Lisa said, "has there ever been any follow-up on that pastor's wife from Dayton?"

"Ruth," Felicia reminded them. "Nope. It's as if she disappeared into thin air."

"So bizarre," Lisa said. "You'd think if she'd been kidnapped or killed, some trace of evidence would have shown up by now. And if she ran away, like some people said, you'd think they could find a motive at her house, or a credit card, or some smidgen of a lead."

"Only on TV," Jennifer said. "On *CSI* they can solve a case in less than an hour. But in the real world, some never get solved. I think this may be a secret that we never get the answer to."

"I propose we have one less secret," Lisa said cryptically. She must have seen their inquisitive looks because she continued quickly. "The July Fourth picnic is coming up. Let's tell our husbands about our get-togethers. I really want Joel to know you guys, and I'm tired of having to gloss over where I am every other Tuesday."

Felicia realized it would be nice to be able to tell Dave about the PWs, and she did want him to know the others' husbands. "I'm in," she said wholeheartedly.

"I think it's a great idea," said Jennifer. "As long as they don't think they can join us here every other week."

They laughed.

"They can sit in booth 26 if they do," said Mimi, pointing to their least favorite booth, near the door, which let in frigid air in the winter and hot blasts in the summer. "But yes, let's do it. We can get a few picnic tables together that day so our kids can meet, too. Although you might wish you hadn't, once you get a load of my monkeys."

"Megan is a little doll," Felicia said. Mimi had brought Megan to one of their lunches a year or so ago when she couldn't get a babysitter.

"Yeah, well, you try to get a comb through that doll's ratty hair while she's screaming bloody murder and let me know if you still feel that way," Mimi said, smiling.

Gracie came to drop off the check, dramatically handing it to Jennifer. "Mrs. Trump, I believe this is for you."

She started to walk away, but Lisa touched her arm, causing her to turn back around. "Gracie," Lisa said in her sweet, calm voice.

She is such a treasure, Felicia thought.

"We were wondering how it's going for you at church. You know we're here for you if you have any questions or want to . . . pray."

Gracie squinted at her. "You're here for me twice a month, and that's just plenty, thank you. Between your crying and whooping and what all, I think I get enough of you." Her eyes were twinkling, though, telling Felicia there was humor behind every word. "But I'll let you know if I suddenly feel the need to drop to my knees in the middle of my shift while you're here. 'Course that would mean a slight delay on your food, and I know how you PWs are about getting your lunch."

The bell over the door rang and Felicia saw Seth come in. *Now there is someone who can relate to going from completely antichurch to gung ho for Christ.* She waved him over.

"Hi, ladies," he said, arriving at the table. He looked at Gracie. "Hey, G, I've got an order to go."

G?

"Do you know each other?" Mimi asked.

Seth looked over at her. "Well, sure. I live right across the street, don't I? This is practically my kitchen, isn't it, G?"

Gracie nodded. "This one needs to learn to cook and save himself some money. I used to dread seeing him drag his old scraggly self in here, but he's been looking different lately. Really turned himself around."

The four PWs exchanged looks. They knew the key to his successful turnaround.

"Gracie," Lisa started, "there is a reason for the changes in Seth. You see—"

Waving her off, Gracie started to back away from the group. "You think I don't know all about this? As much as you four"—she jutted her chin toward the PWs' table—"have been working on me, this one"—she pointed her order-taking pencil toward Seth—"has been working double time. It's like he's getting a bonus or something if he can reel me in."

He will, Felicia thought. *Riches in heaven.*

"And on that note, I'd better get back to work or you all won't have a place to come practice being missionaries no more." She started to walk away, then turned around again. "I'll let you know when I'm ready to make that big walk down the center aisle," she said, which Felicia took to mean her willingness to come forward and accept Christ at the church's altar. "Until then, 'I can do all things through Christ who strengthens me.'"

Seth quickly said his good-byes and the women stood to leave.

"She sure does have a good hold of Scripture for not being a believer yet," Lisa said.

No one memorizes Scripture who doesn't have some semblance of faith. "I think she is a believer," Felicia asserted. "She's just not sure what to do with it yet."

Jennifer began walking toward the cash register. "Guess we'll need to mentor her."

"Mmm-hmmm," came the response from the other three.

After they bid one another farewell and broke away to their own cars, Felicia sat in her sports car and looked at the exterior of Lulu's, the most nondescript diner she'd ever seen. Inside, she could barely make out Gracie, lumbering from table to table. Horns honked as Jennifer, Lisa, and Mimi pulled away. With the engine running and the air-conditioning blowing, she closed her eyes.

Lord, I couldn't have dreamed all of this in my wildest imagination. First you find me three friends in whom I can confide, and then you use us to influence at least two people for you in this simple restaurant. Once again, I am amazed by how your plan unfolds.

A knock at her window jolted Felicia and her eyes popped open. It was Gracie, holding Felicia's black leather purse with the gold-chain strap.

She hit the roll-down button for the window.

Gracie leaned in. "Now don't get so caught up in living for the Lord that you forget the small things."

It was good counsel from a believer.

CHAPTER 50

Mimi

Thursday, June 26

3:31 p.m.

"You got everything? All the pictures from the kids? My medicine? My cane? My socks?"

"Yes, Dad," Mimi said, pushing her father's wheelchair. "I've got it all."

"Did being in that coma make you forget how anal your daughter is?" Mark laughed as he walked alongside the wheelchair, carrying his father-in-law's belongings.

"Oh, hush," she told her husband. "Are you comfortable enough, Dad?"

"I'd be more comfortable if I could have a drink," he said. But as Mimi and Mark stopped walking, he quickly said, "I'm just kidding. Being in a coma wasn't the ideal way to get detoxed, but it worked."

They started to walk again.

Mark and Mimi had discussed bringing the kids with them to pick up Archie from the hospital but finally decided it was better to do it without them. There were still too many things to say to clear the air. So they had called the Taylors, a family in their church who also had children about the same age as theirs. The Taylors gladly offered to watch the children for a few hours.

As they arrived at the front door of the hospital, Mark began to walk ahead. "You two hang out here while I get the car. I'll be back in just a minute."

Mimi watched her husband head toward the parking garage of the county hospital. When he disappeared around a corner, Mimi turned her attention back to her father. She gently patted down the hair on the top of his head. "You've still got that cowlick back here, I see." It was a stupid thing to say, she knew, but she didn't know what other conversation to make. And she certainly wasn't going to delve into anything deep and meaningful in the hospital lobby. It did feel good, though, to touch her father.

"We fixed up Mark's office at home so you won't have to climb any stairs. We put MJ's bed down there and made the room really nice. MJ was thrilled—he's going to sleep on an air mattress."

"You didn't have to do that," her father said gruffly. "I could have just slept on the couch. I've spent so many nights there anyway."

"Not with your ribs fractured the way they are. It really wasn't a bother. You need to take good care of yourself. You've been through a lot with this accident."

"I can't believe Walt's dead," he muttered, shaking his head. Walt was the driver. After her father left their house that day, he'd met up with Walt, a buddy who had started attending AA, but was no more committed to the program than Archie. The two had spent the day hopping from bar to bar, throwing back pint after pint of beer. That night they had decided to drive over to Cheeksville, forty miles away, to meet with another of Walt's buddies. But on the way, Walt crossed the centerline and plowed directly into an oncoming car, killing himself and the two people in the other vehicle, two teenagers out on a date.

"You're fortunate you aren't, too," was all Mimi could say. She didn't want to come off sounding judgmental. But it was amazing that he was the only person to survive. "God's obviously keeping you around because he isn't finished with you yet. He has a plan for your life."

Her dad exhaled loudly. "Well, maybe he does . . . Maybe he does."

The green Ford Freestar pulled around the corner and came to a halt at the front of the building. Mimi unlocked the wheelchair brakes and pushed her father out the door as Mark got out of the driver's side and opened a side door for her father to get in.

They spent most of the drive home in silence. Mimi assumed Mark and her father were thinking the same thing she was: *What do I say?* It was sort of like that thousand-pound gorilla in the room. She wanted to confront it, to get it out in the open, and start things on a better footing, but she didn't know how to begin. *So, Dad, you gonna quit drinking now? Learn your lesson?* She knew that wasn't a way to start an open dialogue.

Finally Mark spoke up. "We're glad you're okay, Dad."

"Both of you?" Archie said.

Turning in her seat to face him, Mimi looked at her dad. It was now or never. And she knew it had to be now.

"Dad, I didn't mean the things I said to you. I shouldn't have said them."

He cut her off. "Yes, you did mean them." His voice wasn't angry; it held a resigned quality.

"No, I—"

"You should have meant them. Everything you said was true. To be honest, I'm kind of disappointed I didn't die."

"Dad!" Mark said.

"Don't say that," Mimi said. "I know you're a good man. It's just that deep down, somewhere, somehow, you got lost."

"I wasn't drinking when you came home."

"I know, Dad. I—"

"When Mark left that day to go to the hospital and left me in charge of the kids, for the first time since I've been at your house, I felt like I mattered. I felt like you trusted me. That really meant something, and

I wanted to prove to you that I could be trusted. That I wasn't some worthless man who couldn't do anything. So I decided to surprise you and make my special chili that I haven't made in years."

Mimi couldn't believe what her father was confessing. She hadn't made her father feel special—she'd made him feel like a charity case. It was Mark who, on a fluke, had empowered her father. And what did she do? How did she repay him? By yelling at him and re-instilling in him the knowledge that he was, in fact, no good.

"I'm so sorry, Dad. I have been terrible to you."

"No, you took me in. I should be grateful. But I'm not stupid. I know you're ashamed of me. Just like your mother was."

It was true. She couldn't deny it. If she did, they'd all know it was a lie.

"You're right," she said after a few moments. "The only thing I ever wanted in my life was a peaceful family. I wanted some normalcy. I wanted a father who was sober and a mother with us who was present mentally. I wanted to be a kid and not have to act like the adult." She started to tear up, and turned away from him.

I still want my dad . . .

"The fact is, I've missed you," she continued, looking straight ahead. "I've always missed you."

She readjusted her seat belt against her shoulder and then pushed her hair behind her ears. A gentle pressure came to her left shoulder. She looked down and saw a large, calloused hand with yellowed fingers reaching for her. Her right hand immediately came up and squeezed his as she turned to look into his eyes. Eyes that were slightly yellowed from age and ill health; eyes that glistened with tears. Eyes that were the most beautiful she'd ever seen in her life.

CHAPTER

51

Felicia

Friday, June 27

9:05 p.m.

"It's been more than a week and Gina still hasn't called," Felicia said, handing Dave a bowl of ice cream and a spoon. She curled up next to him on the sofa and produced a second spoon from her robe pocket.

"Hey!" he said, playfully holding the bowl where she couldn't reach.

"Shhh," Felicia said with a giggle. "You'll wake up Nicholas and then he'll want some, too."

He moved the bowl between them, and they each dipped in a spoon.

"So what do you think is up with her?" Dave asked, referring to Felicia's concern about Gina. "Why would she talk to your mom and not you?"

Felicia savored the chocolate-almond confection. "Well, it's not like she's really *talking* to Mama," she said defensively. "Just that one time, when Li called."

Dave nodded.

He's right. She has talked to everyone in the family but me. Maybe she only talked to them once, but at least there was that one time.

"I just hope she's okay," Felicia said, putting into words the anxiety she'd felt since finding out Gina was pregnant. Every time the phone had rung since then, she'd anticipated it would be Gina needing something. And then every time she felt that, she scolded herself for being so selfish. Ultimately she just wanted to hear that her sister was okay, but deep down she suspected she wasn't. She rarely was. And now she'd have a child to consider, too.

The thought of Gina with a baby reminded Felicia that she and Dave hadn't discussed their own family-planning issues lately.

Ice cream and a Friday night—seems as good a time as any.

She scooped up another bite of ice cream. "Dave," she said, allowing the sweetness to coat her mouth, "I don't know what to do about another baby."

He nodded again slowly, his mouth full, but she could tell he had something to say by the flash of thought in his eyes.

"I've been praying about that," he said after swallowing. "I know I kind of left you holding the bag on that one, and that really wasn't fair."

"No, it wasn't!" Felicia said, glad to hear him admit it. She dropped her spoon into the empty bowl and took it from Dave to place on the table next to her. Then she turned back to him. "I have to tell you, I've really been struggling over this. There just doesn't seem to be a right or wrong answer."

"Me, too," he said. "On most things I feel like I get a pretty clear answer from the Lord. But on this one, it's just been sort of . . . neutral."

"I know—me, too!" Felicia loved it when she and Dave had similar experiences in prayer. Even though this one was not a shared answer, she still relished how they could see God working in their lives in parallel ways. "I don't feel as if he's saying yes and I don't feel there's a no. It's more of a 'do what you want.'"

Dave's tone turned pastoral. "I don't think it's that. It could just be that we need to keep searching our hearts, and his, for what is in his plan."

Felicia thought about an article she'd read in a magazine earlier that week. It was a profile of a conservative Christian family with seventeen children, all born to one set of parents. She was fascinated by the parents' ability to care for that many kids (and stay sane!), and admittedly cringed a bit at the girls' matching prairie dresses and what she viewed as sexist language from the husband about the wife. But all of that aside, what mostly struck her was the answer they gave when the writer asked why they had so many children.

"We feel the Lord opens and closes the womb," the wife had replied. "So we leave ourselves open to what he gives us or doesn't give us."

At first Felicia was taken aback by the brazenness of such an act. Not use birth control? But the more she thought about it over the following days, the more the word *control* kept coming back to her. As she had been agonizing over this decision, she'd recognized she was verging on telling God to give her the "right" answer. Yet that wasn't the same as surrendering to his authority to do what he wanted when he wanted, as the couple in the article had.

The words came out of her mouth before she'd even reflected on them. "Maybe what we should do *is* nothing. Keep doing what we're doing, and if God wants us to have a baby, we will. If not, we won't."

Dave looked into her eyes. She knew he was wondering what they'd done with his wife the control freak. "You'd do that? You'd really just go off the pills and roll the dice, so to speak?"

She nodded eagerly. "We give everything else to God's command. Why not give him that, too?"

The apprehensive look on his face made her laugh.

"Are you afraid we might end up with a basketball team?" she asked, clasping his hand in hers.

His expression softened. "Realistically, I guess we don't have that many childbearing years left anyway."

"You mean *I* don't have that many childbearing years left. Men can go on and on. Just look at some of those old actors and singers who keep having babies with their third-marriage trophy wives. They end up with grandchildren the same age as their children."

He squeezed her hand and looked at her with puppy eyes. "I promise not to leave you for a trophy wife."

"Hey, mister, I *am* your trophy wife," she said, reaching for a pillow to swat him. "And don't you forget it."

They started to tussle over the pillow until Felicia held her finger to her mouth. "We'd better keep it down," she said, accepting one last thump on the shoulder from a green upholstered cushion.

Dave put down his weapon and his face returned to a thoughtful gaze. "Just because we're giving this up to God, you know that doesn't mean we'll necessarily get pregnant. I've counseled a few couples at church who've nearly broken up over infertility. It even happens when you already have one kid."

Felicia thought of Jennifer and the misery she'd endured over her inability to have a baby before she adopted Carys. Although she understood how people like Jennifer felt, especially those who had never had a child, she didn't see herself in that situation.

"I'm not gnashing my teeth about it," she said.

Dave looked relieved. "I thought you really wanted another one and were afraid to tell me."

She spun to look at him. "Really?"

"Yeah. That's why I wanted it to be your decision. Because to be honest, I kind of like things the way they are, just us and the Nickster. But I didn't want to stand in your way if you wanted another one. Seems like it affects you way more than it does me."

" 'Cuz I have to gain forty pounds and go through something that's like pulling your lip up over your head?"

They both chuckled, but Felicia knew what he meant. Having a new baby, with the feedings and the day-to-day care, usually did come down to the mother, no matter how involved the father was.

Felicia was satisfied that they were both on the same page—and amazed by how they both thought the other wanted a baby when neither was leaning that way. She started sorting out the plusses and minuses of having another child, then cut herself off. *God is sovereign. He is in control now.*

She rose to take the ice-cream bowl to the kitchen and get a glass of water. As she did, Dave asked meekly, "I do want to make an addition to our family, though."

Felicia turned to him, wondering what he had in mind.

As if on cue, their cat Bengal jumped from the floor into his lap. Dave smoothed his fur and looked up at Felicia, batting his eyes, as Nicholas did when he wanted something. She knew he was aware of her disdain for the feline in the family.

"Nicholas might be okay as an only child, but *he* needs a brother or sister," Dave said. He held the cat's face and looked into it. "Don't you, Benny?" The cat wiggled out of his arms and meandered off.

Felicia stood shaking her head. Even at forty, her husband still had a boyish quality.

"I give up," she said with a smile and set off for the kitchen.

Dave's droll voice was directed toward her. "That'll be the day."

CHAPTER 52

Mimi

Sunday, June 29

10:02 a.m.

"Watch out! Coming through, coming through." MJ led the way through the church, like Harold Hill leading a marching band.

Mimi was carrying Milo in one arm and holding on to her father with the other. He was moving slowly, with the aid of a cane, but at least he was moving. Everything was still a little rough around the edges, but his second chance at life seemed to be going well. He'd promised to attend AA meetings faithfully—and to mean the commitment this time. He had even gone so far as to ask his sponsor to call him or drop by the house every day. And the best part of all was that he'd finally agreed to attend church with the family. Not every service—"That's a little too much religion for me." But the Sunday-morning services were doable, he'd admitted.

Now here they were for the first church service of his new beginning. Mimi hated to admit it, but there were Sundays in the past when she'd been grateful her father didn't want to attend church. She was afraid of how the church members would react to seeing her less-than-perfect parent. And those times grieved her now. Her priorities had been so messed up! Who cared what people said or thought? This was her father's soul. And she'd forgotten about that—well, she hadn't really forgotten; she'd just chosen not to consider the eternal issues.

But not anymore. Life was too short, and God graciously had given her a second chance to make things right. And she wasn't going to squander it on overconcern for what others thought. She wasn't going to be ashamed of her father—the man God had chosen and allowed to be her father.

They entered the foyer of the church and headed slowly to the sanctuary. They got only halfway before several church members approached them.

"Good morning, Mimi! And who is this?" It was Anne Payton. Her husband was seated in one of the hallway chairs. He waved in greeting.

Mimi smiled brightly. "Good morning, Anne." She felt her shoulders push back proudly as she said, "This is my father, Archie. He's been staying with us."

"A lot of people have been praying for you, Archie. We're glad to see you're healing nicely."

Mimi was taken aback. How did people know?

Anne smiled. "This is a small town, Mimi. People may know everybody's business—don't they, Bill?" she called over to him. "But they also have some good qualities. And one of them is that when they talk, they also pray."

Well, God's just showing up all over this day, she thought gratefully.

"Thank you, Anne," she said, and genuinely meant it. "We've been feeling those prayers. Keep them up."

Anne smiled, then patted Archie on the arm. "You take care of yourself. Your daughter doesn't want to spend any more time in the hospital."

He chuckled and said, "Neither do I."

"Amen to that," called Bill.

Mimi led her father into the sanctuary—walking down the center aisle for everyone to see—and parked him in her usual spot, two-thirds of the way toward the front.

The service seemed to take on a spirit that Mimi hadn't felt in a long time. It was wonderful to sing next to her father and sit close enough to reach over and pat his leg or hand.

When a group of ladies got up to sing right before Mark's sermon, Mimi was surprised to hear one of them ask for Mimi and Mark to join them on the platform.

"You know," began one of the singers, Michelle Sullivan, as soon as Mimi and Mark were standing next to her, "we're not a bad bunch of people once you really get to know us. We're all just a bunch of sinners who need a savior and who need a whole lot of grace to get through this life. We don't always succeed, but we keep trying."

Where is this going? Mimi wondered. She turned slightly to look down at her father. His smile warmed her body.

"Well, we've stood by and watched as the pastor and his family quietly dealt with some difficult issues this past year. They've had it tough—especially with that little Milo." The congregation laughed. "He's the loudest baby I've ever heard." She chuckled. "Anyway, Pastor's always telling us that the church is about a community of believers who are supposed to be there for one another, praying, loving, and helping." She turned toward Mark and Mimi and began to talk directly to them. "It's about time you allowed this church to minister to you a little, like you two have ministered to us."

Mimi didn't know what to say. She glanced over at Mark to see his reaction. He was as surprised as she was.

"Some of the women got together and decided that we were going to start praying for you and your family. So every Thursday morning, while you've been about your business, around seven ladies have gotten together at Anne's house and have been praying specifically for you and for this church. We just wanted you to know that. But also . . ." Michelle waved to a woman sitting in the second pew. "Come on up here, Linda." Linda, a heavyset woman in her sixties, made her way to the platform. "Tell them about your son-in-law."

Linda cleared her throat, obviously nervous about talking in front of the church. "Well, my son-in-law, as many of you know, is the night manager for the Marriott in downtown Cincinnati. I spoke to him about doing something special for Pastor and Mimi here. So every other month, starting next month, a couple folks from the church are going to start taking your kids so you two can have a night out on the town—our treat. You can do dinner or whatever you want, then you'll spend the night there at the Marriott. You two have a full house and schedule, so you need to refill your tanks and spend some time together, just the two of you. This is something we can do for you."

Mimi and Mark looked at each other, dazed.

Finally Mark stepped forward. "Are you serious?"

"As a heart attack!" Bill Payton called out from a pew in the back of the sanctuary. The crowd erupted in laughter.

"You do understand that whoever watches our children would have to watch MJ and Milo, too, right?" Mimi asked, smiling. "They're part of the deal."

Everyone laughed again.

Michelle turned toward the congregation. "That's right. We hadn't really figured on those two."

"I don't know what to say," Mark said.

"That's a first," another man called from a pew in the front.

Mark laughed good-naturedly along with the group.

"Well, thank you so much," he began. "I think I can speak for Mimi as well when I say this is a wonderful gift you're giving us. We appreciate it more than you know."

Mimi looked across the sanctuary at the faces—faces she'd too often judged, and had too often not given enough credit or grace. She felt shamed and blessed at the same time.

Then she looked down again at her father. She had almost stopped believing she'd ever see him in a church. Yet here he sat. Miracles did still happen.

Her father winked and gave her a quick thumbs-up, then looked down as if studying his bulletin.

Then she lowered her eyes to the altar in front of her. It had felt the tears she'd cried and had been witness to the prayers she'd offered up to her heavenly Father.

God had been so good to her. He had heard her cries for help and grace. He had answered her pleas for mercy and for her family. He had shown up and had proved faithful again. Even when she hadn't deserved it.

Mimi knew the future wasn't going to magically become easy. She knew her father's road to recovery—*her* road to recovery—was going to be a long, difficult one. There were going to be setbacks and times when impatience and frustration won out. But she prayed those times would be brief and forgettable. Above all, she knew God would continue to show up and would continue to offer grace. And how thankful she would be.

CHAPTER 53

Lisa

Sunday, June 29

11:01 a.m.

Lisa stood in her pew, halfway back on the left side of the sanctuary, singing and swaying to the rhythm of the praise music. Ricky was sitting behind his drum set, at the front, on the same side, keeping time and singing along to "Shout to the Lord." Callie was standing next to her with her hands raised and eyes closed. Joel was on the platform, one arm raised to heaven.

Tingles spread over Lisa as she gazed around the sanctuary. Forty church members, spread out around the room, were in various postures as they sang out in worship to their Lord. The spirit was strong and alive—something that she had felt was missing from the services for more than a year.

"'Power and majesty, praise to the king . . . '"

A lump formed in Lisa's throat, forcing her to stop singing. Still swaying, she lifted her hands, and let the tears flow freely. *Thank you, Jesus. Thank you.* She whispered it over and over.

Everything about the service seemed to feel renewed and spirit filled.

The chorus ended, but the group still hummed and praised, as Ricky continued to tap the cymbal and the keyboardist played chords. The spirit was too strong to stop the worship part of the service yet.

After a few moments, Joel stepped to the pulpit. He lifted his hands and smiled widely. "God is here this morning."

Shouts rang out across the room. "Yes!" "Praise him." "Thank you, Jesus."

"We're not a perfect church," Joel continued, raising his voice. "But we're covered by the blood of the lamb!"

More shouts filled the sanctuary. "Yes, Lord!" "We love you, Father." "Yes, yes."

He moved his hands, motioning for everyone to take their seats.

"Three Sundays ago, this church made a very difficult decision and took some disciplinary action. It was painful—for all of us." He stepped to the side of the pulpit and waved his hands across the sanctuary. "We lost a lot of our members—folks we genuinely loved and cared for."

Lisa glanced around the room. In those last three weeks, the church had lost a full three-quarters of its members. They had never had a large church, but she'd always felt it was a good size.

It was odd to see the seats so empty. Now there were forty members left. Not large by any stretch. But they all wanted to be there. She saw Bonnie Bentz seated across the aisle from her, draped in a purple wrap and fanning herself with the morning's bulletin. Don Angle and his wife, Marcy, sat next to each other farther down from Bonnie. The Markins family sat in front of her. Good people. Faithful people who loved God and his work.

The few Tom "moles" weren't there that morning—probably they'd had enough and realized it was never going back to the way it had been and that they weren't going to be able to control or bully or manipulate the pastor anymore.

Forty people. She wasn't sure how they were going to survive, but she realized size really didn't matter as long as the church members were alive and vibrant.

"Those who left—we need to commit to pray for them, to not wish ill of them," Joel continued. "We need to continue to love and treat them as God would have us treat them. Amen?"

In a chorus, the group all shouted, "Amen."

"This isn't a time to harbor bitterness or anger. They will be judged on their actions—as we will on ours. As the remnant people, let us be found faithful and obedient in this."

That may be easier said than done, Lisa realized. The rumors about her family had continued—although, admittedly, they'd become fewer. Now the comments were mostly about Lisa and Joel playing favorites, or that Joel had cussed out one of the church members who'd left, or that Joel was power hungry and now was able to do whatever he wanted in the church. They were ridiculous statements that anyone thinking logically would realize were lies, but still hurtful all the same.

"We need to take care of some family business today," said Joel. "Our church has been hit hard, and it's going to take some time for us to heal. Healing doesn't just happen overnight. We can't expect things to be smooth right now, or we'd be fooling ourselves. I've heard from a number of you over the past several weeks, and you've been filled with fear over what has happened. Not fear over the discipline. We all agree that it needed to be done. But now many of us are filled with the anxiety and worry over how we're going to pay our bills—because we need the tithes—and how we are going to grow—because we lost so many of our attendance. We wonder how we're going to survive—but we will! I can assure you, we will. Because God has brought us this far, and he didn't bring us this far to leave us alone. He will be faithful to us. He will protect and bless us."

Lisa felt that tingly feeling again—the spirit of God was in this place. Her eyes fell on her husband as he continued to encourage them. They had been through so much together. Marriage issues, parenting issues, church issues. He had grown through them all. They both had. And they were still standing.

He's a good man, a good leader, she thought. All of a sudden her eyes filled with tears and her heart swelled in her chest—she felt so proud of him!

She knew this wasn't the end of their church troubles. As long as they were doing the Lord's work and involved as pastors in the local church, they were going to encounter attacks and rumors and other trouble. That was part of the job description. But sitting there among the faithful, she was also convinced that this was exactly where God had placed her family. They had been refined by fire. They—and their church—would continue to be refined, but oh how beautiful they would be on the other side of that refining.

Callie gently poked her mom and passed her a note.

I ❤ you and Dad. And I ❤ God.

In that moment, as her husband spoke, and her son was at his drum set, and her daughter sat next to her, Lisa realized anew that they were going to be okay. It was all going to be okay. Not easy, maybe not even smooth, but okay.

Thank you for my family, she prayed. *Thank you for watching over us and not ever giving up on us. And thank you that we have a good church where we can worship and serve you.*

Lisa put her arm around Callie and pulled her close, kissing her on the side of her head. "I love you, too, baby girl. I love you, too."

CHAPTER 54

Felicia

Monday, June 30

1:28 p.m.

The phone. Again.

"Hello?"

Felicia's greeting was met with silence.

"Hello?" she asked again, growing impatient.

It was a tiny voice, like a stone that had been chipped away from a boulder. "Feef?"

Gina.

"Gina! I'm so glad you called." She realized she meant it. "I've been so . . . I've wanted to—"

The voice came stronger this time, but choked. "Fifi, I need your help."

A chill ran down Felicia's spine. She could tell this asking for "help" wasn't Gina's typical request for money. She sounded vulnerable and weak, not the unabashed Gina she knew.

"What is it, Gina? Are you okay?"

"Can you just come?"

Felicia asked her address and Gina gave her directions from the I-71 freeway. She recognized the exit as one she'd passed every day when she used to commute to Cincinnati.

"I'll be right there."

Thirty-five miles later, plus cell phone calls to Dave and Lisa (who said she would call Mimi and Jennifer) for prayer, Felicia pulled up to Gina's apartment building in northeast Cincinnati.

She walked to apartment 4G, unsure of what she might encounter when she opened the door. Drugs? A battered Gina? Some thugs holding her captive for money?

Instead, her knock produced just her older sister, wearing a torn Van Halen concert T-shirt and elastic-waist shorts. Her shoulder-length black hair—the same color as Felicia's—was disheveled, as if she'd just gotten out of bed.

Gina didn't raise her head when she opened the door, simply uttered a quiet "Hi."

Felicia gently lifted Gina's face to hers. Her olive skin was stained from crying, and her eyes were bloodshot.

Before Felicia could say anything, Gina reached around her with both arms. It was more than a hug—it felt to Felicia as if Gina were hanging on to her for dear life. Gina was drowning and Felicia was her buoy.

"Hey, now," Felicia cooed, rubbing Gina's back as she sobbed over her shoulder. "It's going to be all right."

She had no idea what "it" was, but she didn't know anything else to say.

With Gina attached to her, Felicia had a chance to peruse the room from the doorway. No Li, she noticed, and there wasn't much to distinguish the place as a home. A card table and two chairs made up the dining area, while a few pillows on the floor appeared to be the living room.

Felicia spotted an ashtray filled with cigarettes. She felt a momentary rise—*surely she's not smoking while she's pregnant*—but then assured herself they were probably Li's.

Gina's tears calmed slightly, and she eased away. Then she led Felicia into the apartment and shut the door.

Felicia set her purse on the floor. "What's going on, Gina?"

Gina sniffed a few times and wiped her face on her T-shirt. "Let's go sit over there," she said, pointing to the folding chairs.

Once she was seated at the table, Felicia could see in the kitchen. Beer bottles were stacked on one counter and soda cans on the other. A box from a frozen pizza was the only sign of food she saw. Alarm rose in her for Gina's unborn child.

"I see you looking around," Gina said accusingly when Felicia's eyes turned to meet hers. *Ah, the same old Gina is still in there somewhere.* "If you're wondering if all of this stuff is mine, well, most of it is."

Gina must have seen the displeasure on Felicia's face because she quickly added, "I'm not pregnant. Anymore, I mean. I lost it."

Felicia felt the anger leave. "Oh, Gina, I'm so sorry. I had no idea. No wonder you're—"

"No, that's not why I called you here. I lost it a few weeks ago."

Waves of emotions were crashing through Felicia's body. *Something was more important than the miscarriage?*

Gina took a sip from a Pepsi can on the table. Making a face that told Felicia the soda was flat, Gina continued. "Li's gone. Left me here. By myself." Her face tightened, and she started to cry again. "Can you believe he would do that?"

Felicia was confused. First Gina and Li were a couple of nomads, making their way to Ohio from California. Then they were happy parents-to-be. And now they were broken up. All in a few months?

"Why did he leave?" Felicia was afraid to ask but knew she had to.

Gina sighed deeply and swiped at her wet face. "He found out about me losing the . . . the baby."

"What do you mean 'found out'?"

Her face a mixture of defiance and defeat, she blurted out, "Don't get on your high horse with me about this, Feef. I was doing . . . what I thought I needed to do. I'm not like you. I had to do it."

"Do what?" Felicia's heart was in her throat. Had Gina aborted this baby?

"I lied to Li. Uh, not exactly lied. I just didn't tell him. I didn't tell him about the miscarriage."

"You let him think you were still pregnant? Why?"

Gina's face fell. "It all started when I took the pregnancy test that week we moved here, right after Dave's party."

Felicia saw that image of Gina and Li in a cloud of smoke in her garage. She took in a sharp breath. "Gina! You were smoking pot when you knew you were pregnant?"

"I didn't know . . . really." Her response told Felicia she suspected it, but Felicia decided to let it go. Any damage the drug could have caused the baby was a moot point now.

Gina went on. "I told Li right away about the pregnancy because I wasn't sure what to do. And he was *so* excited. I couldn't believe how excited he got, Feef. He'd always said he didn't want kids when we talked about it. But, whew, as soon as he found out he was having one, he sure changed his mind fast."

Felicia smiled at his eagerness. Maybe he would have been a decent dad after all—maybe the baby would have somehow motivated him to get his life in order.

"And then the next week—I was just getting used to it all—I felt a pain and saw blood. Li was at work, so I took the bus over to the clinic. The doctor checked me out and told me I'd lost it."

She dropped her face again, but Felicia still wasn't sure which loss she was mourning—the baby or Li.

"I'm sorry," Felicia offered again.

Gina took another deep breath and raised her head. "I decided not to tell Li. I had this weird feeling, I can't explain it, but I knew if he found out, he'd leave. And"—she waved her hand toward the empty room—"I was right."

They sat in silence for a moment. "So how did he find out?" Felicia asked.

"I started my period, the first one since then," Gina responded. "I tried to hide the tampons, but he saw one in my purse. And when he asked, well, I had to give it up."

Felicia told herself to temper the impatient tone she often used with Gina, but she heard it anyway. "At what point were you going to tell him? What kind of plan did you have?"

Gina's eyes narrowed. "I didn't have a plan. Not everyone plans every second of every day like you do, Felicia."

The indictment stung, but after her recent struggles with letting God be God, Felicia knew Gina was right. She did overplan, and she thought people who weren't like her were incompetent.

"I shouldn't have called you." Gina started to rise from her chair.

Felicia waved her back down. "No, no, I'm glad you did. We're sisters."

The reminder brought a wry grin to Gina's face. "Huh. We're about as alike as two strangers on the street, you and me."

Gina was right. "I know," Felicia said. "You can choose your friends, but not your family. You're stuck with us."

They burst into awkward, but knowing, laughs, breaking the tension that had poisoned the room.

Then Gina seemed to remember her situation, because her expression transitioned from pleasure to pain. "I'm scared, Feef," she said, looking away.

Felicia had never heard Gina say anything timid or insecure in her life. Even when they were kids, Gina refused to cry when she got hurt at the playground or someone called her a name.

"But you've always been the strong one, the one who took the path less taken," Felicia said, hoping to console her. "What do you have to be scared of?"

Gina faced her again. "My future. My life. What am I going to do now? Do you realize I've never not had a boyfriend? Every time I've ever broken up with someone, I've always had my eye on the next one."

Although Felicia was distressed for Gina, she couldn't help but notice how much more she could relate to this open, less impervious version of her sister.

"You know," Felicia said, "I always secretly admired how you approached life. I couldn't ever be a free spirit like that. About anything. No matter how much I try, I can't seem to let go."

Gina looked at her, wide-eyed. "You've got to be kidding. You were the one who did everything right—went to college, married the quarterback, got a great job and made lots of money. And now you're a pastor's wife! How could I ever match up to that?"

Felicia shifted on her chair. She had done all those things. "But where is there a rule book that says success means one thing? Remember that old saying, 'God doesn't make junk'? I think that's true. Some of us just take longer to learn how to let him lead us."

Although she wasn't sure if her mini-sermon was intended for herself or Gina, the resolve Felicia felt and the contemplative look she saw on Gina's face told her they both benefited.

The effect didn't last long. "But here I am, stuck in Ohio by myself, with nothing," Gina whined. "And no one."

"You have me." Now Felicia was the one with tears. "Gina, you're not alone."

Gina shook her head. "No, Feef, I can't be part of your world. The church and all. And now they know I smoked pot. And by the way, I hated that stuff. Li loved it, so I tolerated him doing it, but I really wasn't into it."

Felicia was relieved by her unsolicited explanation.

Gina continued. "Anyway, I'll never be able to be around your church people with them knowing I did that. They'll always be looking down their noses at me—the brown girl from California who does drugs. What a stereotype!"

"First of all," Felicia responded, "they wouldn't look down on you." She knew that wasn't entirely true—she'd felt some people judge her—but it was in most cases. "And who cares anyway? We all have stuff in our lives. That's why we go to church, to learn how God wants us to deal with it. And second," Felicia added, "no one knows about it but Dave and me. Everyone thought it was just cigarettes." She thought for a minute. "Well, except Charlie, but everyone thinks he's crazy anyway, so they wouldn't believe anything he said. And who knows? Maybe you'll discover there's some good stuff in church. Just like you're afraid they'll stereotype you for being Hispanic, maybe you're doing the same to them—judging them because they're Christians."

Wow, Felicia thought for a moment. *Have I done that to our church members, too?"*

Gina didn't look convinced.

"Come move in with us for a while. We have plenty of space. Just until you decide on your next adventure, of course."

A slow smile crept across Gina's face. "Are you sure? I am family, you know. You didn't choose me."

Felicia stood. "I may not have gotten to choose you as a sister, but I'm choosing you now . . . as a friend. Let's go home, my friend."

CHAPTER

55

Herman's Park

Friday, July 4

11:47 a.m.

Mark squeezed their minivan into a small space between two cars on the grass and parked.

"All right, kids," Mimi said, unbuckling her seat belt. "Everybody grab something and carry it with you. Dad, would you take care of Milo? I'll get the chairs and diaper bag."

"Got him," her father said.

She stepped out of the van and smoothed her red-and-white sundress. She could see past the cars to the park where Red River's annual Fourth of July picnic had just started.

Was it just two years ago when we were here and I threw up all over Kitty Katt's outfit and shoes? she thought, amused. She'd been pregnant with Milo then. Thankfully, there was no pregnancy for her this year. *Maybe for Felicia? Let her be the babymomma for a while, if it's meant to be.*

She threw the diaper bag over her shoulder and took two chairs, while Mark doled out all the picnic stuff to the kids. MJ was in charge of carrying the bucket of Clucker House chicken. When Mark had suggested they stop off on their way to the park, Mimi started to complain, but then stopped. *This is a battle I am not going to win. So I might as well learn to enjoy it. Well, maybe not* enjoy. *Tolerate.*

"I'm glad you decided to join us today, Dad," Mimi said. And she meant it. She knew they were never going to be a "normal" family, but they could appreciate the "normal" that was theirs. And with her father holding up his end of the agreement and staying sober, she felt they had hope for a loving, respectful relationship. Plus it was fun to watch him enjoy time with his grandchildren, especially Milo. He loved that crazy kid—he didn't even mind changing his diapers, which was just as well for Mimi.

As they all walked closer to the picnic area of the park, she started to scout for the other PWs. She was actually looking forward to having the husbands join her and her friends. They were still going to meet as PWs at Lulu's, but at least this could open other opportunities for them to socialize. And finally, she and Mark could start having more consistent date nights—okay, who was she kidding, they could start *having* date nights—and unload the kids on one of the other couples. *Heaven,* she thought—*as long as it doesn't lead to me being pregnant again.*

She spotted Lisa and Joel at one of the large tables in the center of the eating area. Lisa had covered the entire table with blue-and-white-gingham tablecloths and looked as though she was making Ricky and Callie stand guard so nobody else took their space.

Lisa saw her, too, because she waved wildly for Mimi's gang to join them. "Over here," she called out. Lisa looked beautiful, better than she had in a long time. Her shoulder-length hair was pulled back in a barrette, and she wore a white T-shirt and white shorts that showed off her figure.

Well, that's one way to lose weight—endure a church split.

But most important, Lisa looked at peace. Joel stepped over and said something in Lisa's ear, then kissed her.

Mimi could hear Felicia behind them yelling for Nicholas to slow down. Then she spotted Jennifer and Sam walking toward Lisa from the opposite side of the park. A woman wearing a large U.S. flag T-shirt followed, pushing a carriage. *That must be Jo Jo.*

Perfect timing. *Don't know how we did it with all our kids in tow. We can mark that one down as a miracle.*

As soon as everyone arrived at the large table, the kids dumped their stuff and started to play with one another.

"Hello, everybody!" Lisa clapped her hands. "Welcome to our first PWs and their husbands and families get-together."

Mimi saw a confused look pass over Mark's face.

"What's she talking about?" Mark whispered.

"Mark," Mimi said, dumping the diaper bag and chairs and walking to Lisa, "this is my friend Lisa. You know her husband, Joel. They pastor at the Assemblies of God church here in town."

They all went around the group with the PWs introducing their husbands and children.

"Gentlemen," Jennifer said, "we have a confession to make to you. Every other Tuesday, when we mysteriously disappear and you think we're off to the market or a meeting or a doctor's appointment or something, the four of us get together for lunch and fellowship. These women have walked me through some dark times and some wonderfully joy-filled ones. They've been my lifeline, my sanity. They have been true sisters in Christ to me. And I know they all feel the same."

"Great," Dave said. "When do we eat?"

Felicia punched her husband in the arm. "That's it? We tell you this secret part of our lives and you're just interested in eating?"

"What secret?" Dave said. "We knew where you ladies were every other Tuesday."

Mimi's jaw dropped. "Is that true?" she asked Mark, who barely hid a smile.

He shrugged.

"How did you guys know?" Jennifer asked Sam.

"It's a small town, Jennifer," he said. "Everybody knows. And Cheeksville isn't exactly a whopping metropolis either."

"You mean," Lisa said, "for three years we've been secretly driving forty miles out of town so nobody would know our business—and everybody knows our business?"

Joel laughed. "That's about it. Well, not everybody. But the ones who did know thought it was kind of fun."

"But," Mimi said, feeling a little miffed, "why didn't you ever say anything? And why didn't we ever hear anything from anybody else in town?"

"Because everybody knew it was supposed to be a secret. Plus, we knew that time was important to you. And because of that, it was important to us. As a matter of fact, there were quite a few Tuesdays while you were meeting that the four of us were meeting, too."

Mimi's father let out a loud guffaw. "That's great!"

Joel hugged Lisa. "We hope you're not too mad?"

"No, I guess not," Lisa said.

"So now that means you don't have to drive forty miles to get together anymore," Sam said. "You can get together here in town."

All four women vigorously shook their heads.

Give up Lulu's? No way.

"That's our special place. Too much has happened there for us to leave it," Mimi said.

"And much will continue to happen there," Lisa said. "We've got a waitress there who needs to see women role-modeling Jesus."

Gracie.

This year, Lord? Mimi prayed silently. *Will it be this year that she'll truly find you?* Between the PWs working on her and Seth there, Mimi felt confident that God was going to do a great work in Gracie's life.

You don't give up on us, do you, God? You keep seeking us, keep wooing us, keep loving us.

Mimi's eyes caught a Hispanic woman walking toward them. "Gina?" Mimi asked Felicia.

Felicia turned to watch the woman approach them and nodded.

As Gina came closer, Mimi could see the L.A. look. Her brown top was a little too low, high, and tight. She wore big hoop earrings. The only resemblance she had to Felicia seemed to be their identical silky black hair.

How different they look! Mimi thought. There stood Felicia, starting to look more like a Midwestern than a West Coast woman. On her feet were white Keds, and she wore a white polo and blue capris.

Felicia introduced her sister to everyone. Mimi was so proud of the PWs as they all immediately welcomed Gina with warm hugs.

"Can we eat now?" Dave said, tapping the cardboard top of the Clucker House bucket.

"Yes, fine," Felicia said.

Everyone looked around to see who was going to pray.

"I'll pray," MJ piped up.

Mimi and Mark shot looks at each other. *Oh, no. What's our child going to do this time?*

"Are you sure you want to do that, son?" Mark asked in his no-you-don't-really-want-to-do-that-*do*-you tone.

"Yeah." MJ stepped onto the table bench.

Mimi bowed her head, frantically saying her own prayer that MJ wouldn't embarrass them too much.

"Dear God, thanks for this day and this food. Thanks for my friends and my family. Thanks that you love us."

That's sweet, Mimi thought, starting to relax. *He's doing great.*

"Please be with everybody at the picnic and keep them safe. Thanks for bringing my grandpa to live with us . . ."

Mimi started to feel a lump form in her throat as she felt Mark's hand reach out to grab hers.

"And please don't let my mom be too upset when she sees that I broke her favorite candy dish at home. It really was an accident and I didn't mean it, and help her forgive me and not ground me . . ."

What?

Mark's hand squeezed hers.

"And help her remember that Jesus loves us when we forgive each other. In Jesus' name. Amen."

The group let out a collective laugh as MJ presented a wide grin to his parents, then hopped off the table and ran.

"I'm going to get that kid," Mimi said.

"You've got to give him credit," Joel said. "He figured it was better to admit it here in the midst of witnesses."

"Oh, sure, and the whole forgive as Jesus forgives was purely coincidental," Mark said, picking up a plate.

Everyone filled their plates and sat to eat.

"I still can't believe you all knew about Lulu's," Mimi said, buttering her corn on the cob.

"So how's the church doing?" Mark said to Joel, sitting across the table from him.

"Better than it's ever been," Joel replied. "We have a lot of healing to do. But God is faithful, and we're going to make it."

"You look good," Mimi leaned over and told Jennifer. "And your mom looks good."

"I think we're on our way. Mom has agreed to get some help. That will be a huge plus for her and for our relationship. And in other news, I officially turned in my resignation as church secretary."

Mimi saw that Lisa and Felicia had started to pay attention to what Jennifer was saying.

"Well, it's not as if you need the money," Felicia said.

"Right," Jennifer said, scooping up a pile of baked beans on her plate. "We're going to hire someone. I don't need to work anymore, and anyway, with two kids now to care for, I'll need more—"

"Whoa, whoa!" Mimi dropped her fork. "*Two?*"

"Don't you hold out on us," Felicia said.

Jennifer squealed and nodded vigorously, her strawberry blond ponytail jerking up and down behind her. "A young woman came to the Fortress and wants to place her baby for adoption. She's agreed on Sam and me as the adoptive parents."

"Excellent!" Lisa said.

"Oh, Jennifer, I'm so happy for you," Mimi said and hugged her.

"Thanks."

"And don't forget. MJ is still available for adoption."

"It's been a wild three years, hasn't it?" Jennifer said.

"It has indeed," Lisa said.

Mimi thought about everything that had happened to her and her friends in the past three years. Pregnancies, miscarriages, church splits, alcoholic fathers, near infidelities, death, and, most important, friendship.

"We've learned a lot, haven't we?"

"Mmm-hmmm," Jennifer said. "And it's been really exciting to watch Lisa's vision for the other wives blossom and grow. I hope that group finds the kind of friendship with one another that we've found."

"God has been so gracious to us, hasn't he?" Lisa said. "As difficult as the journey is, he provides reinforcements along the way. Going through this past year, I don't know how I would have made it without you all. The times when I wanted to give up on the church, you were there for me, standing strong and praying me through. What would we have become had we not taken a risk on one another and become vulnerable?"

"There's no place I'd rather be, PWs," Jennifer said.

"Oh!" Felicia said. "That reminds me. Ally called me the other day wondering what she should do with all of Kitty's clothes. She told me that Norm had kept everything of Kitty's and she wanted to get rid of it." Felicia laughed. "She said"—Felicia went into a high-pitched, giggly imitation of Ally—"'Like, I've never seen so much yellow in my entire life. Hee, hee, hee. I told him I was never going to wear that color, which is actually a good thing anyway, because I don't really, like, you know, look good in yellow.'"

"Poor Ally," Lisa said. "She's just young. We were that way once."

Mimi, Jennifer, and Felicia all leaned back and stared.

"Okay," Lisa said, retracting. "Maybe not exactly like that. But for some reason, she looks up to us. And she's going to need some women who have walked the same road she's now on."

"I never thought," Mimi admitted, "that we'd be having this conversation about Norman Katt's wife. Kitty would never have come to us for advice or wisdom."

"Maybe she would have, after a while," Lisa said. *Always the optimist. Always offering grace. Just like our Savior.*

"So what did you tell her?" Jennifer asked.

"I told her to box them all up and give them to you to donate to the shelter," Felicia said.

"All those women there are going to look like they're wearing uniforms," Jennifer said.

"Um, speaking of . . . ," Mimi interrupted them.

"Hello!" Ally was leading her husband, Norman, over to their area. She was dressed in a fitted red, white, and blue sailor outfit. *Okay, that's cute,* Mimi thought.

As soon as Ally was close enough to the group, she announced, "Everybody, I need your undevoted attention." She giggled, then wrapped her arms around Norman, who gazed at his young wife, very obviously adoring her.

"Normy and I have an announcement to make. We're going to have a baby Katt!"

Mimi looked across at Felicia, who was barely able to contain herself. Mimi slightly lifted her finger, mentally willing Felicia not to burst out laughing.

Lisa was the first from her seat. "Ally, that's wonderful news!"

Mimi and Jennifer jumped up and quickly went around the side of the table to offer their hugs and congratulations as well.

Finally Felicia rose, tears in her eyes from suppressing laughter. "Ally, we couldn't be happier for you," she said and kissed her cheek. "Just wondering, do you have a name picked out?"

About the Authors

Ginger Kolbaba is editor of *Today's Christian Woman* magazine, a publication of Christianity Today International, and author of numerous books, including *Surprised by Remarriage: A Guide to the Happily Even After* (Revell). She lives with her husband, Scott, in the Chicago suburbs. Visit Ginger at www.gingerkolbaba.com.

Christy Scannell is a freelance writer and editor, and a college journalism instructor. She and her husband, Rich, a newspaper editor, live in Southern California. Visit Christy at www.christyscannell.com.